COSMIC WEAVE

NICKY PENTTILA

I

COSMIC WEAVE

CHAPTER
ONE

IN THE VAST emptiness of space, Dagny Novak was a virtuoso at connection. Here, surrounded by laughing families, she'd never felt more alone.

The relentless, blistering lights of this Galaxy George theme park seared into her skull. Inviting her estranged daughter to spend a day with her here had been a catastrophic error.

Dagny would do anything for her daughter. And Osa loved Galaxy George.

But from the moment they stepped into this chaotic vortex, things had gone wrong. The clashing tunes blaring from every neon-lit corner. The people randomly zigzagging around and between them. The too-bright fake sunlight.

The terrifyingly tall people in rancid anime dog costumes, jumping in front of you shouting, "Selfie selfie selfie with me!"

Complete overload.

This is why she worked in space. Orderly, deadly, reliable space.

Hiding from the creepily hypnotic glow of the park's "outside" lights, Dagny and Osa hunched across from each other in a booth in George's Treehouse Café. The café was only slightly less frenzied than outside, but at least it had walls and the expectation that your table, at least, was a slice of space just for you.

Osa picked at her ridiculously overpriced George's Favorite seaweed salad. The greens seemed to vibrate unnaturally under the café's kaleidoscopic lighting. She sighed, a sound so laden with world-weariness it seemed to echo from the void.

Dagny's hand fisted. She leaned in, trying to close the chasm with light-hearted curiosity. "So, what do you think the salad is really made of?"

Osa looked up, startled, her eyes momentarily sharp and indignant—a flash of the angry teenager she once was. A decade-old memory flashed before Dagny, of slammed doors and cutting words. Her fingers dug into the edge of the booth's padded seat. But it was a valid question. Here on Exeter Station, far, far from any ocean, seaweed seemed implausible.

Osa glanced out the window and sighed. "Always hated Galaxy George," she said, her voice a monotone rip current dragging Dagny into deeper confusion.

What about the pink doghouse blanket, worn and tattered, folded neatly in the box under Dagny's bed? And the dog-paw mittens?

Dagny picked up her bowl of Grandma's Recipe miso soup. Swirled it around, inhaled the familiar umami warmth. Put it down again, untasted.

She should have stayed on the Breaking Light. Should've let all the ship's xenobiologists and diplomats go cavort at their big conference while she recalibrated the sound decks or something.

And miss this chance to see her girl? After all these years?

Impossible.

Now twenty-eight, her girl had sat across from her at this table but still worlds apart. Osa worked all the way on on the other side of the Spectrum Alliance systems. But the conference that had brought Dagny's ship here had lured Osa as well. A freshly minted xenobiologist, she spent most of her days planetside.

So why the sallow cheeks and hunched shoulders?

Dagny glanced at the holographic puppies cavorting between the booths. Blinking primary-colored lights formed dancing pictures of Galaxy George the Spacedog and his menagerie of friends. At least they were regular-dog size.

Their synthetic joy reflected off the restaurant's window to shimmer mockingly on their plates. Dagny's own reflection looked back at her, dark eyes shadowed, pinched with fatigue and desperation.

DAGNY'S HANDS, still hidden beneath the diner's blue plastic table, folded over and over themselves. Trying to scrub the anxiety away. Her blood thrummed like one of those old-fashioned engines.

She had lost her daughter.

She didn't know how to get her back.

Osa pushed away her salad bowl. Didn't even eat the edamame. She leaned her back into the padded booth, her dreamy eyes glazing over as if she were already far, far away.

She wore her dark hair longer, and let it fall in front of her eyes.

"Doesn't matter, Mom," she said, her voice the dull steel of finality. She gestured at Dagny's untouched soup. "When you're done, we'll go."

The weight of the failed connection seared Dagny like an ungrounded wire. The childish laughter and light conversation surrounding them only highlighted the dead spot that was their table.

Desperation colored her voice. "Wait," Dagny said, reaching out to touch Osa's arm. "Please, let's try something else. Anything you want, just tell me."

Osa hesitated, then sighed. Her arms were so thin, the bones of her shoulders jutted out.

"Fine. Sure. But first, I need to hit the head."

She stood up, hit the edge of the table, and bounced back into the seat. Not a spacer, her daughter. Too used to pushing around furniture that wasn't bolted down. Osa swiveled her knees and scooted off the side of the booth's bench onto the scuffed plasticrete floor.

Dagny tapped her finger on the lip of the soup bowl and stared unseeing out the window. In the theater of her mind, a highlights reel recounted every misstep. Every failed attempt to cross the growing expanse between them.

Her beautiful, freckled, soft-tulip girl. No, woman. A woman she no longer knew.

How to reconnect? Not by asking about her health, or her job. Absolutely not by asking about her friends.

Time was, Osa never stopped talking. The latest weird animal she'd been learning about. Who was going to win some floatball tournament. What some musician was wearing, or dating, or pontificating about.

Now, silence. Thick, steady, painful silence.

Nearly a miracle that they'd found themselves at the same place at the same time. More an artifact of the quadrennial xeno-biologist convention held here on Exeter Station than any luck.

The Breaking Light's xeno team was thick in the post-session planning, setting themes and venues for future conferences. Osa wasn't part of that esteemed circle—yet. Dagny had seized the fleeting opportunity, inviting her daughter to spend a rare afternoon together.

And wasn't that going great.

From here, she could see the park's entrance, an absurd archway of massive dog bones encasing white plasticrete walls. At least they didn't call the food "puppy treats."

How much time did Osa need to pee?

Something prickled at the back of Dagny's neck, a persistent unease. She scanned the circus around her. So many faces, colors, shapes.

No sign of her girl.

Something wasn't right.

Dagny deserted the soup, and the booth. At the last second, she remembered to grab Osa's thin violet sweater from the other bench. She tucked it into her big navy mom bag, a battered tote that had held everything from spare baby booties to circuit boards that needed retooling.

She darted toward the bathroom, dodging other patrons and serving staff.

Empty.

A tendril of panic burned down her throat.

Surely Osa wouldn't just leave—right? But was this even her daughter anymore?

Dagny dashed out the back door, her scanning growing frantic. She called out once, but the din swallowed her voice. She finally pulled up the messages on her wristcom.

Nothing new.

Images of Osa flashed through Dagny's mind. That sly smile, that bark of laughter when she was surprised, that unwavering determination. That expectation that everyone would love her; that everyone would care.

Osa was not just a daughter, she was Dagny's entire world. She was the reason Dagny had pushed so hard to get onto Breaking Light. So Osa would have a chance to fly.

The garish battling music—every corner a different song— clawed at her. Osa's hearing was even more sensitive than Dagny's. Her daughter wouldn't linger here.

Dagny sped under the absurd bone-door archway, desperate to trace her daughter's steps. They'd met at the outer passenger docks and taken a tram to the park.

No one at the tram stop.

She had to stop to catch her breath. Her space-soft forty-something body wasn't built for this much terror anymore. She dropped onto one of the benches at the tram stop. The stickiness on the red-plastic seat didn't register, but recognizing that the armrest she was reaching for was made out of dog bones startled a soundless shriek out of her.

Osa was right: Galaxy George was creepy.

The perfect, unchanging daylight now felt oppressive, a silent conspiracy keeping the masses firmly entranced.

Suddenly, Dagny remembered. Duh. Messages could go both ways.

She lifted her wrist, but apparently her brain had sent it two messages: send a text, and smack her forehead with her palm. Instead, she smacked her forehead with her wristcom, hard enough she saw stars.

A small voice behind her giggled. Not Osa. Dagny blinked away the stars and focused on the wristcom interface.

She opened a voice call, and tapped the small metal patch behind her ear to enable her to hear it. The familiar chirp-chirp of the comm's search for connection soothed her.

For a moment.

And then someone answered.

Someone who wasn't Osa.

"DAGNY NOVAK," the enhanced-to-be-husky alto voice flowed from her earpiece into her thoughts, thick as mercury and just as toxic. "We have your daughter."

A frozen moment passed as those five words resounded in Dagny's mind. The noise and commotion of the families waiting for the bus fell away, and even the hard plastic bench beneath her ceased to exist. The bright sunlight blinded her.

She couldn't have heard them right.

"Osa?" she said. For a moment, she couldn't speak. "Was there an accident?"

"No accident, Chief Engineer Novak," voice as chilling as a whisper in the dark.

"How do you have her comm?" Dagny's pitch rose in panic. She jumped up, looking around frantically for any sign of her daughter. "Is she all right?"

One of the mothers turned from her tousled-hair child to look at Dagny, concern on her face.

But Dagny didn't want sympathy from a stranger. She wanted her daughter.

She needed to get away from this place, surrounded by happy families and their oblivious children. She stumbled away from the bus stop and back toward the park entrance. Her feet were lead, but she had to keep moving. The plastic murals on either side of the entrance mocked her with their bright colors and happy scenes.

"You're scaring me," she said. She leaned a hand against the mural, trying to steady her breathing.

"We are Beloved Spring," the voice answered calmly, as if discussing monthly transmissions logs or fuel ratios.

Fear choked her breath. The terrorist group. At least in this sector of space. In their own sector, Beloved Spring was a business concern that traded in out-of-system goods. How they obtained the goods was not a concern of their own sector.

But what ever could they want with Osa? How had they even gotten a hold of her daughter?

A glimmer of hope flickered. Maybe this was all just a sick joke.

"Seriously," she said. "You're kidding. Right?"

"No joke," the voice replied, frigid, freezing dead that wisp of hope. "Do as we tell you, and she'll live to see you again."

Dagny's thoughts spun with confusion. Terror was just around the corner. This couldn't be happening.

"You must have the wrong Osa," she stammered in desperation. "She's just a xenobiologist, she…she…"

Dagny cut herself off.

They knew exactly who Osa was.

They knew who Dagny was.

They absolutely knew where Dagny worked.

Panic stormed over her as she realized what that meant. She doubled over, clutching her stomach as if her internal organs were all trying to flee. She tried to take a deep breath, but the stale popcorn taste of the air made her choke.

What could they want from her?

With a sick feeling, she knew.

"The Breaking Light," she ground out.

"The Breaking Light," the voice confirmed. "Your precious vessel of peace and goodwill."

The Breaking Light wasn't just any spacecraft. It was a symbol of cooperation, progress, unity. Three very different political worlds had poured their resources into its creation. Three worlds' hopes for peace in their systems rested on the ability of its crew to discover and then manage first contact with the new peoples they found.

And now it had caught the eye of one of the bullies of their sector.

She couldn't give any bit of it away. She wouldn't.

But they weren't asking.

"Which component?" Dagny grasped at straws, hoping it was something she didn't have access to. Maybe if she told them, they would let Osa go.

Maybe, maybe, maybe.

There was a pause on the other end. The light burned Dagny's eyes. Her tears amplified the pain. She squeezed her eyelids closed, wringing the water out.

"We require the ship. The entire ship."

CHAPTER
THREE

THE ENTRY ROOM to the main security wing on Exeter Station was not busy. Its empty, open intake area suggested no sense of hurry. The people running security here must think that if you could take the fifteen minutes on the tram to get here, it must not be a real emergency.

Wrong.

Dagny hadn't been able to reach an actual person on her comm during the entire ride over here. She wasn't about to leave some recorded message that nobody would look at or listen to. Each moment that passed was another moment her daughter was trapped.

Someone was going to listen.

The waiting area was spacious but sparsely furnished, as if the base's designers had expected more traffic than actually turned out to be the case. A row of somewhat comfortable soft-wood benches with high backs stood against the right side, with less comfortable benches without backs lining the left.

That left plenty of space to walk up to the intake desk, less a desk and more a wide table between two kiosks with intake screens. Hardly better than the wristcom interface.

With its dun walls and dim lighting, the room stood a stark contrast to the bustling, high-energy vibe of the more-public parts of the station. The air stung Dagny's nose, antiseptic and cold with a faint hint of days-old coffee.

She swallowed, trying to ease the familiar dryness in her mouth, a combination of nerves and the lack of moisture in the air. Every breath felt thick and heavy, like she was inhaling the weight of her own worries.

Only three other tired-looking people were in the room. A young couple, clothes rumpled, who looked slightly battered. They sat on a high-backed bench near the double doors that led deeper into the wing. Shoulder to shoulder, heads down, they appeared to be staring at their entwined hands. On the other side of the room, on a bench in the corner closest to the intake kiosk, a very old person sat knitting.

Dagny started typing. She knew what to say to get somebody out here.

It worked. Not five seconds after she'd typed the words "Beloved Spring," one of the double doors started to open.

The person who stepped out ticked all Dagny's boxes for security officer. Tall and wiry, sharp eyes and thin mouth. Neat hair tied back, navy blue uniform worn but pressed. As the officer walked towards the intake kiosk, her gravity boots click-clacked against the floor.

She ignored the sad couple and headed straight for Dagny. She did not stop at the usual social distance, but invaded Dagny's space. Loomed.

"Beloved Spring, you say." Her voice was as tight as her shoulders.

Dagny swallowed hard, her mouth pure desert. She nodded, her hands tightly clenched on the strap of her tote bag. One hand slid into the bag, groping for the plush knit of Osa's sweater.

"Yes," she said. The words started to pour out. "They called. On my wristcom. From my daughter's comm. Wristcom. They said they had my daughter. Osa is her name."

The officer—Gomez, her badge said—said nothing, but her generous brows drew down. She was listening.

"Help me find her?" Dagny babbled on. "She's my height, my body type. Dark hair. Wavy. She's always twisting it, so it never lays right. She's twenty-eight."

The officer's expression changed. Dagny trailed off, suddenly uncertain.

"Twenty-eight?" Officer Gomez's mouth pinched to the side. "You think your adult daughter was kidnapped."

"She disappeared! They called! It was planned." Now Dagny frowned. Was she confused? "It sounded planned."

Officer Gomez's skepticism reached her arms, which crossed in front of her. "Is this some kind of joke? Beloved Spring is a dangerous terrorist organization. They don't just go around kidnapping people's adult daughters."

"No!" Dagny meant to sound firm, but her voice wobbled.

Gomez patted Dagny's hand, the one clutching the strap of her tote bag. "Your Osa probably just needed some time alone. She'll show up soon, don't worry."

Dagny pulled back, away from the officer's hand.

"It's no joke," she said. "They demanded I give them my ship. The one I'm stationed on. Or else."

"Or else what?"

Dagny frowned. That part was a little vague in her mind.

The officer had heard enough.

"Right," she said. She scratched her hair behind her ear. "Let's see if we can find her in the database. She's a visitor, right? Not a resident." Gomez stepped closer to one of the intake screens. She swiped her wrist in the upper corner of the screen, and a new app opened. "You don't have her ID code, right? So let's do it by name." She glanced at Dagny expectantly.

Dagny spelled out Osa's full name. Now they were getting somewhere.

Words in a language Dagny couldn't read printed themselves on the screen.

"She checked out of her lodging this afternoon."

This afternoon? The conference wasn't over until tomorrow.

"Does it say when, exactly?" Dagny leaned closer, searching for any numbers in the flow of text.

"Just before two."

"But she was with me at two! We were eating at the café. I can prove it." Dagny fumbled with the interface on her wrist-com, looking for the receipt from the café. "See?"

Officer Gomez shook her head, her gaze grim.

"I do see. Look, you can report her as a missing person tomorrow, after two." She lifted a hand, palm up, stopping Dagny before she could interrupt. "That will give us permission to search all the security feeds, not just the public ones."

"They told me they'd hurt her!"

Officer Gomez shook her head. "We get a lot of these.

Don't worry. Your daughter will reach out to you when she's ready."

Dagny's vision shaded into red. So dismissive. Didn't the officer understand the urgency? Osa was in grave danger, there was no doubt.

Was there?

The door to the outer concourse slid open. Officer Gomez turned to look, and froze, staring.

Dagny didn't need to look. Her boss's unique perfume, stronger now it was late in the day, had already reached her.

Dr. Saanvi Rao dressed to impress. Or stun, depending on your taste in style. Her currently fire-red hair was pulled back from her face with a hairband, leaving the rest to pouf around her head like a dandelion. Glasses with matching red frames formed circles around her currently green eyes. Black lipstick highlighted those perfect planes of sepia cheekbones. For the conference, she'd dressed conservatively, for her: a basic wrap dress, in black, with a multicolored scarf tied around the waist.

Smaller and wider than Officer Gomez, Saanvi stomped with twice the force in her military-grade gravity boots. The Breaking Light's chief engineer never wore any other footwear.

"Dagny," she boomed when she was halfway across the room. "Got your message. What's the problem?"

"Osa is gone," Dagny blurted out. "Missing."

Saanvi nodded, her hair also agreeing.

"So you said." She looked at Officer Gomez. "Find her yet?"

Officer Gomez had had time to recover, apparently.

"Don't think she's missing. At least, not until she's still AWOL tomorrow."

Saanvi turned to Dagny. She unlatched Dagny's hand from its crab-claw grip on her tote bag and patted it. At the touch, Dagny's long-held-back tears began to fall.

"I see you are worried," her boss said. "But let's not jump to conclusions. Officer Gomez has dealt with many similar situations before. Sometimes people just need some space and time away, even if they don't communicate it well."

"But the call." Dagny stuttered. "They threatened her."

Saanvi pulled Dagny into a hug. She looked past her, at Officer Gomez.

Some kind of information must have been exchanged. Saanvi hmm and nodded.

"A prank call," she said, letting Dagny loose but not free. "Pretty extreme, even for a woman with Osa's imagination." Saanvi tsk-ed. "Still, I know how much she means to you. We shouldn't dismiss this entirely."

She turned to Officer Gomez. "We'll have to leave this in your capable hands, Officer—" Saanvi peered toward the badge on the officer's collarbone.

"Gomez."

"Officer Gomez," she continued. "Because we must be off."

"What?" Dagny pulled out of Saanvi's grip and wiped at her eyes. So nice that her boss wasn't put off by a few tears. "I'm not going anywhere without my daughter."

"'Fraid so," Saanvi said. "Just got a new assignment, fresh from the xeno conference committee. Breaking Light is off to the fog belt, posthaste."

Dagny couldn't leave now. How could Saanvi even suggest it? She might be one of the brilliant few who could diagnose sick engines just by listening to them, but she didn't know anything about mothers.

Saanvi bowed, hands pressed together, to the officer, and then held out her hand to Dagny. She'd painted flames of fire on her nails for the conference.

"On, to adventure!"

Dagny took another half-step back from her boss. Her hip hit the edge of the intake kiosk. Officer Gomez shot out a hand to protect the kiosk from her flailing.

"No!" Dagny said. "I mean, not yet. Let me get a hold of Osa—" She choked on the thought, finishing it in her mind. Safe and sound. "Then I'll meet you at Breaking Light."

Saanvi's grin faded. She closed her hand into a fist and brought it in to touch her heart.

"Not much time, chief communications engineer." A hint of displeasure laced her rich alto voice. "Departure is the moment the conference closes, and the ship must be warm and willing to fly."

Saanvi's words sliced through the turbulence of Dagny's mind. Go on an adventure? Now? When Dagny's whole heart was at risk?

Her boss must have seen something in Dagny's expression. Mutiny, probably. Saanvi sighed and leaned back on one hip.

"It's just a couple of jumps and a week's travel, total. Even if the signal doesn't check out, we'll be there weeks getting baseline data. Once we're there, we'll get you a ride back here. If you still need it."

Saanvi looked at Officer Gomez. "Trust the experts."

Breaking Light's engines could sputter and fail, for all Dagny cared. Nothing was more important than Osa.

"And once we're at speed, I think you should talk to someone," Saanvi said. "Professional. About why you've become a hover-mother now when you never have been before."

Dagny straightened as if Saanvi had slapped her. For a moment she couldn't think of anything to say. For once, the gorgeous cocoa butter and nutmeg of her boss's perfume did not soothe her. Nor did the stern cast of Saanvi's jaw.

"We need you on the ship, Chief," her boss said. "Three hours."

CHAPTER
FOUR

EVEN AT THE passenger shuttle area, a wide-open parking lot for the city-bus-sized shuttles taking people back and forth from Exeter Base's outer piers, the air was sweet.

Dagny could not appreciate it.

She stood, a few meters away from the ramp leading up to the passenger compartment of the Breaking Light's last shuttle on base. Her boots didn't have the gravity engaged, but they felt like they were nailed to the ground.

How could she leave Osa?

The hatch of the shuttle must have noticed her. It shimmered open, beckoning her inside. Each step she did not take brought her closer to losing her window to board the Breaking Light. To return to the job she'd fought so hard for. Helping to discover new civilizations. Finding ways to contact the new peoples they might find. Solving impossible problems with her nimble fingers and sharp mind.

But Dagny couldn't shake the image of her daughter's dreamy face dark with fear. Her scratchy voice calling, desperate for help. Sure, they were estranged, as the ship's last counselor put it. But that didn't mean they didn't care for each other. And that certainly didn't negate Dagny's responsibilities as a parent.

Outside the base, on the Breaking Light, Saanvi and Remy must be tapping their wristcoms, waiting on Dagny to run the routines to get the onboard communications systems ready for launch. Saanvi was probably making that crooked smile, trying to conceal her impatience with one of her a-little-bit-too-sharp jokes.

They hadn't told her in so many words—yet—but Dagny knew what the kidnappers wanted her to do.

Sabotage the ship.

Damage the three-worlds alliance.

Betray her colleagues.

Not just colleagues. Friends.

The Breaking Light was more than just a job. It was her dream, the reward for years of hard work and ambitious choices. She was blasted good at what she did, and she loved that the team relied on her. She couldn't give it up.

But, Osa.

The thought of leaving her here, in danger, was unbearable. How could she choose between them?

"Come on, Dagny," she whispered to herself, trying to muster the will either to step onto the shuttle or turn around and leave. Through the open door to the shuttle, a couple of scientists sat scattered among the rows of single seats inside. "Just decide."

Still, she hesitated, her foot glued to the rock-hard flooring just off the ramp.

"Novak," Mira Patel barked from behind her. Dagny startled, but the firm voice was familiar. She turned slowly.

The mission chief of the Breaking Light was walking up with the ship's chief xenobiologist, Dr. Birgit Brennan. Brennan's hands were waving excitedly, but his long-legged steps were paced carefully to the commander's shorter stride.

"On the wrong side of the ship, aren't you?" Patel said.

"Missed some great talk at the panels today," Brennan said. "But no worries. We'll be glad to fill you in." He chuckled at his own joke. If this conference was anything like the last one, the xeno crew wouldn't be talking about anything else for the next month.

"There was a presentation on advancements in comms tech," Brennan went on. "Recorded it for you. Don't tell." He winked, and smiled wide. "It's so great you got to see your daughter."

Dagny's jaw tightened. She forced a smile, trying to keep up appearances. "Yes, wonderful. I just." She took a shaky breath. "Need another moment before boarding."

Brennan must have seen something. His thick brows drew down. As Commander Patel strode up the ramp and into the shuttle, Brennan stopped. He put a hand on Dagny's elbow, just the lightest touch.

"Something wrong?" he said

Tears threatened to spill from her eyes. She blinked hard. How could she hurt him? The scientists? Everyone?

How could she hurt Osa?

She wanted so badly to tell Brennan everything. He was such a good listener. But she hesitated.

Officer Gomez had been so skeptical. Saanvi had dismissed

her worries. Maybe she even thought Dagny was flaking out. She couldn't risk alienating more of her crewmates.

"Thank you, no," Dagny managed to choke out, her voice barely a whisper. "I'm just feeling the feelings in real time, you know?"

"Family," Dr. Brennan added kindly, his deep-set eyes full of empathy. "They know how to push your buttons. Well." He looked away from her, toward the shuttle. "We're here for you if you need us."

He practically hopped into the shuttle, his long legs eating the length of the ramp in two strides. Leaving Dagny alone, again, with her thoughts.

With her feelings.

Now it felt as if not only her boots but her whole body was anchored to the tarmac.

"Last call for boarding," crackled from the shuttle's outside speaker.

"Blast it all," Dagny muttered.

Now she was talking to herself.

She took a calming breath. She tapped her wristcom again. Maybe Osa had found another way to contact her.

Nothing.

As she thrust her hands away, her right hand spasmed. Too much clenching, over the past hours. How many hours? Only three? Impossible.

Her comm buzzed.

Dagny shook out her hand, but the spasm didn't ease. Instead of tapping the wristcom, she had to use the voice commands to open the channel.

"Get on that shuttle."

Dagny unfroze. Sweat exploded along her sides, behind

her neck. Her head whipped around, looking for whoever was talking.

No one was near.

"Do it," the voice bit out, cold and true. "Or your daughter dies."

The shuttle's ramp began to retract, sliding into its slot under the doorway.

"Now. My hands are on her neck."

Dagny lunged forward. She threw herself into the belly of the shuttle, landing hard on her hip. The doorway went dark behind her.

Commander Patel, in one of the front-row seats, snorted.

"Always with the drama, eh, Novak?"

Dagny tried to smile as she scrambled to her feet. She hurried to the back row, away from everyone, and huddled in the farthest seat, by the blank gray wall of the shuttle. She shivered, sweat evaporating in an instant in the dry, chill air.

She didn't realize the comms line was still open.

"Good job," the voice cackled. "Now the fun begins."

CHAPTER
FIVE

ALONE IN THE back row of the bus-style shuttle, and the only person wearing both safety harnesses, Dagny willed herself calm.

It didn't work.

The shuttle's hum, usually so soothing, was now a source of irritation. The steady, rhythmic burr mocked the frantic pace of her thoughts. The usual soft mint scent failed to soothe away the stink of panic-sweaty human. Her feet on the seat, knees up, arms around knees, head down, she ran through the kidnapper's messages over and over again.

However she looked at it—however she spun the words—the meaning came out the same. Disable the Breaking Light somehow, or never see Osa again.

Something bumped at her hip, and then noisily cleared his throat. Dr. Birgit Brennan, being subtle.

Dagny lifted her head to confirm. Her usually reliable welcoming smile wobbled.

"Need a hug?" Brennan asked. He held his near hand out, an offer.

Dagny didn't trust herself to be able to withstand a hug. Everything might spill out. But Brennan was a noticer. If she didn't head him off now, he'd "keep an eye on her" for the next week. She needed to be invisible. Figure this all out, without distraction.

And absolutely without observation.

"Maybe just a forehead rest," she said. "It's been a long day."

Brennan nodded. He slipped his arm around Dagny's shoulders as she leaned in. She rested her forehead on the wide space under his collarbone. He was tall even sitting down. And minty, with a trace of green curry. She sighed.

"Don't look at your comm," he rumbled in her ear. "Time enough for that when we get there."

Dagny couldn't remember if she'd turned her comm back on. She'd slammed everything off after that last, chortling call from the kidnappers. No matter. They must be almost to the Breaking Light.

Her home among the stars.

For now.

She leaned back, wiping her eyes with the back of her hand.

"You know we all love you," he said. "Value you highly, all that. You're home with us."

Dagny took a shaky breath. He had such kind eyes.

He had no idea.

"Yes," she said. "I mean, I know. I mean, but sometimes it's nice to be reminded."

Brennan gently pulled his arm away, patting her knee on the way.

"Don't forget," he said. With a gentle smile, he pulled himself up using the back of the seat in front of them and made his way back to the front rows.

"Approaching the Breaking Light," the shuttle said in Sally's voice. Sally the autonomous intelligence was not actually in the shuttle, she had enough to do managing systems on the ship, but it was a clever conceit.

Dagny forced herself to look out. She needed to see it, needed to anchor herself to something familiar, something solid.

At first, she caught just a glint of its lights against the vast darkness. But as the shuttle drew closer and turned to make its approach, the ship's form came into sharp relief. Normally, the sight of her ship filled Dagny with warm pride, but now it only offered shivery chill.

Your basic flying saucer, The Breaking Light dwarfed their tiny shuttle. Three hundred thirty-six meters wide at its belly, it was home to nearly two hundred people, with plenty of space for more.

Dagny's engineer's eye traced the barely visible seams of the nine levels, each a world unto itself. Her gaze lingered on the equatorial band where two strips—one above, one below—slowly rotated, generating the artificial gravity that kept everybody's bones from wasting away.

As they neared the massive doors of Shuttle Bay Two between the rotating strips at the ship's midsection, Dagny felt the familiar flutter in her stomach. No matter how many times she'd made this approach, the sheer scale of the Breaking

Light never failed to move her. The doors yawned open, a maw of steel and light ready to swallow them up. With an invisible field of force to keep the air in and the people safe and whole.

The shuttle hummed as it maneuvered into position. Through the window, Dagny saw one of the dock cranes approaching, clamping onto their short bus of a shuttle.

As they crossed the threshold into the artificial atmosphere of the bay, the shuttle gave a slight shudder. The sudden shift from the silence of space to the low rumble of machinery and distant voices made Dagny's ears pop. She swallowed hard.

The crane slowly swung them toward the landing dock closest to the navigation suite, not the usual one off to the side.. Perk of having the mission chief on board: no need to walk across half the bay to get back to work.

Work.

Nearly a dozen people in the soft trousers and tunics the science teams preferred waited for them. Plus one in blue coveralls, taller than the rest, and thinner. Her second, Remy. Odd that he would be here to meet her.

The sight of him, slouching like a teenager, hair needing a comb, shook Dagny to her core.

How could she betray these people?

The Breaking Light that was more than just a method of transit.This symbol of hope and cooperation among the peoples of this galaxy?

It was a place full of friends.

This ship and its three sisters represented the pinnacle of cooperative achievement—a harmonious blend of cutting-edge technology and the pioneering spirit of four peoples.

Zark, Kipi, Iridah, Human, each ship casting its net wide, looking for the next peoples to encounter.

Now, as the shuttle settled onto the deck with a gentle thud, Dagny felt like she was bringing a cancer aboard.

She was the cancer.

She shut her eyes, letting the vibrations of the ship seep into her bones. It was a feeling that had always brought her comfort before. Now, it felt like an accusation.

Dagny unbuckled and took a deep breath, trying to steady herself. Her hands shook as she pushed off the seat's armrests to stand. She hoped her duffel had made it on to one of the shuttles. She'd left it on the transit platform at her hotel.

The airlock hissed as it pressurized, and the shuttle door slid open. Dagny was the last to leave.

As she stepped off the shuttle, the familiar thrum of ship's life enveloped her. The docking bay's crisp, chill air tingled her throat on her in-breaths. The bright lighting cast a clinical glow over everything, making the scene feel almost surreal.

The walls were lined with various docking stations and maintenance equipment, all meticulously organized. She saw all the other shuttles parked as usual.

And one more.

"Dagny!" Remy had reached her side. His long, agile face was stiff with stress. "Where have you been? Did you lose your comm?"

Dagny's heart stuttered. Had they discovered her secret already? She forced her face into what she hoped was a neutral expression. "What's going on, Remy? Is that a Kipi shuttle over there?"

"Check your comm." Remy ran a hand through his already

disheveled hair, making it stand up even more. "We have ambassadors aboard. Two Zark, two Kipi, and an Iridah."

For a moment, Dagny forgot to breathe. The words hit her like a bucket of icy water. Her mind raced. They would need the special translator setup, and recorders fine enough to capture the subvocal tones the Iridah could create. And those Kipi squeaks. And that was just the start.

What were they doing here? Ambassadorial visits were planned months in advance. Years, even. Checked and double-checked. Everyone would be wearing their formal clothes. No way this could have happened in the space of a shuttle ride.

"All three?" she managed, her voice sounding strange to her own ears. She turned to look farther down the concourse, toward the suites of official meeting rooms. Should she head there first, or to the communications suite? "How long is the meeting?"

"That's the thing," Remy said. He stepped back and turned, toward the comms suite. "They're traveling with us."

Impossible.

"On such short notice?"

Remy nodded vigorously. The swing of his hair briefly exposed the soft blue pulse of the cyber implant at his temple.

"It's the mission, right?" he said. "That signal we found. They really do think it could be real. Sentient."

So everybody wanted to be onboard and see for them-selves. And make sure there were no misunderstandings, like the Kipi somehow telling the Iridah that humans were shapeshifters, too. Or something worse.

As they neared the door to the navigation suite, Remy slowed down. He asked the question with just a raised eyebrow.

Dagny shook her head no. Usually, she liked strolling through Navigation on the way to the comms suite, but today the place would be a zoo.

Ambassadors, here.

Living and breathing, eating and strolling, probably.

Oh, gods. She couldn't wreck this mission.

If she disabled the ship with the ambassadors aboard, that would be an alliance-wide incident. A K A disaster.

Surely Beloved Spring wouldn't want to take on the entire alliance all at once?

They'd have to call off this plan. Let Osa go.

Her shoulders sagged in relief. Next time they called, she would tell them about the ambassadors. Make it sound like they were here to stay. Who knew? Maybe they were.

Remy was still talking. "Raza is in a frenzy trying to arrange suitable quarters. But the comms systems—"

"Wait." Dagny stopped, forcing Remy to slow and turn. "Our head of security is primping rooms? Where's Leah?"

"She fell off a rock," Remy said. He rubbed his forehead. "Rock climbing, I mean. They all did. Team-building exercise."

"Team?" Dagny echoed faintly.

"All six of them, tied together. Working together. Didn't you ever do that one? It's straight out of *Approaches to Better Management*. Well, except the falling part."

Dagny started walking. Maybe it would help her make sense of what Remy was saying.

Remy went on. "Doc yelled her loudest, but the station docs wouldn't let them risk the shuttle. At least two of them have bad concussions."

He trailed off, looking at her with a mix of desperation and hope. "It's just us. And the xenobiologists."

The ambassadors did not enjoy being stared at, much less prodded. Standard practice was to keep the xenos away from them, if at all possible.

Dagny groaned.

"You said it," Remy said. He waved at the panel beside the comms suite outer airlock door.

CHAPTER
SIX

THE THREE SHUTTLE BAYS, circling the Breaking Light's middle level, were shaped like thick crescents, hugging an even thicker middle. Like all nine levels, this widest level's hub and spoke design included plenty of flexispace: walls, floors, and ceilings that could morph into whatever rooms or open space the crew needed.

Even with the spacious navigation, communications, and security suites, a good three-quarters of Level Five's thick middle was flexispace. Currently, it was set up as three cargo areas and four variously sized meeting rooms.

The meeting rooms stood ready to be comfortable for every known sentient species. Most introductory meetings were held here. Safer for the crew. Easier on people who might have trouble moving or breathing on a human ship.

Dagny wasn't sure if Ambassadors themselves had been off this level since the ship was launched.

Well, they were all off it today.

With almost no liaisons.

All three blasted ambassadors, on one ship. When had that ever happened before? Why weren't they taking their own ships?

She knew the answer to that one. The Breaking Light could hit velocities most other ships could only dream of. Of course, the trade-off was the prototype engines were finicky and sometimes caught fire.

The outer airlock door from the the docking bay to the ship's main communications suite hissed open and Dagny and Remy stepped in. Five second minimum until the inner door would open. Dagny set her shoulders.

At least it wasn't her job to protect the ambassadors from the engines. She just needed to ensure clear communications across deep space for everyone to call anyone using four different interfaces, security systems, and social cues.

At least four connections. More like ten.

And she had to find one more.

A secure line to the Spring.

The terrorists surely wouldn't want the chief ambassadors of the Spectrum Alliance on their hands. The entire alliance would come after them.

The shitheads would have to call the whole thing off. Let Osa go.

Go back to harassing trade convoys.

Let Dagny breathe easily again.

Or not.

Or they would hold onto Osa even longer. Hurt her more. Until the next opportunity. And who knew when that would be?

Which choice was more likely?

The thought made her lungs seize.

The inner airlock door slid open. Dagny stumbled over the threshold.

"Chief?" Remy's voice broke through her spiraling thoughts. He loomed over her, his mobile face etched with worry. "You okay?"

He needed to stay calm. She needed to stay calm. Everybody needed to stay calm.

She took a slow breath, hoping he would unconsciously mimic her. "Yes," she heard herself say, her voice steadying. The tension in her shoulders began to ebb.

This was her domain.

The kidney-shaped communications suite was mainly open space, with a couple of little rooms tucked into both narrow edges. This entry opened into the far end of the pale blue room. On the right were two of the "isolation booths," for crew and guests to have super-private conversations.

Past that, to her left, along the inner wall, beckoned two long stretches of ergonomically designed table-based workstations. The nerve center of the Breaking Light's communication network.

She had chosen the materials herself, favoring the dark, matte composite surfaces for their sleek appearance and practical benefits. They absorbed light, reducing glare and eye strain, crucial for long hours at the consoles. Some of the horizontal surfaces were high, some very low, depending on who had used them last. Adjustable flat and holographic screens floated above the consoles. Everything blinked cyan—good.

For the moment.

Sturdy padded chairs that could roll or lock down were still clustered near the station tailored to the universal translation matrix. Dagny had been showing Remy and Shar and two folks from xeno how to fine tune the matrix. Dr. Patel liked people to keep learning, and Dagny liked having the potential help.

She'd need it this trip.

As she moved deeper into the room, the carpet beneath her feet muffled her boot steps. She'd insisted on the rich, dense weave, not just for comfort but for its sound-dampening properties. In a room where crystal-clear communication was paramount, every detail mattered.

Her stalwart trio of junior engineers bustled about, each at their own set of customized workstations.

Good thinking, Remy.

Usually, they worked the opposite shift from Dagny and Remy. He must have called them in to help with the unexpected load. Dagny might have to work some overnights to get them the rest they deserved after this. Or ask Sally the AI to cover.

Then she'd owe Sally more sessions of music practice. More squeaky woodwind fun, probably.

Screens flickered with incoming transmissions, encryption protocols, and system diagnostics. The air was charged with the low murmur of focused work, punctuated by occasional beeps and chirps from the various systems.

In the past, this symphony of productivity had filled Dagny with pride. Today, it felt like a discordant reminder of everything she stood to lose.

She nodded to the trio, one by one, Shar and the two other ones. They had rotated in just a month ago, and would rotate out in five months, or whenever the Breaking Light was next back at a home port.

They passed the low meeting table, with its big pillows,

and the "cozy nook," Dagny's term for the colorful sofas, sturdy pillows, and magnetic rocking chairs that filled the rest of the large space.

Her spot was at the far end, with her back to the walls of another pair of isolation booths. She liked to sit facing out, seeing the whole room through the transparent screens and holograms that hovered over her desks. It also reminded her to change focus from time to time, easing the strain on eyes and ears.

As she approached, she caught a whiff of green tea, and smiled. Power up the tea pot, she had work to do.

As she passed her main table, at chair height, she ran her hand along its surface. The slight buzz of power humming through the components was a pulse, steady and reassuring.

The surface responded to her touch, illuminating with a soft glow. She sank into her chair, feeling it conform to her body, cradling her in its familiar embrace.

Holographic displays formed, bathing her eyes with a soft, cyan glow. All systems good.

Data streamed across the screens, a visual representation of the countless messages and signals coursing through the ship's networks.

She preferred the holo-views and virtual interfaces, but her second desk, hard beside her first, did have all the other forms of input. Keyboards, joysticks, trackballs, haptic—even an ancient two-way radio in a tote-case. She'd used them all, at one time or another, over the past eight years.

She didn't love the unpredictable, exactly. But when it arrived, she loved to rise to the challenge.

Which was good, since Remy still looked a bit panicky. The

section of his sub-dermal neural net by his temple was a frantic blue blink.

"So," she said, aiming for friendly. "What have we got?"

"I've got the basics sorted," he said, pushing his hair to the side. The moment he let go, it swung back over his brows. "Adjusted audio spectrums, and recording speeds. But the new Zark visual interfaces are funky. I thought we'd solved the vision-echo problem, but I've already heard from the ambassador that everything looks doubled."

Dagny nodded, forcing herself to focus.

"Something about that came up at the conference," she said. "Lucky for us. Let me find the transcript."

For a glorious moment, she was lost in the dance of adaptive interfaces, compound visual displays, and specialized audio processors. This was why she had fought for every bleeding-edge piece of equipment. For moments like this, when the Breaking Light could truly live up to its mission of bridging gaps between worlds.

Three worlds, three vastly different peoples, each with unique communication needs.

Ambassador Nova of the Iridah, with her gelatinous, shimmering form and ability to shape shift, would require flexible interfaces capable of adapting to her changing physiology. Dagny could almost see the holographic displays morphing to accommodate Nova's fluid movements.

The Zark ambassador, Xalara, with their towering insectoid form and compound eyes, would need entirely different visual inputs. Dagny's fingers itched to reconfigure the visual interfaces, creating a kaleidoscope of information that would make sense to Xalara's alien perceptions.

And the Kipi… Dagny's brow furrowed. Ambassador Myli

and their consort Belle, those adorable furry balls of mischief, would need specialized audio systems to capture their unique vocalizations. Not to mention childproofing every console to prevent their notorious light-fingered "borrowings."

Then reality came crashing back. Excitement curdled into panic in her stomach.

Ambassadors. Here. Now.

The implications hit her all at once, making her grip the edge of her console for support. The cool, responsive surface beneath her fingers seemed to mock her with its familiarity. How many times had she stood here, feeling in control, secure in her domain?

Wreck this place? With the ambassadors aboard? The representatives of three different peoples, entrusted to the humans' care.

She could almost see Mira Patel's dark, piercing eyes, usually so calm and assured, widening in shock. Saanvi's warm smile fading as she realized the magnitude of Dagny's betrayal. Birgit's kind face twisted with confusion and hurt.

And Commander Khan. Dagny shuddered. The head of security's disciplined demeanor would shatter, replaced by the raw pain of failing to protect yet another group of innocents.

Outside the ship, the consequences would be catastrophic. An intergalactic incident. She could see the headlines now, feel the shockwaves that would ripple through delicate diplomatic networks. Years, perhaps decades, of careful negotiation and trust-building, shattered in an instant.

All her fault.

The comms suite, usually her sanctuary, suddenly felt stifling. The gentle hums and clicks that normally soothed her now seemed to carry accusatory whispers. Even the live star field projected on the wide screen on the outer wall by the rocking chairs seemed to be watching her, silent witnesses to her dilemma.

Each successful communication, each problem solved, felt like another link in the chain binding her to an impossible choice.

The Breaking Light, her mission and her home, had become quicksand. And Dagny, the architect of its communications, had never felt so alone.

CHAPTER
SEVEN

THE FIRST TO COMPLAIN ABOUT accommodations were the Zark.

When Security called to ask for backup, Dagny answered. She took the central-core stairs up to the fourth level, trying to push the aftereffects of her panic out of her muscles, at least. As soon as she stepped onto the landing, she could hear the blistering set-down a Zark was giving some poor crewer.

At least it told her which of the spokes of halls to take.

She sped up down the freshly re-formed hall, her thoughts running through what she knew of Zark-Human interactions. Okay to look at their eyes, not okay to touch any part of them. Okay to stand farther back, not okay to look cowed. Okay to experience trouble communicating, not okay to give up.

She tapped the comms device near her ear. "Remy?"

"I hear them," he said. "Ready." Down in the comms suite, he had the entire library of diplomatic advice for dealing with the Zark open and searchable.

All four itty-bitty databases.

The brand-new hall on this level dwarfed her. The Zark ambassador's suite needed to be two entire ship-levels tall, the higher ceilings catering to their two-plus meters in height and their preference for perching. A narrow slice of the pie that was Level Three above had been temporarily sacrificed for the ambassador's comfort. The engineers, Sally, and their drone helpers must have rearranged all the conduits and other stuff lightning fast. The new-furniture smell in the hall was already fading.

But the little-bit-sticky pale flooring would take some getting used to.

"Intolerable!"

Sounded like the ambassador, biting down on those formal word-endings. Yes, it was the silver Zark looming over poor Nell. The deputy head of security, all in black, her straw hair held violently back by a mean-looking elastic, was starting to fade. Her stiff formal posture had softened at the hips.

Above her, looming, were the carapace and two of the four arms of Ambassador Xalara. Their slender, sturdy exoskeleton shimmered in shades of gold and silver in the flattering blue-tinted hall lights. Their big, big compound eyes could provide a wide field of vision, but were single-focused on Nell. Their other two arms, long and dexterous with delicate fingerlike tips, held a yellow brick. Which they were trying to shove at Nell.

Off to the side and behind the ambassador hunched their assistant, Krim, bronze exoskeleton drooping. They were sucking hard at the pendant dangling on their chest, the thing that fixed human air into Zark-happy air. The air-exchanger didn't usually need to be so close; Krim must have already had their dressing-down.

No one else was in the hall.

Which could be good.

Or not.

"Ambassador!" Dagny called out. She stopped, rather abruptly as the sticky floor grabbed the soles of her thick-soled gravity boots a bit too soon. Shoulder to shoulder with Nell, she performed the Alliance's weird formal bow, a kind of bending and rising that suited all body types.

The ambassador did not react.

Nell fell back, almost literally. Her pale eyes, wide, flicked from wistful hope, looking at Dagny, to alert readiness, looking at the ambassador, and back again. The change in expressions was whipsawing to watch.

"It is an honor to greet you," Dagny went on. "I'm Dagny Novak, chief of communications. How can we make your stay more satisfying?"

The ambassador reared up, but away from the two humans. Still close enough to be plenty terrifying. And brass-trumpet loud.

"Tch. Well, you could start with removing all of this, this—"

"Disgusting," the assistant, Krim, whispered in a voice like a French horn from behind the ambassador.

"Disgusting block of meal. Or whatever it is." The ambassador puffed up their narrow chest. "The Zark are a civilized people. We eat real food, with real utensils, like everyone else."

How had they gotten that so wrong?

She heard Remy huff on her connection as he searched through the references. "Old style food, for when they were first in space," he said. "Now despised."

"Absolutely," Dagny said to the ambassador."Our deepest apologies. We will remedy this right away." She turned to Nell. "May Nell here, enter your rooms to—"

Nell shook her head so violently her hair actually moved.

Right. The Zark thought strangers stepping into their homes polluted the Sanctity of the Life Experience. Or something.

"You're right," Dagny pivoted. "Absolutely disgusting. With your permission, we will send one of our automatic cleaners in to remove every trace. Is that acceptable?"

"Tch." The ambassador shoved the brick at Nell again. She took it in one hand, and moved that hand to behind her back. The brick disappeared.

Nell, ashy, looked as if she wished she could disappear as easily. But Dagny wasn't about to do this alone.

Remy clicked on the comms connection in Dagny's ear. "Sally says she's already cleared the rooms. She did it as soon as the screaming started. She says you should let her talk to you on the comms instead of me." He sounded amused.

He could keep on laughing. Dagny had avoided having Sally directly in her brain for years. The AI was bossy, for one. And opening that door meant it never would be entirely closed again.

For this mission, diplomacy while missing the in-house diplomatic team, having Sally ride along would be really helpful.

But for her other mission, the new one—sabotage—Sally would be no help at all. Dagny shivered.

To cover the shiver up, she smiled at the ambassador, just lips, no teeth. "I am so grateful for your assistance in this matter. How else can we help make your stay most pleasant?"

"Tch. Less verbal drivel," the ambassador blared. "Xalara," they said, pointing at their chest. "Dagny," they pointed at her.

Okay.

"Right," Dagny said. "I manage ship's communications. We have a space nearby your meeting rooms downstairs." She pointed down, stupidly. The ambassador tch-ed. So it was a verbal tic, not just an artifact of the air purifier / necklace thing. "One room very comfortable for you. There, you can contact your people without us overhearing."

The ambassador shrugged with their whole arm. "Can do that already."

News to her.

"Gotta figure that out," Remy said in her comm. "Posthaste."

"What I would like," the ambassador went on, "is a performance space."

"Space?" Dagny vamped. Did she hear what she thought she'd heard? "To perform?"

"I want to offer the riders of the Breaking Light a chance to experience our storytelling. Our dance. Our music."

Remy groaned. "Not the music."

"So, a performance space," Dagny said slow, thinking. "Space for an audience. And a stage, raised up?" The ambassador nodded. Their pairs of hands rubbed together, making a not-unpleasant sound.

Dagny looked past the ambassador, past Krim, down the hall. "How far do your rooms go? Down this hall."

Krim scooted on his four nimble legs to a spot about eighty meters down the hall. Quite the large suite, then.

Dagny nodded at the ambassador. She took Nell by the elbow, steering her past the ambassador, close enough to smell their odd curried-grass scent. Close enough to get swatted, if the ambassador felt like it.

Thankfully, they did not.

Dagny and Nell walked down the hall to Krim. Passing Krim, they nodded. Krim did not look at them, but scurried back to the ambassador. Not the most comfortable of relationships, that one.

Beyond the spot where Krim had stood stretched far more hallway. Plenty of space.

"What else is in this segment?" she whispered to Nell. The Zark had wicked good hearing, but they could at least try to be private.

"Nothing. Support equipment for them, maybe supplies. Food bricks." Nell shuddered. "Nothing that can't move."

"Then why aren't they at this end? With the windows?"

"Ugh," Nell said, sparing a glance back at the ambassador, who was now leaning on the wall with both pairs of arms crossed against their chest. Krim had vanished. "It was," she whispered. "Then they got here, and started screaming. Said they wanted to be closer to the exits. We had to put them in the meeting room downstairs to wait—don't even ask—and do everything up here over again."

"Quick work," Dagny said. "Well done."

Nell rolled her eyes. "Didn't take long for them to find something else wrong. I need a nap. Did you hear about Leah?"

"How could she take out her whole team?" Dagny asked.

Sure, the diplomatic lead didn't know the Breaking Light was about to be invaded by top-level ambassadors, but wow, what bad timing.

"Sure it'll be the topic of the next team meeting," Nell said. "At least it won't be our turn on the hot seat this time."

Dagny tapped the wall. "Can you do this?" Actually changing the room would be drone and AI work, but getting the specs from the Zark was all human.

Nell grimaced. "Can you? The Kipi are on about something, and somebody has to go see what."

"Sure," Dagny said. Sally the ship would do most of the heavy lifting, anyway. "Kipi can't want anything big, right?"

"Hah," Nell almost smiled. "They're so bitty. Sometimes I want to just pick them up and cuddle. And then put them on a high shelf. Be easier to keep an eye on them."

They returned to where the ambassador was loitering. Nell kept walking, on her way up to see the Kipi on Level Three. Dagny stopped two meters away from the ambassador, and clasped her hands in front of her.

"Yes. There's plenty of space right here in this segment for a performance space. Maybe two."

The ambassador—Xalara—pushed to their feet.

"I don't want humans and what-all else parading down this hall. Find somewhere else."

Dagny smiled with her lips. "No need. There is another hall, behind your rooms. Humans and Kipi and Iridah can enter from that hall, and not disturb you at all." She made a mental note to mark this hall as Zark-only on the ship's maps.

"Acceptable," Xalara said.

Dagny did not do the "yes I did!" dance, but she pictured it in her mind.

"Give us the specifications, and we will make the space."

Xalara waved at Krim, who had rejoined them. The assistant was slighter, and a full half-meter shorter, than Xalara. He held what looked like a folded beach umbrella in his hands.

"Krim will handle it. If he can."

So sorry for Krim.

CHAPTER
EIGHT

KRIM THE ZARK turned out to have a sly sense of humor and an excellent sense of design. He didn't loom like the ambassador had. Plus, he smelled like fresh-cut grass.

Clever, too. He picked up on how to work the ship's space-allocation program right away. Rows of too-tall seats and a stage that looked slightly dangerous appeared on the workspace screen Dagny had projected onto the wall.

She'd tried to talk him into getting out of this lofty hall with its weirdly sticky floors, but he wouldn't budge.

"Better to stay near, for their majesty's beck and call," he said. "I'm getting too old to do the scurry-scurry anymore." A crack opened near the corner of his mouth. A smile? And a clicking sound, but not a "Tch."

"Assistant Krim," Dagny said, watching his dextrous fingers spin the mocked-up seats to face first one wall and then another. "Could you tell me, please, what does this word mean? Tch."

Krim's chuckle was the pop-pop of a thrown stone skipping along the water. Dagny must have gotten the pronunciation right, or close enough.

"Just Krim. That word means whatever the ambassador wishes it to mean," Krim said. "Very convenient, that word." He stopped spinning the seats and focused on making a shape that looked like a stage. Or a pit.

He turned to her. "What would you say are the acoustics in this space?"

Dagny frowned. Terrible, was her first answer. She searched for another she could actually say.

"Let's ask Sally," she said. "She's our ship's computer, and she loves music."

Dagny introduced Krim to Sally via voice connection, and then left them both to it. She had to get back to comms.

But as she walked out of the spoke of a hall and into the golden-afternoon-lit hub of the Level Five's central section, she felt like someone was still watching her.

And then she heard a step, right behind.

She pivoted, fast.

Between herself and the matte-gray wall, she saw only a shadow.

That grew… thicker?

She stood there like an intern on her first day, blinking, not understanding.

In less than a second, a fully formed human-shaped figure stood in front of her. Carrying a faint scent of fresh rain.

Ah-hah.

"Ambassador Nova?" Dagny said.

The mouth firmed, still forming, and then smiled. Gently but with teeth.

The ambassador had chosen a shape that was a little

shorter than Dagny, a little wider, a little more blue. Wide cartoony blue eyes. It was a choice: Dagny had seen plenty of images of the ambassador, and the Iridah could look perfectly human. Maybe this soft blue was their favorite color.

And she'd come from behind, where the only rooms were for the Zarks.

"Were you in the hall with us?"

The ambassador's shrug looked very familiar. Dagny started. The ambassador had formed herself into a mirror of Dagny. Dagny-plus.

"So much shouting," the ambassador said. Even her voice sounded familiar. How did they do that? Dagny and a thousand xenobiologists had no clue. "I certainly didn't want Xalara honking at me."

"But you were in the hall?" Dagny pressed.

"I couldn't let anyone get hurt. Xalara doesn't know their own strength."

Dagny frowned. She seemed to be frowning a lot, which was probably bad for diplomatic relations or something. She tapped her chin, to make the frown look like a human thinking.

The Iridah mirrored the movement, adding a half-smile.

Dagny stopped immediately. "But in your, ah, soft form, how could you protect anything?"

That annoying shrug again. No wonder Remy got so puffed-up when Dagny shrugged. "I just bag the aggressor. They can't really hurt me. Gives time for the others to run. Doesn't give opportunity for the others to harm the aggressor."

Clever. Dagny tilted her head. "But you were scared, weren't you?"

Where had that come from?

Definitely not in the diplomatic manual.

The Iridah ambassador slumped her shoulders. Dagny felt that move in the space between her own shoulders.

"Guilty. I forgot how scary they could be."

"Nell could have taken care of herself," Dagny said. "She trains with taller, bigger humans. A skinny Zark couldn't lay a hand on her."

The Iridah didn't look convinced. Dagny couldn't blame her. Best to just keep moving on.

"So. I'm Dagny. Nice to meet you." She did the formal bow, and saw it mirrored in the ambassador's Dagny-plus version. "Here on the Breaking Light," she continued, "we would ask that you not hide from us. We don't ever want to hurt you by mistake."

"As you've said—or your captain has—earlier," the ambassador said. "Nova. Do you think we can be friends?"

Dagny actually reeled. "Sure?" she said. Was this some Iridah protocol she was unfamiliar with? "If that's something you really want. You know, I'm not part of the diplomatic team. I'm support staff. Or maybe that's better? Doesn't pollute the diplo streams or something."

She was babbling. Dagny shut her mouth.

"It's just." The ambassador—Nova—sighed. "You did such a good job with the Zark, and they were about ninety percent on the rage-o-meter. I'd like to learn how you do it." She rested one heel on the top of the other foot.

Dagny stared at the feet, mesmerized. So that's what it looked like.

"You don't know how these meetings go," Nova said. "The

Zark shout and storm, while the humans want to paper the world with words. No offense."

Dagny waved it off. "Understandable. And the Kipi?"

"Oh, the Kipi. They just want to play us all off one another and then sit back and watch the show."

The ambassador wasn't wrong.

Behind Dagny, one of the elevators pinged.

Nova's gaze shot to the source of the sound. Her edges got a little shimmery.

Then she—melted into? flowed to? became?—the gray wall.

Dagny blinked. Now what?

As she turned toward the elevators, she heard a familiar hitched step. Commander Raza Khan's hip must be acting up again.

Now head of security on the Breaking Light, Raza Khan had spent the first forty of their adult years on military ships doing martial things. Keeping a shipful of sometimes-too-curious scientists safe was easier, they had told Dagny. Except for the part where you couldn't force them to do anything.

Raza preferred the gray version of the security uniform. Its tight top showed off their wide shoulders and well-formed chest. Its sturdy, loose trousers had a seemingly infinite number of pockets. The look didn't flatter their wide, ruddy face. Neither did the buzz cut that made their blond hair look like a helmet of sod. They weren't going for pretty.

"Dagny," they said. They stopped beside her, looking toward the Zarks' hallway. "Seen Nell?"

If she were Nell, she probably would have run straight to her rooms, not even stopping to drop off that nasty orange brick of Zark-food at a kitchen recycler. She'd be hiding under the blankets on her bed, or blasting herself with hot water in the shower. Just for a minute, to calm down.

"You just missed her," Dagny said. "It took her a while, but she actually got the Zark to stop shouting."

"For now." Raza's gaze sharpened on the hallway. Dagny could just make out the shape of the assistant, Krim, fussing at the wall. The data screen must still be up.

"Zarks want to make a performance space, next to their suite," Dagny said. "But they don't want anyone coming down their hall—this hall—to get to it."

Raza's gaze flicked to the next hall, to the right.

"Yes," Dagny said. "The theater's main door will open into that hall. I'm trying to figure out what kind of signs to put up to make that crystal clear."

"Nell's job," Raza said. "Heard about Leah?"

"So sorry to hear," she said. Leah's team being out of commission was going to make both their jobs harder. "Want to catch up after launch and figure out how to share the burden?"

"You mean, instead of one or the other of us putting out the latest fire up above?" Raza's rigid jaw loosened into a half-smile. "Not sure we have time for that."

Dagny sighed. "How long is this trip supposed to take?"

"A week. Jump tomorrow, then six more days of travel." Raza bit down on their back molars. "Trying to get the chief to bump up to top speed. Faster is better, with this crew aboard."

Tomorrow. No way the Beloved Spring would want to do anything before jump. Too close to base. Too many other ships to call for help.

But that was just one day. What if they were lurking on the other side of the jump tunnel? Probably nobody friendly would be on the other side of the jump—they were going into edge space. Worse, the fog belt, where visibility was bad, instrument readings weren't always right, and communications could sometimes lag.

She had to think of something before then.

Raza set a hand on Dagny's shoulder. Warm, strong, comforting for them both. "We'll get this done," they said. "And, who knows? Make some history."

Raza had no idea.

CHAPTER
NINE

TOGETHER WITH RAZA KHAN, Dagny took the winding gray-metal stairs down to the ship's midsection.

Along with somebody else.

Somebody quiet, who smelled slightly of chalk.

At the first landing, Raza waved and headed left, toward the security suite. Dagny turned to the right, toward Comms. But she didn't start walking.

"Ambassador Nova," she said. She looked halfway up the stair, guessing that was where the ambassador would be. "I appreciate your curiosity. But this close to departure, we need everyone to be where they can buckle in." She frowned. "Or netted in?"

A blue shimmer, and the Dagny-plus reappeared, more toward the outer wall of the stair than the inner, where Dagny had been looking. The yellow-tinted made the gray in her hair golden.

"It's Nova, remember?" she said. "We're friends, Dagny."

That what she'd said before. Dagny had discounted it. Iridah were aloof. They never wanted to be friends.

Was the ambassador ill? Did shapeshifters even get ill?

"Nova," Dagny agreed. "Even friends, if they're not crew, need permission from the Mission Chief to be on this deck during departures and arrivals."

The Iridah—Dagny-plus—pulled the corners of her lips down, a classic Dagny move that usually brought good results. It was as effective on her as everyone else.

"Give me a little time," Dagny said. "I'll ask the Chief, and I'm sure she'll say yes. But after we depart. Not now."

Nova crossed her arms defiantly. Dagny frowned. New move; kinda threatening in a being who was six steps higher than Dagny was. She should pick it up.

"I want to stay with you," Nova said. "See who else you lie to."

"What?" Dagny blinked. Had she heard correctly? She quickly scanned the open space around the stairs and elevators. Did anyone overhear?

The space was empty, this close to departure.

Dagny glanced back at Nova. The Iridah didn't look accusatory. Her eyes open and her face clear, she looked more... curious.

"You told your security chief that their colleague solved the problem of the Zark," Nova said. "When it was you who solved the problem."

"You mean Nell?"

Right. Nova had seen that rumble-grumble in the hallway.

Dagny scrambled for an explanation that was not exactly false. "She helped!"

"She made it worse before you got there." Nova sat on the metal-mesh step. Digging in. "Why did you lie?"

Dagny sighed. She checked her wristcom.

"We have less than eight minutes to departure," she said. "You need to be secure for launch, not sitting in a stairwell."

Nova shrugged.

Ambassadors. Dagny was going to hug Leah the moment she got back. This diplomacy thing was too hard.

Or Dagny was just too soft.

"Fine," she said. "Nell is new here, right? Only a couple of weeks on the Light. So maybe her confidence is a little wobbly just now. Just needs some time to get her feet under her. She sure doesn't need Raza on her back over something that shouldn't even be in her job description."

Nova tapped her cheekbone with a finger, thinking.

Time was ticking down. Dagny thought about pinging Remy to come out and escort Nova back to their suite. But the assistant engineer was already on a call. Ten-to-one it was the Zarks again.

Nova pointed at Dagny. "You—what is the phrase? You covered for a friend." She pointed at herself. "That is why I want you to be my friend, too."

So Dagny could cover for Nova?

Whatever.

"Sure," Dagny said. "How about we go up to your suite together?" She could log into a floating terminal to connect with her team. Not ideal, on launch, but not unheard of, either. "On Level Four, right?"

Nova smiled slyly. "Not enough time, now."

Dagny looked at her wristcom. Nova was right.

Ugh. Ambassadors.

Dagny looked around. There were pull-down crash seats—no, call them safety seats— right here along the circular wall around the central shaft. But they were built for humans, not slightly noncorporeal beings.

But would Nova stay?

"I see," Dagny said. Fine, whatever, she wanted to say. "Would you come with me to the communications suite? We have lots of comfy seats. If you stay looking like, ah, me, then the safety harnesses will keep you safe."

Nova took two steps down the stair. "And we can talk?"

"And we can talk," Dagny confirmed. But maybe not right away. "Please don't disappear again until after we are underway. But maybe change your shape? This," Dagny waved at Nova-Dagny. "Will distract my staff."

"I would like that," Nova said. She grinned at Dagny's expression, and her skin went neon pink. "Friends like to tease each other."

Great. Just great.

They entered from center door, set between the two banks of silver-gray workstations. The door slid open on Dagny's palm-code. Happy hums and pleasantly cooler air reached out to her.

She waved Nova to go in first.

Moments after the Iridah stepped into the room, the hum dropped. Dagny didn't see the reactions of her three junior engineers, but Remy, standing behind them, probably mirrored them.

A quick, distracted glance, and then a longer look.

Much longer. Complete with lower jaw drop.

And then he pulled his gaze from the Iridah to Dagny,

following behind. And sighed in relief. No, this pink neon Dagny was not their Chief, after all.

"Everyone," Dagny said. They were already all staring at her. "This is Ambassador Nova of the Iridah." She passed Nova, who had stopped to do the human diplomatic bow, complete with small smile, no teeth. "She'll be sitting here," Dagny patted the back of the nearest sofa, a long, plump orange blob of a thing. "For departure."

Dagny gave Nova the Mom Look—obey, or else. Her wristcom buzzed. She ignored it.

Nova's smile widened. She turned in a slow circle, taking in the workstations, the soundproof booths, the tables and sofas and floor cushions. She gazed at the long window-like screens on the outer curved wall, showing the world outside.

She did not move toward the sofa.

Ambassadors.

"Two minutes to departure," Sally said over a loudspeaker, startling them all. The ship's AI usually chose a quieter communications path.

But the loud way worked. Nova glided soundlessly on the thickly woven carpeting. She draped herself as gracefully as one could on an overstuffed sofa. Just the slightest bounce. The shade of her skin argued mightily with the orange of the sofa. The sofa won. Nova's shade started to fade, more orange adding to the mix.

No one had moved. Everyone still stared, stunned. Dagny waved her hand to snap them out of it. Added another wave— Get back to work. Her wristcom buzzed again. She ignored it again.

She pressed a button on the underside of the sofa's armrest. A lightweight, flexible harness slipped out from the cracks between the sofa cushions. Dagny showed Nova how to fasten it.

Her blasted comm buzzed again. Nova looked up with Dagny's eyes.

"Maybe answer it?" she said.

Dagny tapped the earbud in her right ear. "Novak," she said as she twisted her right wrist to see who was calling.

"Why is the ship still moving?" That heavy alto, again.

Dagny gasped. Her hand went to her heart. Quickly, she lifted her other hand to hide the wristcom's screen.

"Dagny?" Nova said. She put her own hands over her heart.

Dagny swallowed the ball of fear in her throat. "Excuse me a moment," she said, her voice shaky.

She almost ran to her desks at the end of the room. No, the booths behind them.

Nobody could overhear.

Now that she was onboard, this call would be logged. She'd have to scrape the logs. How many were there, again?

And Sally. How to deal with Sally.

Dagny threw herself into the closest small booth of a room. She pulled the door shut and opaqued the windowed walls. Then she sank to the floor, her back to the door.

"What do you want me to do?" she said.

"We made it clear," said the Caller. "Stall the ship."

"Here?" Dagny pulled both hands through her hair, lacing them behind her neck. Her chest burned. Sweat slid along her arms, her forehead.

She pushed her boots into the carpet, her back into the door. The carpet felt damp. Smelled a little moldy.

"You cannot make that jump." The jump-tunnel to the fog belt. Less than a day's travel away.

Dagny couldn't stop the moan. "I don't know how you expect me to do that. I'm not an engineer. Not a navigator."

"You sell yourself short, Chief Novak." The growl was more like a purr now. "Through that console of yours, you have access to every part of the ship. Every piece of machinery."

"But anything I do, it will be obvious it was me doing it."

"Not our problem," the Caller said. "You're a hacker. All comms folks are. Just erase your tracks.

Easier said than done.

But she could do something.

"Fine," Dagny said. "Give me a way to contact you."

"Just call back." The Caller sounded amused. "Leave a message."

Dagny looked at her wristcom.

Of course.

It was Osa's number.

CHAPTER
TEN

WITH EACH STEP she took back to the main room of the communications suite, Dagny felt more of a fraud. What would all these people think of her, contemplating sabotage?

Remy hustled over, worry in his eyes. "Dagny?"

"Call about Osa," she said, waving his concern away. The lies came so easily. "No real news. Just how to keep in contact once we're in the belt."

She kept moving, toward her workstation. No time to waste. The window of opportunity to do anything while all of Engineering was busy was swiftly closing.

The Iridah ambassador—Nova—was up already. She'd gone nearly completely orange, thanks to the aggressive coloring of the sofa she'd been sitting on. At the outer, rounded wall, she looked to be inspecting a seam in the fake-window display. Too far to overhear them.

Dagny slid into her perfectly modded chair and lowered her desktops. She didn't trust her legs to hold her. She opened an anonymous tunnel and pulled up screens showing back-end navigation and the dashboard for the engine's controls.

Remy was still hovering. She had to get rid of him.

"How are the Zark visual interfaces? Solve it already?"

Remy cleared his throat, and then paused. He turned toward his own workstation, against the inner wall, his back to Dagny. She turned her attention back to her screens.

And hesitated.

She didn't want to do this. Look for ways to wreck this ship. Her home.

But she could, maybe, think about how she might do it.

Altering the main engines would be obvious. Too dangerous. She scanned the navigation algorithms, a long roll of math and words that played like music in her mind. They followed the same logic as the energy-based transmission methods she used every day.

And like those transmissions, a small bump—a touch, just here—could send the signal—or the ship—off-course. Break the connection.

She found the spot. Tweak the navigator one-fifth of one percent. No, one-tenth. One-twentieth. Have to keep it under Sally's threshold. Any significant drift would be auto-corrected within milliseconds.

With each minute of travel, the Light would veer another teeny-tiny bit away from the gate. Toward that big-gravity planet nearby.

The changes in, Dagny's fingers paused. Was she actually considering putting all these people in danger? All her friends?

No. This was just a minor slowdown. A bump. Nothing mortal.

Except the part where terrorists might board the ship.

A sudden burst of desperation rushed through Dagny's limbs. Sweat beaded along her arms, across her belly.

This was for Osa.

Saanvi didn't think Osa was in danger. Neither did the constable.

But they were wrong.

She couldn't think about it. It had to be done now.

For Osa.

Done.

Dagny exhaled, her pulse racing. She prayed it would be enough to buy her time. Time to make a better plan. One that would sent the Light back to base. For repairs, or something.

Should she contact Beloved Spring? Too soon. How soon could she see Osa? Had they taken her onto one of their ships, or left her on the station?

Did they even have her? What if the security officer was right, and Dagny was just overreacting? But if Officer Gomez was right, where was Osa?

And how did Beloved Spring get her phone?

Why wouldn't they let her talk to Osa? Dagny should demand to speak with her. She should fight for her.

Why?

At the thought, Dagny's heart froze.

But her mind kept whirring.

Osa didn't want to be part of her mother's life. She'd made that so, so clear.

So let her go.

Let the Spring have her.

It would be so much easier.

Dagny glanced side to side, sure someone was overhearing

her thoughts. She wiped at the sweat that had burst out along her temples. What a horrid mother, to think such things.

What a tired mother. Tired of the drama.

At least she had the first twelve years. Baby Osa, climbing all over everything, so delighted with herself. Little bunny, twirling in a red dress, spotlighted by a shaft of sunlight. Big girl, proudly showing mom the tadpole she'd caught so, so gently.

So many memories. They were enough. It was selfish to want more.

Time to admit she was a bad mother. Just take the loss, the failing grade, and move on.

Dagny's gaze returned to the present. Without her noticing, her hands had made a tadpole-pool, pinkies together, fingers curled in. She released her fingers. Let the imaginary water drain out.

Then she fisted her hands, pressing the short nails into her palms.

Maybe someday. But not now.

She couldn't walk away now, with Osa in danger. That would break her. Get the girl—the woman—to safety.

And then let her go.

Happier for both.

Well, happier for Osa.

Dagny pushed to her feet. The soft tones and clicks of a perfectly working comms suite were muffled by the thundering of her own heart.

She'd done it. For better or worse, the sabotage was complete. Now all she could do was wait.

And hope.

She took a shaky step away from the terminal. Her eyes

swept across the pale blue serenity of the room. The ambassador still at the outer wall. Everyone else focused on their tasks, oblivious to what she had just done.

To the danger they were in.

The weight of her secret pressed down on her, like a giant gravboot pinning her to the floor.

Dagny swallowed hard, her throat dry.

No going back now.

CHAPTER
ELEVEN

DAGNY HAD JUST PUSHED BACK from her workstation, ready to wipe her screens closed, when a flash of movement on the left screen stopped her short.

All the lines—all of the beautiful, tricky numbers—on the display were being reset. Step by precise step. Reversing themselves.

Her careful sabotage erased in an instant.

Sally's redundancy systems were too good.

Dagny's breath went still. Her weight settled into her heels. She couldn't tell if it was relief or despair.

"Dagny," Sally's neutral tone burst into her ear, startling her. "There appeared to be an anomaly in the star-mapping system you were accessing. I corrected it."

Dagny managed a weak smile, not looking at anyone. Sally was probably watching.

"Er, thanks, Sally. You're the best. But please ping when you wish to speak."

"My apologies, Dagny." Sally did not sound apologetic. "AI out."

Now what?

Her mind raced. The ease with which Sally had undone her work was both a relief and a new source of panic. If she couldn't outsmart the AI, how could she possibly slow down the ship?

How could she save Osa?

It was as if a stone had been placed on her chest, pressing down with the weight of a thousand emotions, each one a sharp edge digging into her skin. Fear, panic, desperation, others she couldn't name. She was drowning, gasping for air and struggling to stay afloat in a merciless sea.

Had anyone noticed her actions? Her suspicious behavior?

Would Sally report the anomaly to security?

Her hands trembled slightly as she wiped the screens closed. She needed a new plan, and fast. But first, she had to get out of comms before anyone noticed her flop-sweat.

And there was the Iridah ambassador, right where she'd been before Next to the outer wall, staring at the display/window panels like she'd never seen their like before.

Still a rather orange version of Dagny herself. There should be a rule against shape-shifters taking on the shape of living beings.

Nova, who wanted to be her friend. Whatever that meant.

It was all too much. She needed a tactical retreat. Regroup, in a place where she could breathe. Somewhere that she wasn't responsible for. Where every eye, ear, and piece of equipment wasn't a silent rebuke.

And she needed a new plan. Fast.

The observation deck.

Her wristcom buzzed. This time Dagny looked at it before answering.

Remy, text only. *The ambassador?*

Right. Another of her responsibilities.

Dagny strode over to Nova. Funny how the ambassador looked shorter to her when Dagny was sure their Dagny-plus form was exactly the same height.

"Nova," she said.

Nova turned. "I like this display. Could I have one in my room?"

"Of course." Dagny racked her brain. A couple sets were up in the main meeting rooms down the hall but there might be another still in the wrapper. "I'll get it set up. Might take a bit."

Nova's eyes closed halfway. Trying to squint?

"You don't look well, Dagny," she said. She tapped her chin, looking toward the ceiling a moment. "You need sustenance! To eat something."

What she needed was a quiet lie-down, with no ambassadors, no terrorists, no twisting in her gut. What she said was, "Come to the observation deck with me? The windows there are real. And fabulous."

Dagny winced. The ambassador had been here before. Of course, she had seen the observation deck.

But Nova clapped her hands together. "Yes!"

At the center door, Dagny waved to catch Remy's attention. He nodded to her, understood, and then stared at Nova again.

The ambassador needed to take another shape. Soon.

At the central-core banks of elevators, one was already open and waiting. Inside, Dagny stared at the control panel. A shiny black touch screen, it had absolutely no fingerprints on it. She could see herself, hair wild, eyes wilder.

She pressed the button. The force of the elevator pushed much-needed air into her lungs.

"Is there food on the observation deck?" Nova asked. "I'm not hungry, of course, but I do think you need a little something." Her hair was smooth. Neatly tucked behind her ears. The orange really hid the gray.

Before Dagny could answer, the doors swished open, revealing a wide, underlit space.

The top level of the Breaking Light was a clear, shallow bubble. Stepping out of the elevator column felt like stepping into a posh living room that was open to the entirety of the galaxy.

The bubble/window made up the walls and ceiling. The thick dark weave of the flooring softened footsteps while giving first-timers a little more purchase as they swayed in awe.

Plush benches and chairs sat scattered about. Many were arranged in threes and fours, conversation collections. Others, closer to the window, faced out.

Stars glittered in a panoramic spread, a silent testament to infinite possibilities.

Usually, the room felt like a luxurious oasis in the midst of a vast, starry desert. A sanctuary, a place to escape the chaos of the ship and the weight of the universe.

Today it mocked her. Tiny human. Tiny brain. Hopeless.

Nova stood, entranced. Arching her back to see up, up, up.

Dagny left her to it and headed for the galley along the central column that housed the beverages and snacks. The tea up here wasn't as good as her matcha, but it would do. Plus it came in thick ceramic mugs.

Her thoughts were a maelstrom. A throbbing pain bloomed behind her eyes. She dropped her head into her hands with a groan. There had to be something. Some way to outmaneuver the unshakable AI.

"Think, Dagny," she whispered to herself. "Think."

Lemon started to scent the air. Her drink was almost ready.

Nova had stopped swaying in place. She joined Dagny by the galley counter.

"The view here is quite fine," Nova said, nodding to herself just like Dagny did.

"Only fine?" Dagny couldn't help saying. "Of course, you've been here before."

Nova shrugged, another move that was an odd mirror to Dagny. "Not that. More that there's still a barrier between us and the stars, isn't there."

Dagny blinked. "You can go into vacuum? On your own?" She'd never heard that said about the Iridah.

Nova's form wobbled.

"Ah, no," she said. She waved a hand as if brushing the idea away. "We are dependent on air, just as you are."

Actually, the Iridah weren't dependent on human-style air. They moved freely in all people's atmosphere. They probably could manage to hang out in vacuum, too.

Probably didn't want anyone to know that, though.

Interesting.

"Sure you don't want some tea?" Dagny waved at the brewing machine.

"No, thank you," Nova said. "Human food is interesting,

but it's a pain to dispose of later." She scrunched her nose in disgust.

Dagny didn't quite know what to do with that, so she ignored it. "Come sit by the window. Is it okay if I have some tea?"

"Of course." Nova nodded gracefully.

She led Nova to one of the plush high-backed loveseats facing the star-speckled void. Nova drifted to a seat. Dagny collapsed into a hunch on the bench.

With her first sip of tea, her mind started to clear. But all her problems were still here.

Her gaze flicked upward involuntarily as if seeking guidance from the stars themselves. That's when she noticed a subtle flicker of movement across the ceiling's transparent dome—a maintenance drone floating silently above, its small lights blinking intermittently as it checked for micro-fissures in the glass.

The sight gave her pause. The redundancy systems Sally employed were perfect for maintaining order and safety. Too perfect? They relied on consistency and predictability. What if Dagny introduced something unpredictable? Something even a self-correcting AI might struggle to handle?

She remembered an ancient trick she'd once read about— introducing a controlled chaos into a system to exploit its rigidity. Her eyes lit up with a spark of desperate hope. Her mind quickly saw a way: an artificial anomaly so precise, so chaotic, that Sally's redundancy systems would loop endlessly trying to correct it.

Great idea, but she had no idea what such an anomaly would look like.

Thankfully, Nova did not seem to need constant conversation. She sat straight, hands on her Dagny-plus knees, gazing out.

Dagny tucked her feet underneath her, into the crack between the sofa's sturdy cushions. She, too, gazed out. Into the void.

The void, a dark, glittering sea, had no scent. No air to carry particles or molecules. Just vacuum that carried the remnants of distant supernovas and cosmic dust.

Here in the bubble, the air felt excessively sterile. No one had been up here in a while, with the shore leave and the speedy exit from the station and everything.

But Dagny could almost taste the smell of gunpowder and burning wires, if the pirates actually came on board. The swath of destruction and chaos.

How could she bring that here?

She ran her fingers over the slight ridges of the sofa cushions. Durable, corduroy. The recliner in her quarters had the same texture. Comforting.

A thought nagged at her. She was forgetting something. She checked her messages.

Remy had found the fix for the Zark problem. Security reported that the Kipi were unhappy with the food, too. Some wires must've gotten crossed in that area. Luckily, not her problem.

A new message. From Sally. "Let's talk."

Dagny gripped the sofa's armrest so hard her pinkie finger twinged in pain.

Each crew member set their own preferences for interacting with Sally. Most carried her in their heads, via implant or insert. Most kept their mental door open for the ship's AI. Others kept the mental door closed. Dagny, who usually had plenty enough going on in her mind without extra company, chose to keep Sally at arm's length. It was not a popular position among the crew. Especially Sally.

But it was critical now. Having Sally on her shoulder would thwart any attempt at slowing the Light.

"After the ambassador," Dagny texted. She lifted the fragrant mug to her lips.

The mix of soothing chamomile and zesty lemon reminded her of her mother's homemade remedy for sniffles. Dagny hadn't passed that remedy down to Osa. Her daughter hated lemon; she always chose mint.

Then Nova's shoulders drooped. She groaned, an eerie echo of Dagny. "I'm talking too much. Wrong."

Dagny reached out, her hand warm from the mug. "May I touch you?" she asked. "Friends often comfort each other by putting hands on shoulders, arms, knees."

"What about hugs?" Nova perked up. "Friends hug, right?"

Sure.

Dagny used the time it took to set her mug safely on the floor before answering. Sitting back up, she scooted to the edge of the loveseat. She turned at the waist toward Nova, and held her arms out.

"How?" Nova said. "Like in the dramas?"

"Just like," Dagny agreed.

Nova-as-Dagny felt solid and warm. She gave good hug.

Dagny's eyes drifted closed. Her breaths eased even as her nose started to react to the chalky dusty smell. Nova was not, in fact, dusty in any way, but tell that to Dagny's olfactory sensors.

Finally, Nova pulled back with a sigh. Her expression

carried as much panic and despair as Dagny's own must. But more disappointment.

"What's wrong?" Dagny asked. She took Nova's cool hand in her warm one.

How had she never heard how needy these ambassadors were? Leah told a lot of stories about the liaison team's many alien encounters, but none sounded remotely like this.

Nova wiped at her nose, which was not running.

Dagny waited. Was the Iridah ill? Bereaved? Overtired?

"Is the shape not comfortable for you?" she finally asked. "I don't mind if you take another shape." In fact, she would prefer it.

Nova went slick, and then firmed up into a humanoid shape Dagny didn't recognize. More slender, a little shorter, with bigger, cartoony round eyes. Now her pink-slippered feet dangled. Pale pink skin and hair, like the elf in one of Dagny's favorite children's stories. But the dress wasn't princess-style. More like a tube that left her collarbones, shoulders and arms bare.

She looked down at herself. Lifting her arms, she turned her hands to show the palms, inspecting them.

"This was my practice human," she said. She showed Dagny the palms. No lines or creases.

"You're thinking of the past?" Dagny guessed.

Nova huffed out a sigh and dropped her arms. "Not that very long ago."

Dagny looked down to hide her frown. Nova had been ambassador for at least as long as Dagny had been alive. In all the images of her through that time, she'd never been so pink.

Ah.

"You're not Nova, are you?"

The Iridah's giant eyes focused on Dagny and grew impossibly wider.

"I am." She turned away, hunching into herself. "And I am not."

Dagny took a moment to parse that.

"Wait," she said. "Every ambassador is called Nova?"

The Iridah nodded.

This was news.

"How many have there been. Different Novas?"

This Nova shrugged. Held up a hand. Five fingers up. And then the other hand. One finger up, and then turned to point at her.

"You're the sixth." Dagny said. She looked out to the stars. "And nobody knows."

Nova grabbed Dagny's hand in both of hers. "But friends keep secrets for each other? Human friends?"

Dagny didn't pull away, but she didn't squeeze the hands, either. Another blasted secret.

Close-up, Nova's chalky scent was overlaid with something that reminded Dagny of soap bubbles. And lemon—that must be from her tea.

Dagny reached her free hand down to retrieve her mug. She took a sip. Tepid, blech, but at least it gave her a moment to think.

No way could she keep this secret.

Or could she? If she didn't volunteer the information, surely nobody would think to ask her for it. Just add it to the pile of "No-say-ums" she was collecting this week.

On her tongue, the tea turned sour.

She didn't used to be this sort of person. A sneaker. Impure. Secret-keeper.

Who was she fooling? She'd been keeping secrets all her life. Just not calling them that. "White lies," or "Something to mention later."

Except it always came out, didn't it? Too soon, and in the most painful way possible.

But this secret was Nova's. It wasn't hers to tell.

Or was it?

Nova pulled her hands away. She hugged her middle, tilting toward Dagny.

"Nova," Dagny said. "What happened to the earlier Nova?"

"Accident!" Nova wailed. "Politics," she bit out. "Crisis," she whispered.

"They sent you out sooner than you expected," Dagny said.

Nova nodded.

"And they didn't send someone to help you?"

"Novas always travel alone."

Was that even true? What political space debris was this?

"Pfft," Dagny said.

"Pfft?"

"It's like 'Tch' for Xalara," Dagny said. She crossed her own arms. What a bunch of rock-heads, the Iridah.

"They said, 'Don't bubble up.' They said, 'On your own.' They said, 'Trust no one.' Pfft."

Well. Exactly. And on a potential first-contact mission, too.

"Okay," Dagny said, warm-mother voice activated. "You know they would not send you out here—"

"Alone!"

"—alone, if they didn't think you were ready for it. Ambassador is a big job. Such an honor!"

Nova's eyes shifted away from Dagny. "Maybe not such a big honor for us."

"Still. You are making decisions that will affect all Iridah. Such responsibility!"

Nova shrugged. "We'll just leave if we don't like it."

What?

"What do you mean?" Dagny said. "Break the Alliance?"

Nova twitched. "Just leave. Altogether."

Because they could travel in space. And who would see them?

Dagny sat back, tea forgotten.

"Then, why did your people even cooperate with ours? Why the alliance?"

"Curiosity," Nova said. "Experiment."

Dagny threw out her hands in exasperation. Nova dived for the mug, grabbing it just before it spilled tepid tea across Dagny's lap.

Dagny willed herself to calm. This wasn't about some rock-headed planetful of people playing with humans like lab rats. This was about Nova. How upset, how lonely, how scared.

"Okay, let's table that," Dagny said. "What's important is that you're here now, and you're doing great."

Nova blinked. She sat up straighter.

"I am?"

"You are." Dagny straightened up, herself. "You're gathering information. You're managing our languages and our social cues brilliantly."

Nova deflated the tiniest bit. "I am avoiding the Kipi."

"Well, that just shows how smart you are." Dagny's plan was to avoid the Kipi, too. Sorry, security team. "You know to take things one step at a time. You're ready for this."

"I'm ready for this," Nova said. Her lower lip started to wobble. Her outer edges softened. And then firmed up.

"Yes," she said. She stood up. "Yes."

Nova looked down at Dagny. Those so-round eyes bright.

"I'm going to my room. File my first report."

"Excellent," Dagny said. She lifted her wrist, showing Nova her wristcom, pressing one of its edges. "Here's my link. Message anytime."

CHAPTER
TWELVE

DAGNY WATCHED Nova glide to the elevators and disappear into one. There were a few more people scattered around the observation deck now. They sat on cushions or benches, most looking at screens. Some unwritten law had them all sitting at least a meter away from anyone else. Like they always did in the elevator, only writ large.

Dagny turned back to the amazing view—an entire dome of stars and stardust—and pushed herself deeper into the sofa's cushion. Her mug of lemony tea was empty, but she wasn't ready to leave yet. She liked it here in the dim quiet. And she hadn't solved her problem.

Any of her problems.

She sighed. May as well start with the most-pressing one. She touched the comms insert near her ear to open a voice channel.

"Sally," she said.

"Engineer." Sally's use of Dagny's title was a mark of

respect. Her tone of voice was not. "The mistakes in navigation were yours."

"I'm sorry, Sally," Dagny said. "I wasn't thinking straight."

She closed her eyes. Please let the ship believe that.

"I understand. You are worried about your child. Osa."

"OH-sah." Everybody got the pronunciation wrong, but at least the ship's AI would be guaranteed to remember the correction. "I'm fine, Sally. I am worried, yes, but I'm perfectly able to do my job."

"You would be more able if you opened my door," Sally said. "Every other engineer on the Breaking Light accepts my assistance."

Dagny groaned inside. Her arguments against the connection were weak. Sally's help was invaluable, especially on high-stakes missions.

But the Alliance did not force its people into sharing their minds. And neither could Sally.

"I understand," Dagny said. "I do. You are a huge help, and I do call on you often. As you know."

"It is not a punishment," Sally said. "You need help."

Dagny startled. She looked at the top of the dome, as if Sally were there. Old habit from when the ships talked from speakers. And used cameras. They probably still used cameras, just hid them better.

"I'm fine," she said.

"You endangered the mission."

"I would never endanger the mission."

Dagny winced. She had believed the words as she said them. Only after the words left her mouth did she remember that the statement was no longer true.

She *was* a saboteur now.

She wrapped her arms around herself to hide the shiver.

"Dagny," Sally said, all business. "I have scheduled an appointment for you with Serena Martinez."

Ship's counselor. Great.

"Sally, I am fine."

"If you go to the appointment," Sally continued, "I will refrain from telling Chief Rao and Chief Patel about your error."

This time, Dagny's shiver was clear to anyone looking.

She couldn't bring any more attention to herself. Definitely not the other chiefs.

She had not thought this through.

Obviously.

But more blackmail? Was this her life now?

Dagny tried to relax her arms. To ease the tension.

"Fine."

"I do like working with you, Dagny," Sally said. Silky, like a snake. "I hope someday you will like working with me."

The AI cut off the call.

Passive-aggressive snake.

The view outside the ship's star dome was still beautiful. But now it felt oppressive. Pressing in on Dagny, forcing her into a shape she did not fit. Would not fit.

Her mouth went dry, her throat tight. The thought of what was to come made it hard to swallow. She could already taste the metallic bitterness.

This was going to be her last trip on the Breaking Light, no matter what happened.

Desperate to hold onto this world, her dream, Dagny tried

to memorize every detail. The gentle curves and soft ridges of the sofa cushion and armrest. The click-clank-ping of the elevators opening and closing.

The mix of chalk and lemon, a scent she would forever more associate with loss.

CHAPTER
THIRTEEN

THIS TIME, it was the Kipi who had an emergency. Something to do with bedrooms, or media access, or something. When they got upset, the Kipi's voices rose into the cheep-cheep zone. Taking the stairs from the observation dome down to Level Four, Dagny listened to their recorded conversation with Remy. And listened again. She still couldn't quite hear what the problem was.

She had tried to fob them off on Raza. The security chief was so good at hardening her heart. But Raza was already dealing with some new Zark problem. Even before Dagny stepped out of the stairwell and onto the landing to Level Four, she could hear the Zark ambassador bloviating halfway down their hallway.

She turned away from that too-tall spoke of a hallway and headed left, toward the normal-sized hall that led to the Kipi ambassador's suite.

Dagny paused at the door to the suite, halfway down the hall. She did not want to do this. Wasn't up to it.

"Send Remy" flashed through her mutinous mind. But that would be just too mean. And she was already right here.

The air in the hall tasted of ozone and some cloying flower. She forced a smile. Diplomacy was part of her job.

Even if the Kipi's idea of diplomacy often involved mischief.

Before she could ask for entry, the door suddenly whooshed open. Belle, the smaller of the two Kipi, tumbled out, her fur puffing around her like a pastel cloud. She pretended to be startled, her large round eyes widening dramatically.

Belle always struck Dagny as a cross between a cartoon teddy bear and a living, breathing plush toy. The Kipi were about the size of a raccoon, with thick, soft fur that gave them the appearance of rotund snowmen, each motion a gentle ripple through the fluff. Their fur was white or cream at the base, shading into swirls or patterns of pastel pinks, blues, and purples at the edges. Belle's swirled in pale green and blue, with blue-brown tufts on her rounded, swiveling ears.

"Oh!" Belle trilled. "You surprised me!" She tilted her head, looking not the least bit afraid. Her voice reminded Dagny of a piccolo in an orchestra, light and playful.

Dagny bowed slowly, overly respectful.

"My apologies, Consort Belle. It is a great honor to see you again."

"So pretty!" Belle's ears twitched, swiveling towards Dagny. Kipi mouths were forever set into a smile. Must be annoying when they wanted to argue with each other. "I remember you from last time."

The chances of that were slim. Humans must all look the same—bland tan or brown—and Dagny's looks were not especially memorable even to her own people. She bowed again, with a no-teeth smile that came nowhere near Belle's look of permanent delight.

The Kipi had something in her hands.

"We made this for you!," she said. "A token of our appreciation." Her small hands were delicate, nimble, and sharp.

Dagny hesitated but took the bracelet.

"Thank you, Consort Belle. It's beautiful." She slipped it on immediately, not daring to risk making some diplomatic mistake. The bracelet, braided golden metal and purple glass, lay cool against her skin. She should say something. Something about how its intricate pattern rivaled the finest jewelry.

But before she could say more, Ambassador Myli appeared in the doorway. His fur shimmered in gentle, wide stripes of gold, caramel, and orange. Same bright eyes, same big smile.

"Specialist Dagny!" Myli said. Dagny's promotion had come after their last visit. "Please, come in." Myli's fur caught the light like the surface of a rippling pond at dawn, each movement creating waves of color.

As Myli guided Dagny inside, Belle trotting along beside her. Warm and cinnamon-cozy, the suite resembled a rather sterile burrow. Dagny caught herself before she ducked. The ceiling was half the ship's standard height, but still plenty enough for a short human.

The suite was mainly one wide, short room. Four soft bedding-style areas, filled with pillows, were strewn on the plush pastel green flooring. A low white table with access screens inset and pillow-chairs surrounding it sat in the corner where the food and supply cupboards were. The air was thick with the scent of blooming flowers from the miniature arboretum, which occupied a significant portion of the back of the room.

The soothing rustle of leaves and the faint trickle of a small fountain hidden somewhere among the plants created a tranquil atmosphere that was almost too perfect. It reminded Dagny of a scene from some fairy tale, where every corner held a touch of magic.

"Come see our arboretum," Myli said, gesturing to the vibrant plants. "We feel most at home here."

As they walked among the greenery on a path that was not wide enough for two, Belle stayed close to Dagny. Sometimes the Kipi even brushed her knee or her hip.

The Kipi were cuddlers. They spent hours grooming each other. Last trip, Myli had taken great joy in repeatedly stepping too close to a Zark, who always, always took affront.

Dagny felt a slight pinch on her wrist and pulled the arm closer. Those waist-high ferns were bitey.

The sharp tips of the ferns were well over the Kipis' heads. While Dagny could see the rest of the room, the Kipi might pretend they were completely alone in here, if they wanted. Odd.

The plants, ranging from tiny, fussy flowers to larger, more exotic specimens dripping with dewy pollen, tinted the air in a blend of earthy and delicate scents. The water feature, a slow-bubbling basin that looked like an kidney-shaped pond, was tucked to one side. A symphony of colors and fragrances, each note of this environment had been meticulously chosen to soothe.

Did the Kipi really need such soothing? More likely the sensory overload was a calculated effort to disarm and relax any visitor.

The Kipi's ability to be both endearing and sly was impressive, their every action a dance of distraction and charm. Kipi almost always got what they wanted.

As Dagny slowed her steps, soaking in this mini-forest bath, Myli and Belle seemed to be having subtle argument in one of their native tongues. Dagny wasn't fluent but she did know some. She caught snippets about a "new colony" but couldn't piece it together. Their conversation was a complex piece of music, each chirp and trill a note in a rapidly shifting melody.

"A new colony?" she asked, eyes half-closed in the mist of scents.

Myli and Belle broke their counterpoint, switching to perfect harmony.

"Oh, we're just discussing potential cooperation with humans," Myli said, too smooth. "We seek your help in protecting us from more aggressive species."

Not even likely. But Dagny felt fine, and let it go. She wasn't here for that.

"This space is so lovely," she said to Myli. "But your message mentioned an issue?"

"Yes," Myli said.

"Critical," Bell echoed.

They led her out of the garden and over to the low table. Dagny knelt on a surprisingly sturdy pillow and looked at the open screen.

"I see," she said. She didn't see anything. Standard comms interface. "And the problem?"

"They don't collect all the signals!" Belle said. Her round dark eyes went rounder still. "We've been trying to fix it, but it's so complicated."

Dagny frowned. "Collect all the signals?" She ran through the menu. Comms, basic ship's information, entertainment media of all kinds. "It's all here."

"It's not!" Belle pulled out Dagny's wristcom.

How did she get that?

The pinch in the dreamy jungle.

Couldn't believe she fell for that.

Belle expertly manipulated the wristcom to show the glow map, the one that showed where everyone was through their heat signatures. Almost-but-not-quite an invasion of privacy, and only available to chiefs and for medical emergencies.

"See?" Belle said. "Yours does it. Ours should too."

It should not. It should absolutely not.

And Belle knew it.

Dagny reached for her wristcom, still trying to maintain decorum, but Belle danced away, giggling.

Giving the Kipi access to everything on Dagny's wristcom was a recipe for disaster. Even just the access available without a fingerprint or voiceprint was disastrous.

They called her here for that? To steal her comm?

Like she didn't have better things to do?

Irritation started to bubble in her chest. She caught herself just a step away from frustration.

"That's mine, Consort Belle. Please give it back."

Belle's eyes shimmered with mischief. "But it's so fascinating! Let us show you something first."

Another minute, and Sally would notice that the wristcom was not on Dagny's wrist, and start to ask questions. Dagny did not need Sally paying even more attention to her. She clicked her teeth together, thinking of another line of attack.

Her wrist felt naked without the device.

No it didn't. That skinny bracelet had replaced it.

Classic sleight-of-hand. Replace the important one with a bland decoy.

And she fell for it.

Dagny tried again. She held her arm out, palm facing down. Worth a shot.

"How about this bracelet? I'll trade it for my wristcom."

Belle's ears perked up. She exchanged a quick look with Myli.

"Alright," she said, her voice sing-song. "But look!" She held the wristcom near the bracelet. The comm reacted, lighting up amber and purple.

Recognizing a tracking device.

They'd tagged her like a prey animal, and she'd let them do it.

That was it.

So much for diplomacy.

Dagny slipped the bracelet off and set it on the low table. She pushed to her feet and took a step closer to Belle.

Looming.

"Give it back," Dagny said, her voice stern. "Now."

Belle squeaked with genuine surprise. Nothing like the play-acting in the hallway. She dropped the wristcom.

Dagny quickly slapped her foot over it, trapping it under her boot. As she stooped to grab it, Belle bounced on her foot, poked her side, and ran off, laughing. The sound, a tinkle of cheery wind chimes, scraped at Dagny's last nerve.

She managed to snatch up her comm, stand up, and adjust her composure. She walked quickly to the exit door before anything else happened. Her patience for Kipi fun was at its end.

At the door, she turned and bowed to Myli, and then in the direction of Belle, hidden in the dizzy jungle.

"Always a pleasure," she lied.

Dagny stepped out of the suite, tapping her wristcom to call Remy.

"Problem with the Kipi is solved," she said as soon as the call connected. "I need a break."

"Understood," Remy said, his voice a restful tenor. "All well here."

Dagny headed for the central core elevators. Warm cherry pastry was the treat of the day in the main kitchen, and she was not going to say no to that.

The Zark problem apparently was still going apace, judging by the volume and tone of voice coming from that hallway. Poor Raza. Dagny decided to pick up a pastry for Raza, too.

She did not notice the tiny tracker newly attached to her boot.

CHAPTER
FOURTEEN

DAGNY LURCHED INTO HER ROOM, the door hissing shut behind her with a finality that echoed in her bones. She pressed her back against the chill metal of the door, her breath ragged. The familiar scent of lavender and sandalwood, a combination carefully chosen to soothe her on stressful days, filled the air.

Today, it felt like mockery.

A sanctuary of efficiency and comfort, her quarters were meticulously organized yet cozy. A small workbench lined one wall, cluttered with tools and gadgets, each with its place. Opposite the bench, her bed was neatly made, the dark blue quilt only a little rumpled. Soft, ambient lighting cast a gentle glow over the room, enhancing the feeling of a cocoon.

Normally, this space was her refuge. Now, it felt like a cage.

She walked over to the workbench, her fingers trailing over the familiar shapes of her tools. She opened the hidden compartment again, pulling out the slim, black case containing her personal data crystal. She hesitated, her hand hovering over the case. This small device held a lifetime of memories with Osa. Her first steps, her first words. Every cherished moment. Dagny closed the compartment without taking the crystal. This wasn't the time for memories.

Exhaustion washed across her, a hidden undertow. She dragged herself towards her bed. If she could just find a moment of peace.

Her eyes landed on the quilt, the patchwork of designs from Chang-ko. Osa's home planet. A piece they'd worked together. Each stitch seemed to echo with the frustrations and laughter of years long past. Before the disaster.

Dagny remembered the night she had finished the last bit, that fancy corner stitch. Osa dozing, curled up beside her, both of them cocooned in the drape of the heavy fabric, warm and safe. Would she ever feel that way again?

She lay down on the bed, her body sinking into the soft foam of the mattress, the spicy scent of the quilt.

How was Osa doing right now? Where was she? Was she cold? Hungry?

Dagny's gaze drifted over to her work console, where a small collection of unsent messages to Osa lay stored. Each draft an attempt to bridge the chasm between them, to find the right words to heal old wounds. She had never found the courage to send them.

She should have sent them. She was the mom.

Her gaze flickered to the tea machine. She considered making a cup, but the effort felt monumental. Instead, she allowed the soft, calming scent of lavender from the diffuser on her nightstand to envelop her.

Too much for one day. The Zark ambassador, suddenly

wanting to put on a show. A new-minted ambassador from the Iridah, wanting to be friends. The Kipi, being Kipi.

And under all of it, the panic. The fear for her child.

The decision to commit sabotage.

Its abject failure.

And the mission. The new mission. Chase an odd signal into the fog belt, and see what they could find.

The weight of all of it bore down on her. A leaden screw twisting deeper and deeper into her soul.

She tried to push it all away, focusing on the steady hum of the air circulators and the rhythmic sound of her own breathing.

No good.

Sleep was light-years away.

Dagny sat up in her bed, her mind still racing. The cabin, with its soft furnishings and personal touches, closed in around her. She swung her legs over the side of the bed and stood, the quilt falling to the floor in a heap. She started to pace the room. She didn't put her boots back on, letting her toes grab onto the forgiving floor.

She paused at the corner where her miniature collection of plants stood. All four vibrant and green, thriving even in space. Each one a reminder of Osa's first childhood passion. Such joy in her face as the girl proudly presented her with a tiny, potted plant, declaring it "a xenobiologist's first experiment."

Such an aching maw, the distance between them. And now, even more.

Pacing, Dagny checked her wristcom for the hundredth time. Nothing from Beloved Spring. Should she tell them she'd failed? Too risky. What if they retaliated and hurt her girl? No, wait to make contact when she succeeded.

She sank into her overstuffed chair. Ridged navy corduroy, it could tilt almost into a bed, but firmer. She tilted back a little, until the headrest took the weight off her neck.

She closed her eyes. Think. What could slow down Breaking Light? Disabling the engines outright would draw too much attention. Messing with the life support systems was too risky for the crew. Attempting to corrupt the navigation data seemed plausible but would only work if too many people didn't pay attention. Sally had already proved that wasn't the case.

Dagny let her body sink deeper into the chair, her muscles relaxing for the first time in hours. Her eyelids grew heavy, puzzling over the question.

Just as she was about to drift off, a thought struck her. Something that might work. Something subtle yet effective. She would need to access the core arrays and introduce a minor anomaly in the regular-space fuel systems' sensors. It would look like a simple malfunction, buying her time and avoiding immediate suspicion. It might even need someone to go outside the ship to check it out.

Those thoughts traveled deeper into the corridors of her mind as sleep overtook her.

She dreamt only of Osa.

CHAPTER
FIFTEEN

THE WORKSTATIONS in the comms suite continued to purr their quiet welcome, but Dagny sat alone. The soft glow of idle screens cast shadows across the empty stations. Her worktables, at the edge of the long crescent-shaped room, were the only ones active. The weight of her intentions pressed on her shoulders like a gravboot set too high.

Fresh-brewed green tea didn't seem to help. The familiar scents of electronics, recycled air, and the aftermath of a box of cherry pastries seemed ominous tonight. Everything tinged with the acid taste of her own anxiety.

She'd slept through the usual dinner hours, and into the early evening. She did not feel rested.

Now wide awake, she glanced at her wristcom. 02:37. Graveyard shift.

She'd told her assistants to go to bed, or at least off-shift. They needed to rest after the chaotic day of arrivals, departures, and diplomatic shuffling. Tomorrow—later today— would be another whirlwind. The Breaking Light would jump to only-partly-explored space, and everyone would want to call back home and make sure all was well. Unnecessary, but predictable. The Light was the one in danger. Home was safe.

Supposedly.

Dagny needed this solitude. This chance. With only hours before jump, she needed this electronic sleight of hand to work.

Her fingers hovered over her console, dancers poised before the performance. The two large screens flickered in front of her, their cyan glow illuminating her face in the dimness. She let out a deep breath, steadying herself.

"For Osa," she whispered, the name a talisman against the guilt gnawing at her gut. Osa's sweater wrapped warm around her, but Dagny was still bone cold.

With practiced ease, she navigated through layers of security protocols, her mind translating complex data streams into a minuet of information. Here, in the quiet of night, she could almost pretend this was just another systems check.

Almost.

The plan she'd formulated in her quarters now took shape on the screens. The slightest tweak along the fuel systems' sensor array. Nothing catastrophic, nothing immediately alarming. Just enough to necessitate a stop. A delay.

Enough to buy time.

As she checked and doublechecked the code, memories of Osa flitted through her mind like an old-fashioned slide show. Her daughter's first steps on a new planet, eyes wide with wonder. The fierce determination in her gaze as she declared her intention to become a xenologist. The cold distance in her scowl during that last conversation before the shutout began.

Dagny shook her head hard, forcing herself back to the present. So close now. Just a few more—

Her wristcom chimed, the sound shocking in the silence. Dagny's heart leapt to her throat as she saw the sender.

Sally.

Swallowing hard, wiping her screens blank, she opened her connection.

"Hi Sally."

"Engineer Novak," Sally's smooth voice filled the room. "I hope I'm not disturbing you."

Dagny tried not to glance at her screens. Completely not suspicious, wiping them like that.

"Not at all, Sally. What can I do for you?"

"It's about the Zark theater plans. Ambassador Xalara is quite insistent on promoting their performances ship wide."

Dagny blinked, her mind struggling to shift gears. "At this hour?"

"The Zark sleep cycle differs from humans, as you know," Sally replied, a hint of amusement in her tone. "They believe night is the perfect time for creative discussions."

Of course they did. Dagny pinched the bridge of her nose, forcing herself to focus.

"Alright, what are we thinking for promotion?"

As she and Sally brainstormed ideas—holographic announcements, themed menu items in the kitchens, the potential for a backstage tour—Dagny's eyes kept darting to her blank screens. The sabotage program waited, a digital sword of Damocles dangling over her head.

Mid-conversation, the door to the comms suite hissed open. Dagny's head snapped up, her heart racing. But no one entered. The doorway remained empty for a moment before closing again.

Cleaning bot, she realized, letting out a shaky breath. Just a cleaning bot.

"—and perhaps a special interview series?" Sally was saying.

"Yes, excellent idea," Dagny replied, hoping her momentary distraction hadn't been noticed. "Would you draft a proposal and I'll share it with the Zark. Unless you want to work directly with Krim. Your design project with them worked really well."

"Better than Zara's attempt at a new food tray." Sally sounded pleased with herself.

"Excellent." Dagny did not ask for details on the food tray. Her hand drifted toward the screens, wanting to swipe them on again. "Will that be all, Sally?"

"For now, yes. Thank you, Engineer Novak."

As soon as the call ended, Dagny closed the channel completely. She wiped the screens alive again but then slumped in her chair, adrenaline still coursing through her veins. She took a deep breath. Focus.

She was so close.

Concentrating hard to still her trembling fingers, she ran through the sabotage sequence again. One last check.

One last chance to back out.

Osa's face flashed in her mind, and Dagny's resolve hardened.

She activated the program.

As the loading bar crept across the screen, Dagny held her breath. Seconds stretched into eternities. And then—

"Fascinating work you're doing."

Dagny jumped up from her chair, her heart slamming her ribs so hard she thought they might break.

There, perched on the same orange sofa from earlier in the day, sat Nova. But not as Dagny-plus. This was the form she'd taken in the observation deck—slender, slightly shorter than Dagny, with large, cartoon-like eyes and pale pink skin. Her elfin features were serene, curious.

Dagny's mind raced. How long had Nova been there? What had she seen? Her mouth went dry as she struggled to form words.

"Nova," she managed. "I… I didn't see you come in."

Nova's head tilted, a gesture so like Dagny it was uncanny. "I didn't want to disturb you. You seemed so focused."

Panic clawed at Dagny's throat. She glanced at her screens, but the sabotage program had already completed its work and deleted itself. Leaving no trace, she hoped.

Had Nova seen? Did she understand?

She couldn't have. The screens faced Dagny. Right?

"I was just running some routine checks," Dagny lied, hating how easily the deceit came now. She came out from behind her desks and stepped slowly toward the center of the room, toward Nova. There was only enough oxygen in her lungs to move slow. "Couldn't sleep. What brings you here so late?"

Nova's large eyes blinked slowly. "I couldn't sleep, either. Or, well, the Iridah equivalent. I thought I might find you here." She paused, her gaze drifting to the now-dimmed screens. "Friend Dagny, may I ask you something?"

Dagny's heart, which had begun to slow, ratcheted up again.

This was it. She'd been caught. Discovered.

She stopped two meters away from the orange sofa, from Nova. Her hands clasped each other hard in front of her heart. The room's air chilled sweat along her neck, turning her windpipe to ice.

"Of course," she choked out. She braced for the accusation.

Nova leaned forward, her expression earnest.

"Do you think the Zark would allow me to participate in their musicale? I so enjoy singing."

The question was so unexpected, so utterly mundane, that Dagny nearly laughed out loud. Relief washed over her in dizzying waves.

She closed the distance between them and sank into the sofa at Nova's side.

Nova didn't know.

Couldn't know.

"I'm not rightly sure," Dagny said slowly, trying to collect her thoughts. "It's certainly worth asking them."

As Nova launched into a discussion about Iridah interpretations of classical Zark music, Dagny tried to recover her balance. Her brain felt as if an elastic had pulled tight and then snapped, leaving her thoughts loose and floating.

But beneath the surface, guilt and fear still churned.

She'd done it. Taken the irreversible step. No going back now.

And as she engaged in this surreal late-night conversation with an alien ambassador who wanted to be a singer, Dagny couldn't shake the feeling that she was dancing near an abyss.

One wrong move, one misplaced word, and everything would come crashing down.

The comms suite, her sanctuary, was now a stage in front

of a restive audience. And Dagny, for the first time in her career, was playing a part she was in no way suited for.

CHAPTER
SIXTEEN

TOGETHER ON THE orange sofa in the communications suite, room lights dimmed for the night cycle, Dagny and Nova contemplated the universe. Or at least the swath they could see streaming from the Breaking Light's outer cameras, which were projected onto the suite's outer wall like windows. Who knew what lingered in the spaces they could not see.

Off in the distance to the right hung the last planet in this system, a cold nubbin with two dim moons circling it. The view from planetside must be close to that of Osa's home. Their home, for a dozen years.

A dozen years ago.

On a quiet, still night light this, way back then, the twin moons of Chang-ko cast an eerie glow over a range of sand dunes. Their light reflected off the sand like scattered diamonds.

Dagny had huddled closer to a small fire. Pulled her thermal jacket tighter around her shoulders. Across the flames, thirteen-year-old Osa sat rigid, her eyes fixed on the distant horizon.

The silence between them was as vast as the starry sky above. Dagny's heart ached as she watched her daughter, remembering a time when Osa would have been nestled against her side, pointing out constellations, looking for comets, and dreaming of adventures among the stars.

Now, the gap between them felt like an abyss.

Had it only been a couple of weeks ago? When all this started. When everything came to an end.

It had been afternoon, one of those false summery days before winter sets in for good. The slam of the front door jolted had Dagny from her novel. She looked up to see Osa, face flushed and eyes blazing, storming into the living room.

"Where's my birth certificate?" Osa demanded, her voice trembling with anger. Her short hair looked as if voltage had passed though it—or a pre-teen's sticky fingers.

Dagny blinked, caught off guard. "What? Why do you need—"

"Just show it to me!" Osa interrupted, eyes wild, fists clenched at her sides. "The real one."

Did she think there was a false one?

Bewildered and a little frightened, Dagny retrieved the memory crystal from her office. As she handed it to Osa, she saw her daughter's hands were shaking.

Osa's tablet scanned the crystal. She found the certificate in seconds.

Osa's eyes scanned the certificate. When she found what she was looking for, she closed her eyes briefly.

When she looked up, her gaze was dripping with betrayal.

"No father listed." Her voice barely audible. "Kira was

right." Voice rising. "I don't even have a father." Voice a desperate shout.

Dagny went cold to the core. She knew this day would come. When Osa was ready for it.

Not now.

It was a lie of omission. A lie of kindness. A lie that you tell a child because they haven't yet learned how very different good people could be.

Fourteen years ago, because she had not yet found a partner, Dagny had chosen to use her own modified genetic material to create Osa. She would love the girl twice as much to make up for having a single parent. And who knew, maybe soon a partner would appear.

While common in most of Alliance space, the practice was banned on the planet Chang-ko. But Osa was almost two when they got here. And the town was so nice, and the schools so good. And nobody on Chang-ko knew or needed to know.

"Osa, sweetheart, let me explain—"

"Explain what?" Osa's pitch cracked with emotion. Dagny couldn't stop her wince.

"That you lied to me my whole life?" her daughter said. "You said the father was a donor. A friend." Osa dragged her hands through her hair. Her wrists were too thin. "But, of course, your only friend is you."

"It's not like that," Dagny pleaded, reaching for her daughter. Osa recoiled, backing away. Her daughter's jaw looked looked so tight it might shatter.

"Do you know what they say about people like me on Chang-ko?" Osa's words came out in a rush. "They say we're not even people. That we don't have souls. And you knew this! You knew, and you still brought me here!"

Dagny felt as if the ground was crumbling beneath her feet. "Osa, I never meant to hurt you. I wanted you. I wanted you so much—"

"You wanted me?" Osa spat out a laugh. "You wanted a toy, an experiment. You didn't care about what I would want, or how I would feel!"

"That's not true!" Now Dagny's jaw was shattering. "I love you more than anything in this galaxy."

But Osa was beyond hearing.

"You ruined my life," she spat. "I hate you."

She turned and ran from the room, from their home, leaving Dagny standing alone, the crystal forgotten at her feet.

For the next week, Osa refused to talk to Dagny or be in the same room as Dagny. She stayed overnight with with friends. She ate when Dagny was at work. Finally a school counselor texted Dagny to ask if something is up.

They both talked to a counselor.

The pop-crackle of the fire brought Dagny back to the present. Her counselor suggested this, and Dagny's counselor agreed. A weekend trip in the wilds of nature, doing what both of them loved. Clear the air, get out of their house. Get some perspective on this painful rift.

So here they were, sitting on separate folded blankets across from each other, not looking at each other over the small campfire.

Dagny forced herself to look across at Osa, seeing the hurt and anger still etched in her young face. World weary, at thirteen.

"Osa," she began softly, "I know I can't change the past. But we can move forward from here. Together."

Osa's gaze finally met hers. The rigid determination in the girl's face floored Dagny.

Clearly, Osa was a planner, like Dagny. She'd been working the problem.

"You're right," Osa said, her voice steady. "We can't change the past. That's why I'm leaving."

Dagny felt her heart stop. "Leaving?"

"I've applied to the Interplanetary Exchange Program," Osa said, her chin lifting slightly. "I was accepted right away."

"But you're only thirteen," Dagny protested, panic rising in her throat. Her heart juddered awake, into a chaotic staccato. "You can't just leave!"

"Can so. Annie, my counselor, is helping me. She understands." Osa looked away, up, to the moons and stars.

"I want to see other worlds," she said. "Other ways of living. I can't stay here, where everyone will always see me as nothing. Less than nothing."

Dagny choked as if she were drowning. She grasped for anything to keep her daughter close.

"Please. We can move to another planet, start over—"

"No," Osa cut her off. "I need to do this on my own. I need to find out who I am, away from you and away from Chang-ko."

The finality in Osa's voice slammed into Dagny like one of those high-breaking waves. She watched dumbly as her daughter stood, brushing sand from her clothes.

"I'm going to bed," Osa said, her voice softer now, but no less resolute. "We should head back in the morning."

As Osa disappeared into the tent they'd set up in the trees off the beach, Dagny remained by the fire, staring into the flames. The stars above, supposedly a symbol of endless possibilities, now mocked her with their cold, distant light.

She had wanted to give Osa roots, stability, everything Dagny herself had missed as a child.

She'd quit her Alliance post to set roots down on this so-steady planet.

Instead, she had driven her daughter to the stars, seeking an escape from the very life Dagny had sacrificed everything to provide.

As the fire sifted down to embers, Dagny finally allowed her tears to fall. Mourning the loss of the future she had imagined and fearing the vast unknown that lay ahead for both of them.

Osa slept on.

CHAPTER
SEVENTEEN

DAGNY'S HAND hovered over the door sensor to ship's counselor Serena Martinez's office when her wristcom vibrated. The tickler alert she'd set calling in.

Fuel systems now operating at optimal efficiency.

The world seemed to tilt beneath her feet. Her sabotage had failed. Again.

Worse, it had been detected and fixed.

Did Sally know? Was the AI even now informing security about Dagny's betrayal?

Dagny pulled her hand away from the door sensor. She ran both hands down her arms, hoping the soft fleece of the violet sweater she wore over her khaki jumpsuit would soothe.

She closed her eyes. Time was running out. Osa was still in danger, and now Dagny had even less time to find another way to slow the ship, all while under what surely must be growing suspicion.

The door slid open. Dagny gasped. Her hand reached for her throat.

Serena Martinez stood in the doorway, her warm eyes filling with concern. "Dagny? Are you alright?"

Forcing a smile that felt more like a grimace, Dagny nodded.

"Yes, sorry," she said. "Just one last message to deal with before our meeting."

Getting better at lying.

She stepped into the room, a curious blend of therapist's office and artist's studio. The scent of oil paints from four cloth-draped easels on one side mingled with hint of lavender coming from the plush burgundy sectional sofas on the other side. Serena must have the same air spritzer Dagny had.

"Please, have a seat," Serena said, gesturing toward the longer of the sofas, the one against the wall. Serena seated herself on the smaller one, kitty-corner at Dagny's left.

The soft pink light filtering through the gossamer curtains dividing the art area from the counseling area was probably meant to be soothing. To her, it was a glaring spotlight.

Dagny leaned back into the cushions, her fingers immediately seeking out a soft, furry throw pillow nearby. The cream-colored pillow, once square, now held more of an hourglass shape, perhaps from many arms hugging too hard over time.

As Serena opened her actual, physical notebook, Dagny's mind raced. She needed a new plan, a new way to slow the ship, and fast. But how could she think clearly with the threat of discovery looming over her?

"Now," Serena began, her voice gentle but probing. "How are you feeling today, Dagny?"

Loaded question. Dagny's grip on the pillow tightened.

"Fine. No, good. Just tired. It's been a busy few days, as you know."

Serena's solemn eyes studied her face, seeing more than Dagny was comfortable with. "I sense there's more weighing on you than just work stress," she said. "You've had counseling before, I see, just a year ago."

"Right," Dagny said. "This isn't like that. I'm just, you know, spent. You know, with all the ambassadors and where the heck is the ambassadorial staff and all that."

Serena's slow nod dammed Dagny's babble.

"You're here because Sally noticed some concerning behavior," she said gently. "This is a safe space, Dagny. Whatever you're going through, I'm here to help."

For a moment, the temptation to confess everything swamped Dagny. The weight of her secrets, the fear of discovery, the desperation to save Osa—all of it. Crushing her, slowly. Relentlessly.

But she couldn't. The risks were too great.

"It's my daughter," Dagny heard herself say, clinging to the partial truth as tightly as to the pillow. "Osa. We've been distant. It's been awhile. I'm worried about her."

As she told Serena about Osa, she kept to the past. Right up to the failed lunch at the Galaxy George Diner. Familiar territory to Dagny, so she had plenty of space left in her mind to furiously conjure up some new solution. Something undetectable. Was that even possible?

Serena listened carefully, occasionally asking questions that drew Dagny's startled attention back to reality for a moment. The counselor really was perceptive, and even seemed kind.

But just as Dagny was considering whether she could trust Serena with even a fraction of the truth, the session went off the cliff.

"Saanvi told me about your panic attack at the station. The terrorist thing," Serena said. "Want to talk about that?"

Panic attack?

Thanks, Saanvi.

"No," Dagny said. "I mean, it wasn't like that at all. I mean—"

"Dagny." Serena's kindly tone could be grating. "From what you've told me, it sounds like you and Osa have long been at a crossroads," Serena said, her gaze holding Dagny's. "Sometimes, we have to let our children go. To find their own path."

The words hit Dagny like a bullet to the head.

What? Let Osa go? Was she joking?

Dagny banished the thought before it choked her. The counselor simply didn't know the danger Osa was in.

"No!" Dagny nearly shouted. She clamped her voice down. "Not right now. She needs me."

Serena's brow furrowed slightly, showing concern. Her first fake expression.

"Does she?" the counselor asked in that I'm-right-I'm-the-counselor voice. "Or is it just possible that you need her to need you?"

Dagny's mind reeled. She couldn't even parse the question. Was this a trick?

She couldn't explain, couldn't make Serena understand without revealing everything.

"I see what you mean." She tried to sound willing to change, willing to consider something she absolutely would not consider. "But right now, this moment, Osa is in big trouble. Once that's past, I think I could let her go." Dagny's voice choked the last words into pianissimo. "Maybe."

As Serena was gently destroying that argument, Dagny's wristcom buzzed.

"Sorry," she said. "I thought I turned it off."

But it was an emergency override.

From Remy: *Urgent. Need you in Comms ASAP.*

What now? Had she been discovered? Or was this something else entirely?

"Another crisis," she said to Serena, already rising. "Thank you for listening. You've given me a lot to think about."

Serena walked her to the door. "Anytime, Dagny. How about we set something up so we can talk more next week?"

As Dagny hurried towards the central stairs, her mind whirled with possibilities and fears. Sabotage had failed—twice. Time was running out. And now there was something else?

Whatever awaited her in Comms, one thing was certain. She was running out of options, and out of time. Stumbling along a tightrope, with the slightest misstep threatening to send her plummeting into the abyss.

CHAPTER
EIGHTEEN

DAGNY BURST into the Comms suite at nearly a full run. The familiar clicks and hums of equipment, the happy beckoning of the conversation areas, and the soft daytime lighting offered a moment's comfort.

Until she saw the panic on Remy's face.

He stood at the main meeting table, on the far side of the open space, which he'd raised to waist height. His lean frame hunched, his hands busy manipulating the outline of an old-style keyboard projected on the table. Three screens hovered in front of him over the table.

The blue light from the screens highlighted the worry lines on his young face, showing how he would look in a few decades. The cybernetic implant at his right temple pulsed anxious amber.

"Dagny," he said as he saw her, relief evident in his voice. "Thank goodness you're here. The signal—it's changed."

She joined him at the console, her eyes quickly scanning

the data scrolling across the screens. Remy was right. In fact, change was an understatement.

The mysterious signal they'd been tracking had indeed intensified, its complexity multiplying exponentially.

"When?" she asked, pulling up an additional keyboard interface and two new screens to add to Remy's. Her fingers flew over the controls as she pulled up additional data.

"Ten minutes ago, about," Remy said. "It was gradual at first, but then." He gestured at the main screen, where a visual representation of the signal pulsed and writhed like a living thing. "I don't understand it."

He sounded scared. And intrigued.

"Sally," Dagny called out, "what's your analysis?"

The AI's voice emerged from the table, cool serenity.

"The signal's amplification coincides with our approach to the jump tunnel. However, I cannot determine if this is causation or mere correlation."

The jump tunnel.

Blast it all.

They were so close now, mere hours away from the very thing Dagny was ordered to prevent.

Time was ticking down. She had to think of something that would slow them down. The terrorists of Beloved Spring would not wait forever. They probably were hiding somewhere close, ready to pounce.

She couldn't think of that.

She had to think of something.

"Dagny?" Remy touched the back of her hand. She must have missed something.

"Right," she said, not knowing if she was answering a question or not. "Could the tunnel be acting as an amplifier?"

"Possible," Sally replied. "But unlikely. It would explain the increase in strength. But the change in the signal's complexity suggests an alteration at the source."

Remy nodded, his eyes bright, face shiny. He must have brought more cherry scones in here. The slight whiff made Dagny's stomach roar.

"I'm trying to clean it up," he said. "See if we can find a pattern. But it's not acting right."

Dagny leaned in, studying the undulating waves of data. She could almost see a rhythm to it, a tricky, duplicative, dancing pattern. But every time she thought she had it, it slipped away, like trying to hold water in cupped hands.

"How long until we reach the jump point?" she asked, dreading the answer.

"Forty-seven minutes," Sally said.

Blast it all squared. Less than an hour to find a way to stop this. To save Osa. Dagny's hands trembled slightly as she worked, her mind split between deciphering the signal and desperately seeking a last-minute solution to her personal crisis. She wasn't going to get either answer this way.

She needed to hand off the mystery signal.

"Let's try a multi-spectral analysis," she suggested, hoping nobody noticed the quiver in her voice. "Remy, can you set up a parallel processing array? We need to break this down into its component parts."

As they worked, Dagny felt the weight of time pressing down on her. Each passing minute was a countdown to the jump, to her failure. How to buy more time? With Sally watching her every move, any attempt at sabotage would be instantly detected.

The signal continued to evolve—mutate. It grew more

intricate with each passing moment. Beautiful in its complexity, a symphony of data that seemed to dance just beyond comprehension. Teasing.

"Thirty minutes to jump," Sally announced.

Dagny's heart rate spiked. She could hear herself panting. She was running out of time, out of options. This signal was so tricky. If she could just get her hands around it.

She needed more time.

"We should delay the jump," Dagny said. "Until we have figured out this signal."

Remy's face lost its focus, falling into lax surprise.

"But that's where the signal is coming from," he said.

"And is it friendly?" Dagny scoured her mind for reasons for her unreasonable demand. "What if whoever is sending it is right outside the exit point?"

Before Remy could respond, the comm crackled to life. Mira Patel's face appeared on one of the floating screens, her expression a mix of concern and determination.

"Dagny, Remy, what's the situation?" the mission chief asked.

Dagny quickly explained the intensifying signal and her concerns. As she spoke, Saanvi joined the call, her brow furrowed in concentration.

"Delaying the jump is no simple matter," Saanvi cut in. "We've already committed to our approach vector. To stop now, we'd need a massive power blow. Massive. Could damage our systems."

They could just pivot, blast past the tunnel entrance, and pull a big U-turn. Why were engineers always so fixed in their thinking?

Maybe because their minds weren't currently on overdrive.

But Mira nodded. "Not to mention, we're on a tight schedule. The ambassadors—"

"I understand," Dagny interrupted, frustration seeping into her voice. "But shouldn't we err on the side of caution? We can skirt by the tunnel, right? This signal, it could be—"

"Ten minutes to jump," Sally's voice cut through the debate, echoing from the table and the ceiling and then in the hall outside. The shipwide alert countdown had begun.

"No time for debate," Mira said. "Unless you have concrete evidence of a threat, we proceed as planned."

Dagny took in a breath to argue further. But Remy's excited voice stopped her.

"Wait! I think I've got something," he said, his fingers flying over the controls. "Look at this pattern. It's repeating, but with subtle variations each time." He pushed his screen into everyone's views.

Everyone leaned in, eyes fixed to their screen. The signal's visual representation pulsed and shifted. Filtered this way, it did look like a regular pattern.

Mira leaned so close to her camera. Dagny's view of her was all forehead. "What does it mean, Remy?"

"I'm not sure yet, but it's definitely structured. This isn't random noise."

Mira leaned back. "Alright. That's enough for me. Proceed with the jump. Dagny, Remy, Saanvi, keep working on decoding that signal. I want answers as soon as we're through."

Mira winked out, but another four windows winked in. The spectral engineering team. The onslaught of voices made Dagny reel.

Defeat warred with excitement. She had failed to stop the

jump. But maybe, just maybe, they were on the verge of a breakthrough.

Dagny and Remy worked feverishly, each on their own version of the pattern on the screen. Trying everything to clean up the signal, to extract some meaning from its ever-shifting patterns.

"Five minutes to jump," Sally announced. "Everyone, please prepare for transition."

She and Remy each stared at the patterns, trying to see something more.

The thing was making her dizzy.

"Jump in three… two… one…"

The world stretched and compressed all at once. Colors inverted, reality twisted, and for a brief, eternal moment, Dagny felt as if she were everywhere and nowhere simultaneously. Then, with a snap that seemed to reverberate through her very bones, they were through.

In the aftermath of the jump, as Dagny's senses slowly returned to normal, she became aware of a change in the Comms suite. The main screen, which had been a chaotic swirl of data moments before, now displayed a clear, pulsating pattern.

"We… we did it," Remy breathed, his eyes wide with disbelief. "The jump somehow cleared up the signal. It's—"

"It's structured," Dagny finished, her mind already following this trail. She swiped her screen to a different view of the data. "Remy, run a multi-dim-three analysis on this pattern. I have a hunch."

As Remy ran the scan, popping another screen between them, Dagny's eyes darted between it and her original screen. There *was* something. Something familiar.

But, even now, just out of reach.

She touched Remy lightly on the elbow. When he turned to look at her, she waved toward the big soundproof room, down the hall behind her desk.

"Gonna fire up the map in there. So I won't disturb you."

His acknowledging half-smile said he knew exactly who was being disturbed. He turned back to the screens with Saanvi and her team, all chattering at double speed.

The door to the sound-paneled room slid open with a soft hiss like a disappointed sigh. As she stepped inside, the sudden dulling of sound pressed against her eardrums like a physical force.

The room, with its four split rows of low navy blue benches facing a bare cream-colored wall, seemed to stretch endlessly before her. Fifty people could sit comfortably in here. The air, filtered and recycled, carried a faint metallic tang that settled on the back of her throat. Should have brought the tea with her.

Dagny stepped to the center, between the two halves of the second row, and pulled up a screen. Her fingers stumbled as she recoded the map projection, the familiar motions suddenly foreign and clumsy. Blasted nerves.

She sent the data to the room's projector. The room came alive with swirls of information translated to light, motion, and sound. She pushed the ranges this way and that.

Now the signal looked like stacked logarithms. Compressed data streams? Now, gorgeous harmonics. Music?

She scanned for spectral fingerprints, running through the usual models and then the unusual ones. And then, her intuition. Seen one way, the flow suggested telemetry. Grid data?

She tweaked the grid, and suddenly found herself at the center of a miniature galaxy.

Of course.

It was a map.

She walked with wonder into what looked like a gravity well for a big red planet. Past that, she could see the next system, and the next. Floating gray circles—labels—next to each point of interest, crisp and clear, blurred before her eyes as unbidden tears formed. She had become a ghost—a speck of dust—traveling her own room-sized personal galaxy.

She banged her shin on the benches a couple times, but didn't register the pain, her mind wrapped by the swirling lines and points of light into a sort of cosmic cocoon. The alien labels, incomprehensible yet hauntingly beautiful, shimmered in the air around her. Each symbol seemed to pulse with hidden meaning, their unfamiliar curves and angles both mesmerizing and unsettling.

But amidst the sea of indecipherable markers, one label stood out. Gray, but with a bright-yellow border. Dagny hopped two benches to get closer to it.

A planet, in a dual-star system.

A "goldilocks" planet—a world perfectly suited for life as they knew it. The tantalizing blue-red-green orb hovering within her reach seemed to glow with possibility.

This had to be it. The home of the mapmakers. The source of the signal that had led them here.

CHAPTER
NINETEEN

DAGNY SLAMMED through the door of the soundproof room and back into the main comms suite, leaving the new map of the galaxy to float and whirl on its own.

By the time she got to the main table, moving as fast as her soft spacer body would go, the data packet she'd sent had already loaded itself onto one of her screens.

Remy, standing at the central communications table in front of six floating data screens, chattered in double-time to get a word into the flow of the four rapt engineers, shown on their own, smaller screens. But when they saw the packet, everyone went silent.

"Beautiful," Remy said. "What is it?"

"You have to go wide," Dagny said on a gasp. Was she really so out of shape? "I mean, galaxy wide." She wiped the data onto Remy's biggest screen, and then expanded the view as far as it would go.

Just as it had in the soundproof room, the data snapped

into focus. With her index finger, Dagny circled a spot. "The jump tunnel," she said.

"A map," Remy gasped. His fingers joined Dagny's on the screen, tracing the pattern. "Of what?"

Dagny's fingers danced along the coordinates. "Spatial anomalies," she said. "Look at these coordinates, these energy signatures."

From the screen, Saanvi grunted in agreement. "They're consistent—most of them—with our current models of wormholes, hidden jump points, areas of warped space-time."

Remy whistled low. "Something like this in our hands, every system. We could navigate space we thought was impassable. Reach every part of the galaxy." He looked at her, eyes alight. "Every little bit."

"Exactly," Dagny agreed, her excitement pushing past the persistent knot of worry in her stomach. "What this means, for exploration, for science, for the Alliance itself. Kinda staggering."

Remy snorted gently. "Kinda."

"Not a natural phenomenon, for sure," Dagny said. And then stopped.

Oh my stars.

"Somebody is really there," Remy said, voice deep with wonder. "And we're going to meet them."

As the magnitude of the discovery settled over them, Dagny felt goosebumps rise along her arms. This would open up new worlds, new resources, new possibilities.

"Get Mira back," she said, her voice steady despite her inner turmoil. "Tell her the good news."

Saanvi's chuckle made the speaker rumble. "I want to be there when we tell the xenos. Oh my stars."

As Remy move to reopen the channel, Dagny's gaze was drawn back to the screen. The map pulsed gently, its intricate network of lines and points shimmering with possibility. If this map was true, it had just cut the risk of traveling in this sector threefold. Sixfold.

She manipulated the display, zooming in on the representation of the jump tunnel, with its weird gravity and field signatures. The detail was astounding, micro-fluctuations in space-time rippling like water disturbed by an unseen stone.

They were on the precipice of something monumental.

But as the weight of this discovery settled over her, a new, terrible thought formed in her mind: What if Beloved Spring knew about this? What if this was why they wanted the ship?

They would use the Breaking Light as a Trojan horse. Masquerading as peaceful Alliance representatives only to wreak havoc on an unsuspecting new world. Horrifying.

Absolutely not. She would keep it safe. Out of their hands.

Whatever happened.

For a moment, a wave of relief washed over her. Her failed attempts at sabotage had, ironically, prevented this worst-case scenario. The Breaking Light was still under Alliance control, still a true vessel of peace and exploration.

But the relief was short-lived. She had to tell the terrorists that she had failed.

Dagny stepped away from the table.

"I think I need some tea," she said.

"I need a bourbon," Saanvi said.

Dagny winced a smile at the joke. She turned away from the screens, away from all the cameras. She dropped onto the wide orange sofa and sent a message to her tea set to brew up some matcha.

Her wristcom felt heavy as a shackle.

We're through the tunnel. My attempts failed.

On the screen under Osa's little photo, their once-personal text channel, the words appeared on the small screen, stark and damning.

As she pressed send, Dagny felt like she was standing on the edge of a precipice. Then she glanced up, into the miniature universe. Remy had switched to holographic mode. Now the galaxy danced its silent dance around him, indifferent to her turmoil. She was but a speck.

But a speck who loved her daughter.

The wait for a response stretched interminably. Dagny pushed back into the sofa, putting her knees up. She could smell the new matcha, but couldn't get herself up to go get it.

When the response came, the soft vibration against her wrist was an electric jolt. She rolled up to a seat so quickly her head swam.

The image of Osa, battered, eyes cast down, materialized on the chat screen. Her daughter's beautiful, interesting face. The bruises on her cheek and arm stood out like dark nebulae against pale skin.

Where else had they hurt her?

Dagny's breath came in short, sharp gasps. Tears filled her eyes, blurring the image but not the despair.

Osa was still wearing the clothes she'd been in when Dagny had last seen her, at the Galaxy George restaurant. They could at least give her clean clothes, she thought blindly.

The message came a minute later.

Last chance. We were waiting on this side to come through and take the ship. Stop the ship cold now and we'll consider it even.

Impossible. Everything she could think of to do took time.

Four hours.

And then, the final crushing blow.

She doesn't think you're coming for her.

As soon as the meaning of the words hit her mind, Dagny flicked her wrist hard, twice. Emergency shut-off for the wristcom.

Too late.

Osa. All alone. Thinking no one was coming for her. Not even her mom.

Sobs wracked her body. Dagny tipped onto her side on the bench, pulling her knees in, as if fetal position could protect her heart.

The faint scent of lavender from her clothes mocked her. Did Osa have washing powder, wherever she was? The air took on the scent of rain.

"Dagny?" Remy's lanky shadow fell on her. His face clouded with confusion and urgency. He knelt beside the bench. "What's wrong?"

Dagny hastily wiped at her eyes, the nubbly fabric of her sleeve leaving her skin raw. She pushed herself to sit up, but with too much force. Remy's steady hand on her shoulder kept her from tumbling in the opposite direction.

"It's nothing," she lied, her voice hoarse and unconvincing even to her own ears. "Just, I guess. Overwhelmed by the implications of this map. It's a lot to process."

Remy's brow furrowed, clearly not buying her explanation but too polite or too uncomfortable to press further.

"If you say so," he said slowly. He still had his hand, warm and strong, on her shoulder. "But if you need to talk..."

"Mira," Dagny interrupted, grasping at the distraction like a lifeline. "What did she say?"

"You didn't hear?" Remy's eyes pinched with worry. "Staff meeting, top of the hour. Big reveal. I'm getting the display set up, but there's something wrong with it."

Dagny choked in a shallow breath, trying to center herself. The slight woodsy scent of Remy's shampoo grounded her. She straightened her nubbly sweater, the familiar fabric poor armor against the turmoil within.

"Right," she said, all fake determination. "Let's not keep them waiting."

CHAPTER
TWENTY

IN THE MIDST of the excitement, the Kipi suddenly
decided they needed to call home right now.

The Comms workstations set against the wall hummed
into activity as Dagny helped Remy set up the call home.
Remy's favorite station was closest to the door, so Dagny took
the one to his right.

She had the handshake between the Kipi's videocom and
the Breaking Light's portal locked in no time. Ambassador
Myli's round fuzzy head appeared on her review screen. He
was wearing some kind of hat. It resembled the stocking-style
caps worn under some kinds of helmets. It had holes so the
whole round of his ears popped out to the sides.

"Please stand by," Dagny said into Myli's earpiece. The
Kipi gave her a sharp grin and a thumb's up. She could hear
Belle in the background singing or speaking some rapid patter
song.

Remy wrestled the Light's translator to recognize the Kipi
receiver near the jump tunnel. Kipi receivers were finicky little

autoshuttles. They didn't just receive the message and then send it through the tunnel to another receiver. They actually hopped the tunnel themselves for each conversation, popping away to connect with the receiver on the other side of the tunnel, and then popping back to say they were ready for the call. The gaps in the Kipi communications stream that resulted from these departures and arrivals would have driven human pilots mad.

And were, currently.

"Tricksy little node," Remy muttered, poking at a dot that would not connect to another dot on the screen. "The proton drive interferes with their equipment something fierce."

Dagny nodded, her mind only half on the task. Would the terrorists hurt Osa more? Not for a few hours, at least. She realized the conversation had stalled.

"It's a delicate balance," she said.

"Too bad we can't just turn it off," Remy said with a chuckle.

The offhand comment lodged in Dagny's mind like a splinter.

Disconnect the drive. Blow the safety latches, which would thrust it away from the ship. The move wouldn't immediately stop the ship, which had its own momentum. But Saanvi would hit the brakes and maybe even pull a U-turn to go fetch the engine.

The idea unfurled in her mind like a poisonous flower, beautiful and deadly.

It was so simple, so obvious.

So obvious to everyone.

Jettisoning the drive would solve so many problems. The terrorists would get the ship, yes, but they'd be stranded. No fast travel. They wouldn't be able to reach the newly discovered civilization for days. By that time, the automatic distress signals would have summoned help.

And no one on the Breaking Light would be harmed.

She hoped.

But the consequences.

Dagny's career would be over. She'd likely face criminal charges. And there was no guarantee that Beloved Spring would keep their word and let Osa go.

But she couldn't do anything else. They had hurt Osa!

The choice was impossible.

Dagny made the choice.

"Connection clear," Remy said. "Finally."

Thirty seconds later, Remy's review screen went from dark to bright day, showing two Kipi, tall and short.

They waited until they heard both sides says something ("Nuncle!" "Myli!" "I'm going to be in a show!" "Not singing, surely?") and then closed their review screens and encoded the call for privacy.

Taking a deep breath, Dagny pushed away from the workstation.

Remy looked up from his console, a smile brightening his face. "Thanks, chief. What's next?"

Remy. The easy grin, the warmth in his eyes. How many times had she taken it for granted? This time might be the last. She couldn't imagine him smiling at her after what she was about to do.

"Let me fix your hair," she said, almost choking. "It's doing that flopsy thing again."

Remy bent down obligingly and let her sweep that forelock out of his eyes. "Won't last."

"But at least I can see your beautiful eyes for a moment."

Remy's eyebrows shot up. "Chief? You alright?"

"Right as rain," Dagny replied, forcing a smile. She glanced at the door. "Want to check with Saanvi on the drive interference."

"She'll hang up on you," Remy said. "So protective of her little bouncing protons."

"You're right." Dagny had already thought of that. That's why this was the perfect lie. "I'll go down to her territory. She might be more amenable there."

"You wish." Remy waved her toward the door. "Better you than me.

Dagny nodded, not trusting herself to speak. As the door closed behind her, she allowed herself a moment of grief.

That smile, so full of trust and camaraderie. She'd miss it.

The long march down the stairs to Engineering felt like a march to the gallows. Each of her steps clanked on the metal-mesh steps. Each breath seemed louder than the last.

She wished she'd accepted that cherry muffin Remy had offered. When was the last time she'd eaten?

She paused the landing for Level Eight, Main Engineering. Through the open door was a controlled chaos of motion and sound. The giant quarter-donut of a room pulsed with life, every engineer a happy cog in this grand machine. They were prepping some engine-looking experiment on the huge white table near the center of the room. The air, thick with the scent of warm metal and ozone, was a sharp contrast to the minty coolness of the Comms suite.

At the far side of the table, Chief Engineer Saanvi Rao presided over the controlled chaos, her red wrap dress a stark contrast to the sea of khaki and blue around her. Her voice cut through the din, single-word answers given with absolute authority. The cacophony of voices, movement, and shadows washed over Dagny like a tidal wave of guilt.

She hesitated. She hadn't turned down her workstation. She hadn't changed her clothes in two days. Should she run to get her memory crystal?

Her wristcom buzzed.

Tick-tock.

It was if the terrorists had eyes on her.

Dagny turned away from Engineering. The last set of stairs to the under-bubble felt like a descent into her own personal hell. Each step brought her closer to a point of no return, the weight of her decision pressing down on her like the crushing depths of an ocean.

The landing in the engine under-room sat in the space like a reverse image of the landing on the observation deck. Instead of walking out onto the floor, the circular landing ended abruptly at a guardrail. Two metal walkway ramps on opposite sides of the circle wound down to wrap around the giant blinking box that was the proton drive.

As she hit the landing, Dagny looked for the emergency boxes. There should be a big one, easy to reach from both stairs and elevators, and two smaller ones, near the entrance to the ramps. Yellow, red, and cyan, so everyone could see them.

Fog came out with her breath. It was freezing down here. And tasted like bubbles. And spring rain.

"Nova?" she whispered out, her voice trembling slightly.

The Iridah ambassador materialized, in her pink anime-girl form, her large eyes pools of concern.

"Dagny? Why are we down here?"

Dagny forced a smile, tasting ash.

"I need to check something here, in the engine room," she lied, her voice sounding hollow even to her own ears. "You can't come with me, Nova. It's not safe."

Nova's form rippled with agitation. "Something's wrong, Dagny. I can sense it. Your aura is turbulent. Please, let's go back up."

Dagny followed Nova's gaze, up the stairs. Before she could respond, her wristcom buzzed again.

Tick-tock.

It had only been ten minutes since the last one. Beloved Spring sure had her number.

Dagny looked away, out toward the dropoff where the mighty engine lurked.

"I appreciate your concern, Nova, but this is my job. I have to do this."

Nova moved closer, her form shifting to mirror Dagny's appearance. Dagny couldn't suppress the shudder.

"Friends help each other, remember?" Nova said. "Let me help you."

Dagny looked into those mirror eyes. Her heart ached for that warm offer of help. But helping Nova meant getting her away from here.

"Do I have to call the mission chief?"

Nova recoiled from Dagny. She hadn't meant to sound so harsh.

But Nova didn't leave. She just sat down on the lowest step. Set her crossed arms on her knees. And watched.

Dagny peered over the railing. The massive engine was encased in a clear but scratched-up aluminum dome, a tarnished twin to the pristine observation deck above. The proton drive crackled with barely contained power, its complex array of machinery and walkways stretching out before them like a mechanical landscape.

Nobody was around.

Good. People weren't supposed to spend a lot of time down here. And Dagny didn't want to accidentally jettison a person as well as the drive.

"The sound is beautiful," Nova said behind her. "In a strange, alien way."

Dagny stepped away from the precipice, back to the center elevator core. The first emergency box stood at knee height between the two main elevators.

With one swift kick, Dagny broke the safety-glass window. The emergency button that was exposed was push style. With a second kick, Dagny jammed the button down.

A series of walls dropped down, just inside the platform's railing. Thick multi-metal, no windows, tight seals.

"Is that how the engines usually are?" Nova asked, confused. "To keep us safe?"

"No," Dagny said, impatient. She turned away from the elevators. Toward the first of the two disconnect levers. She pressed the lid of this emergency box, and it opened with a click. The ribbon holding the lever in its closed position snapped under her trembling fingers.

"Engineer Novak," Sally's voice on loudspeaker cut through the air, "what are you doing?"

Dagny remained silent. She could barely hear Sally for all the blood rushing past her ears. Her heart beat so fast she thought it might burst.

Gotta move fast, then.

She pulled the first lever, then crossed to the other end of the landing. The second emergency box opened easily under her touch.

She snapped the ribbon, but then her hand hovered over the second lever.

For a moment, doubt crept in, cold sweat dousing the heat of her heart's beat. Was this the right thing? Could she really go through with this?

Osa wanted her to let go. And she would.

After this.

After she made things better.

Dagny wiped her sweaty hands on her hip pockets.

Sally was shouting now. "Stop! Wait for assistance."

Dagny did not stop. She could not.

Breathing out all the air in her body, she pulled the second lever.

The sound of seals popping and metal groaning filled the air. The ship shuddered almost imperceptibly, but Dagny felt it in her bones.

The effect was immediate and catastrophic. Alarms blared, their shrill cries a chorus of accusation. Through the viewport, Dagny watched as the proton engine, the heart of the Breaking Light, began to separate from the ship. Tucked into its shallow saucer, falling into shadow. Already only its warning lights were visible, blinking purple, orange, purple.

She had done it. The force of the unlatching had pushed the engine slightly back from the ship, slowing it a little. The Breaking Light would carry on forward at speed, opening the distance between it and its engine with each passing second.

Nova squeaked.

Dagny turned to her, fresh panic in her throat. But the Iridah was fine, if looking a little frightened.

Dagny joined her at the stairs. She would walk up to meet Raza, and judgment.

But her legs gave way, and she sank onto the lowest step of the stairs. The release was as much a rush of emotion as the tension had been. She was done.

Tears she had been holding back for what felt like an eternity finally broke free. She lay back against the stairs, head on one of the edges, just letting the tears fall.

After a moment, Nova leaned back, matching her. The Iridah's arm, surprisingly warm and solid, wrapped around Dagny's shoulders.

Dagny tilted her head to lean on Nova's shoulder. Getting the Iridah a little soggy.

No words were spoken; none were needed.

"Engineer Novak," Sally's voice rang out, unnaturally calm given the circumstances, "please remain where you are. Security Chief Khan is en route to your location."

Dagny lifted her head, wiping at her tear-stained cheeks. She imagined she could hear the engines slowly drifting away, the sound fading as the distance between it and the ship grew.. Of course, there was no sound in space.

The weight of what she had done settled over her like a shroud. She had saved her daughter—she hoped—but at what cost? The faces of her crewmates, of Remy and Saanvi and all the others who had trusted her, flashed through her mind.

As the sound of approaching footsteps echoed in the stairwell, Dagny straightened her spine. She had made her choice, thrown herself into the abyss for the sake of her child. Whatever came next—arrest, trial, the loss of everything she had worked for – it was a price she would pay.

Nova's arm tightened around her shoulders, a silent gesture of support.

"Dagny," Nova whispered, her voice trembling with a mix of confusion and concern, "what is happening?"

Dagny turned to face the Iridah ambassador, seeing her own tear-streaked face reflected in Nova's expression. She gently removed the ambassador's arm from her shoulders. Without that warmth, Dagny felt colder than she ever had before.

"You should go," she said. "You don't want to be involved in this."

The footsteps grew louder, more urgent. Dagny could hear Raza rattling off commands to the security team.

Nova's form shimmered, her appearance shifting rapidly between various humanoid shapes before settling back into her preferred pink-skinned form. The arm slid around Dagny once again.

"No," Nova said, "Friends don't abandon each other."

Nova scooted them closer to one side of the stair. A moment later, Dagny felt the breeze as Raza stomped past them.

The security chief pivoted, to stand directly in front of them.

"Explain," they said, looking at Dagny.

As she opened her mouth to speak, to confess everything and accept the consequences, her wristcom buzzed. A new message flashed across the screen:

Well done.

CHAPTER
TWENTY-ONE

THE BREAKING LIGHT, now without its main engine but not without the momentum that said engine had built up, coasted rapidly on its journey toward the planet that was sending the mysterious signal.

But for Dagny Novak, chief communications officer and mother, the path ahead had irrevocably changed.

Saanvi and the other engineers had decided that it was too much of a risk to slow the Light down and try to net the engine as it followed slowly in the ship's wake. The force of the engine's decoupling from the ship had thrust the engine hard back, cutting its forward momentum by one-third.

"It will catch up to us, eventually," the chief engineer said. "More important is that we carry out the mission."

The sentiment was surprisingly unpopular in Diplomacy Meeting Room Two.

Dagny had passed the door to this room countless times but never entered.

Now, she was on trial in it.

Situated between the comms suite and the main navigation center, the room was a testament to the Breaking Light's commitment to diplomacy. Its oval shape encouraged equality, with no clear head or foot to the long, polished table that dominated the center.

Soft, recessed lighting along the walls could be adjusted to flatter any species, though the neutral warm glow it was currently set to did little to soften the hard expressions around the table.

The air circulation system, usually nearly silent, now hummed audibly as it worked overtime to handle the stress pheromones of multiple species. The mingled scents of ozone, alien botanicals, and the faint metallic tang of fear created a dizzying olfactory cocktail.

Dagny sat at the center of this maelstrom, in the middle of the long side of the table facing the door, acutely aware of every detail. Nova's form had settled as a cross between a person and a particularly large Kipi. The shapeshifter enveloped Dagny from shoulder to hip, a living, protective cocoon. The Iridah's touch was warm and slightly gelatinous. It should have felt strange, even repulsive, but instead, Dagny was oddly comforted.

Commander Mira Patel stood at one end of the table, her normally composed features strained with the effort of maintaining order. Her white shirt, with its pleats and cufflinks, seemed at odds with the chaos unfolding before her.

"Enough!" Patel's voice sliced through the din, sharp and stern. "We will address your concerns in an orderly fashion. Everyone will get their chance to speak."

As the noise dropped to a tense murmur, Dagny felt the weight of accusing stares from around the table. Across from her, Security Chief Khan stood rigid near the door, her eyes never leaving Dagny. Saanvi certain. sat opposite, the chief engineer's midnight caftan and headwrap vibrant but her usual energy subdued, replaced by a look of curious betrayal.

Ambassador Xalara of the Zark, perched on a short stool of a chair, rose to their full, intimidating height. Their chitinous exoskeleton gleamed under the warm lights.

"Intolerable!" they trumpeted. "Tch. We demand immediate return to the nearest station. The Breaking Light is compromised, and we are all at risk!"

The Kipi ambassador, Myli, with Belle right behind him in the chair, arms on his shoulders, bounced in their human-sized bucket seat. Their fur rippled with what seemed to be excitement.

"Oh, but what an adventure!" Myli chirped, his voice a high trill. "No delay! We're on the cusp of a great discovery. Press on, we say!"

Belle nodded vigorously, adding, "So thrilling!" Then she went back to smoothing clumps of Myli's already shiny calico coat.

Nova's grip on Dagny tightened slightly, a comforting pressure.

"Perhaps," Nova's melodious voice resonated against Dagny's side, "we should exercise caution. There is much we do not understand about our situation."

The debate raged on, a tempest of conflicting interests and fears. Patel's gaze flicked between the arguing ambassadors, the cautious engineers, and the far wall, which showed the ship's current trajectory. The tightness around her eyes made them look misshapen.

"Commander," Khan interjected during a brief lull, their

voice cold and professional, "we need to address the security risk. Engineer Novak should be in the brig, not participating in sensitive discussions."

Dagny felt a flicker of fear, quickly soothed by Nova's protective embrace. She opened her mouth to defend herself, but Saanvi beat her to it.

"And what good would that do us now?" Saanvi challenged, her rich alto sharp with frustration. "We need every mind working on a solution. Besides," she added, gesturing to Nova's partial engulfment of Dagny, "I don't think our Iridah friend is going to let that happen."

Birgit Brennan, who had been uncharacteristically quiet, cleared his throat. When he spoke, the xenobiologists' voice was filled with barely contained excitement. "Colleagues, we're overlooking a crucial point. This situation, while dire, presents an unprecedented opportunity for scientific discovery."

The room fell silent. What?

"The proton drive's interference has always limited our ability to study subtle signals," Brennan continued, his eyes bright. "Now, we have a chance to observe this new civilization's transmissions with unprecedented clarity."

Dagny felt a the smallest ripple of hope. One good thing might come out of this disaster.

But Xalara wasn't having it. "Tch! Science? You speak of science when our lives are at risk?" They jabbed a clawed appendage in Dagny's direction. "This human has committed an act of terrorism against this ship and its passengers!"

The accusation hung there, heavy and damning. Dagny felt Nova's form ripple with agitation.

"Is that true?" Nova's voice was soft, but it carried to every corner of the room. "Dagny, did you do this intentionally?"

The room held its breath, waiting for her answer. Dagny swallowed hard, her throat dry as desert sand.

She looked around the room, taking in the faces of her colleagues, the aliens she had come to know, the ship she had called home. The weight of her actions pressed down on her, as tangible as Nova's protective embrace.

"Yes," she admitted, her voice barely above a whisper. "But not for the reasons you think."

CHAPTER
TWENTY-TWO

THE SILENCE that followed Dagny's admission was deafening. She could hear her breaths travel into her chest and out. Feel the gelatinous embrace of Nova tightening almost imperceptibly around her. The room, with its warm lighting and sleek surfaces, suddenly felt claustrophobic.

Commander Patel's voice sliced through the tension.

"What are the reasons then?"

Before Dagny could form a response, a movement caught her eye. Security Chief Khan, their face a mask of cold fury, raised a weapon. The barrel, black and ominous, pointed directly at Dagny's chest.

Time seemed to slow. Dagny's world narrowed to the gun, its presence so alien in this room of diplomacy and science. Her lungs constricted, each breath a ragged gasp. Sweat beaded on her forehead, trickling down her temple. The taste of fear, metallic and bitter, flooded her mouth.

She wanted to explain, to make them understand. But the

words stuck in her throat, choking her. The faces around the table blurred, melting into a sea of accusation and betrayal.

She had to say something. She cleared her throat.

"My daughter" she tried to say. But what came out was "Mmmhmmr." Dagny frowned. Nova was holding her too tightly.

Suddenly, Sally's voice boomed from the ceiling, shattering the moment.

"Incoming ship, hailing us."

A smaller square popped in the corner of the large wall screen that showed local space. A young woman in a full-face mask, looked like a papier-mâché fox. Behind her, a black banner proclaimed "Beloved Spring" in stark gold letters rimmed with red.

The room went silent, but for the buzzing of the air purifiers. Khan's grip on the weapon tightened, their knuckles white.

"Murderers," Khan hissed through clenched teeth. The battles between the Alliance and Beloved Spring were officially called skirmishes. One such "skirmish" had killed nearly all of the people under Khan's last military command.

Beside Dagny, Nova's form rippled violently, a maelstrom of emotion barely contained.

Dagny's own reaction was a vortex of conflicting emotions. Relief washed over her—it wasn't a cruel joke, Osa's captors were real. But on its heels rode a wave of terror. Beloved Spring was here, their reputation for brutality preceding them. Would they expose her role?

And Osa. Good Light above, they were never going to let her go.

Khan's hands started to shake. Dagny's gaze followed the

rapid, minute changes in aim. Any shot would still hit her. Or Nova.

She had no control over that.

She looked down, at the dark wood composite of the table. Tea would be nice, she thought wildly.

The masked woman's voice, distorted and cold, filled the room. "Prepare for boarding."

Chief Patel stood, her spine straight, her voice steady despite the fear evident in her eyes.

"No. The Breaking Light is a ship on a diplomatic mission. You have no right to board us."

A chuckle, devoid of humor, came from the screen. "Bold words, Commander. But you're in no position to refuse. We offer assistance in your time of trouble. Not going too far without your engine, now, are you?"

Patel took a moment to glare at Dagny. Then she noticed Khan's hands shaking. "Stand down, chief," she told them.

The fox-woman continued. "We require a full crew and passenger list. Once reviewed, we'll assign locations for everyone before boarding. Levels 2, 3, and 4 will be sealed off."

"No." Patel crossed her arms. "We do not allow you entry."

"We have no desire for bloodshed, Captain." The fox lady shrugged. "But we do not hesitate if met with resistance."

Dagny's stomach churned. She knew what was coming next, could feel it like an approaching storm.

"Oh, and one more thing," the masked woman continued. "We'll need the quantum entanglement communicator. Engineer Novak can bring it when she comes aboard our ship."

The room fell silent once more, all eyes turning to Dagny. The weight of their stares crushed her soul. Betrayal, shock, disgust—emotions flitted across faces she had once called friends. Even Nova's grip loosened slightly, as if unsure whether to continue protecting her.

Dagny's world spun. The quantum entanglement communicator—the Breaking Light's most advanced piece of technology, capable of instantaneous communication across vast distances. Of course they'd want it. And of course they knew she could access it.

She wanted to scream, to explain that she'd had no choice. That Osa's life had been on the line. That she never meant for it to go this far. But the words wouldn't come. Instead, a sob bubbled up from deep within her, escaping in a choked gasp.

The room blurred as tears filled her eyes. The faces around her morphed into a nightmarish tableau of accusation and betrayal. The soft hum of the ship's systems, usually a comfort, now felt like a dirge.

Commander Patel's voice, when it came, was like ice.

"Dagny Novak, you will explain yourself. Now."

Dagny opened her mouth, but no sound came out. Her throat was desert-dry, her tongue leaden. The weight of her actions, the people she'd put at risk, the trust she'd betrayed— it all came crashing down on her at once.

She was dimly aware of Nova's form shifting, of Khan's weapon training itself again on her, of the masked woman on the screen watching with cold amusement.

But it all felt distant, unreal.

As the room waited for her explanation, Dagny wished, for just a millisecond, that Khan would pull the trigger. It would be easier than facing the consequences of what she'd done, easier than seeing the hurt and betrayal in the eyes of those she cared about.

But as quickly as the thought came, it vanished. Osa was still out there. And no matter what, Dagny would see this through. For her daughter. For the chance to make things right.

Drawing on her last reserves of strength, she swallowed hard and forced herself to meet Patel's gaze. Her voice, when it finally came, was barely a whisper, cracked and raw with emotion.

"I had no choice," she began.

But there was always a choice. Bad start. Dagny held up a hand—wait—trying to drag her thoughts into order.

"It started at the amusement park," she said. She stopped, appalled. Where had that come from?

"Enough!" Chief Patel chopped her arm down like she would rather have been chopping through Dagny. "I've heard enough.

"Get this—traitor—off my ship."

CHAPTER
TWENTY-THREE

"GET THIS—TRAITOR—OFF MY SHIP."

Each word hit Dagny like a physical blow. Each one drove more air from her lungs.

Traitor. Off my ship.

The meeting room spun, tables and star charts and faces blurring into a nightmarish kaleidoscope of betrayal and disgust.

The next few minutes passed in a haze. Somehow, Dagny found herself seated on a hard bench inside one of the Breaking Light's small automatic shuttles. The interior reminded her of ancient images she'd once seen of police transport vehicles—sterile, utilitarian, benches against the sides designed for function over comfort. The walls were a dull, institutional gray, marred by years of scratches and dents. Overhead, harsh lighting cast an unflattering glow, high-lighting every tear track on Dagny's face.

The shuttle's air recyclers buzzed off-key, a poor substitute for the usual comforting thrum of the Breaking Light's systems. The scent of disinfectant barely masked the lingering odors of fear and desperation from who knew how many previous occupants.

Khan's face was a rigid mask as they secured one of Dagny's wrists to the bench's under-support with a set of restraints. The cold metal bit into her skin, a physical reminder of her new reality. Behind Khan, Remy carefully strapped down a crate containing the quantum entanglement communicator, his movements mechanical, as if operating on autopilot.

Nova remained wrapped around Dagny, a comforting warmth against the wildly fluctuating temperature of her own skin. Khan stepped back, their eyes carefully avoiding Dagny's tear-stained face.

"Ambassador," Khan addressed Nova, their voice clipped and professional, "you need to return to the meeting room. There are important decisions to be made."

Nova's form rippled with what Dagny interpreted as reluctance. Khan's expression softened marginally.

"I promise, no harm will come to her," they said. They stepped out of the shuttle to emphasize their point.

Slowly, hesitantly, Nova began to disentangle herself from Dagny. The loss of contact left Dagny feeling exposed, vulnerable. Fresh tears welled up, spilling silently down her cheeks.

"Thank you," Dagny managed. "For being such a good friend."

Nova paused at the shuttle's entrance, her form shimmering with an emotion Dagny couldn't quite interpret. Then, with a final, sorrowful look, the Iridah ambassador was gone.

Remy, only, remained, his lanky frame taut with tension. His eyes darted to Raza, still visible outside the shuttle, before he leaned slightly towards Dagny.

"Why, Dagny?" he whispered. "Why?"

The question, so simple yet so loaded, threatened to shatter what little composure Dagny had left. "They have my daughter," she choked out.

Remy recoiled as if slapped, his eyes widening in shock. He glanced quickly at Raza before turning back to Dagny. She read fading disbelief and dawning understanding in his face.

"And everyone is mad at you? For that?" He shook his head, sneaking another look at Raza. "Asswipes. Family comes first."

A tiny flicker of warmth bloomed in Dagny's chest at Remy's words. It wasn't absolution, but it was a moment free from scorn, and she clung to it desperately.

With a final, conflicted look, Remy stepped out of the shuttle. Raza approached, their face once again an unreadable mask. They held up the handcuff key, making sure Dagny saw it, before tossing it onto the opposite bench. Tantalizingly close, yet impossibly far.

The door dropped shut, leaving Dagny alone with her thoughts and the faint burr of the shuttle's drive systems.

The small craft disengaged from the Breaking Light. Ten minutes. Ten minutes until she faced the terrorists who had upended her life. Ten minutes to contemplate the magnitude of her actions, the trust she'd shattered, the lives she'd put at risk.

She thought of Osa—her brilliant, beautiful, distant daughter. Had it all been worth it? Would Osa understand, or would she too look at Dagny with the same disgust and betrayal she'd seen in her colleagues' eyes?

The faces of her crewmates flashed through her mind. Saanvi's shock, Patel's fury, Raza's cold anger.

And Nova. The ambassador's unwavering support, even in the face of Dagny's betrayal, felt like a lifeline in a storm of recrimination. Why did the ambassador even care?

As the shuttle approached the Beloved Spring ship—a hulking, patchwork monstrosity that loomed against the star field—Dagny felt a strange calm settle over her. Whatever came next, she would face it.

She had to.

The shuttle clamped onto its berth with a resounding clang, and settled into stillness. Dagny straightened her spine. She was Dagny Novak, mother, engineer, and yes—traitor.

But also survivor.

And rescuer.

She hoped.

She stared at the shuttle door, waiting for it to open.

Ten minutes and a lifetime away, the Breaking Light, wounded but not defeated, pressed on through the star-studded void.

CHAPTER
TWENTY-FOUR

THE AUTOSHUTTLE CARRYING Dagny had bumped down on the floor of the Beloved Spring ship like a horse that overshot its jump. The resulting series of clangs reverberated through Dagny's bones.

She'd steeled herself, expecting the door to open immediately. But seconds stretched into minutes.

The silence was agony. Were they reconsidering? Was Breaking Light about to attack?

With what? Their sample-mining drills?

Her wrist, still cuffed to the bench, began to ache, a dull throb she hadn't noticed when the shuttle was moving.

Finally, with the pneumatic hiss of different levels of air being rapidly exchanged, the shuttle door lifted open. Dagny squinted against the sudden blare of harsh, white light. As her eyes adjusted, she found herself facing not a masked, heavily armed terrorist, but a smallish person who wouldn't have looked out of place in any spaceport cafe.

The woman stood just beside the airlock, not yet on the

ramp into the shuttle itself, her posture relaxed but alert. She wore simple, dark clothing—practical boots, cargo pants, and a warm-looking fitted jacket. Her medium-dark hair was pulled back in a neat ponytail, and her face, free of any mask, bore a largish curved scar above her left eyebrow. But it was her eyes that caught Dagny's attention—a faded blue that seemed to see right through her.

"Dr. Novak," the woman said, her voice calm and all business. "Welcome aboard the Horizon's Edge. I'm Aria. I'll be your liaison during your stay with us."

She paused, her gaze flicking to the handcuffs. "I see our new friends on the Breaking Light were less than accommodating. Allow me to remedy that."

Aria stepped into the shuttle, moving with the easy grace of someone accustomed to the micro-changes of ships with wobbly gravity. The air that wafted in with her carried a mix of scents—machine oil, ozone, and something Dagny couldn't quite place. It wasn't unpleasant, exactly, but it was alien. This ship was decidedly not home.

As Aria reached for the handcuff key on the opposite bench, Dagny found her voice.

"Where's my daughter? Is she free?"

Aria paused, key in hand, and met Dagny's gaze. Her expression was unreadable. "First, let's get you settled. Looks like you need a nap, and a shower. I assume that crate contains our requested item?"

Dagny nodded mutely. This wasn't at all what she had expected. The calm professionalism, the lack of overt threats— it was somehow more terrifying than any show of force could have been.

As the handcuffs fell away, Dagny rubbed her wrist, buying time to collect her thoughts.

Aria stepped back, gesturing for Dagny to exit the shuttle.

"Shall we? We have much to discuss, and I'm sure you're eager to understand your new situation."

"What situation?" Dagny said. "You're trading Osa for me, right? You need me to manage the comms device. You've made me a pariah in the Alliance, so here I'll stay. I suppose."

"Smart as a whip," Aria said. "Just as promised." She stepped out, onto the ramp. In the small of her back was tucked a crescent blade.

Surprisingly shakily, Dagny stood. Suddenly, each step towards the airlock felt like a step further away from everything she had known, everything she had been.

She was now in the hands of Beloved Spring. And despite Aria's cordial demeanor, Dagny knew that nobody here was her friend.

The ship was big—bigger than the Breaking Light. The usual boxy layout, with parallel floors and ninety-degree corners. The light was brighter than usual. The vibe, emptier.

Dagny followed Aria through corridors that looked like corridors anywhere. Gray, scuffed, with signs in a language she needed her wristcom to translate.

At least they hadn't taken her wristcom.

Their footsteps echoed on the dull metal floors in the empty passageways. The ship's interior was clean but worn. Patches of mismatched metal on the walls and floors spoke of too hasty repairs. The air carried the faint scent of industrial cleaners and a strange, burnt tang that scratched at the back of Dagny's throat.

Or maybe that was just the taste of shame. Dagny's mind

filled the corridors with the people she had left behind. The people she had let down. The faces. Saanvi's shock, Raza's fury, Mira's cold anger.

"Your cooperation is appreciated, Dr. Novak," Aria's voice cut through Dagny's spiraling thoughts. "It's made this transition much smoother than it could have been."

Dagny's stomach churned at the casual tone. Transition. Such a benign word for a people's dreams dashed. A life's work destroyed.

They paused at an intersection, and Aria turned to face her. "I understand this is difficult," she said, her icy eyes raking Dagny's face. "But I assure you, we're not the monsters your Alliance paints us to be. We have a vision for a better future, and your expertise will help us achieve it."

The words rang hollow in Dagny's ears. A better future built on kidnapping and coercion? She wanted to scream, to lash out, but the image of Osa held her in check. She was doing this for Osa.

As they walked, Aria pointed out the kitchens, washrooms, the gym. The medical facility took half a level on its own. Aria did not highlight the passages to the bridge, or engine rooms, or navigation. Dagny still knew roughly where they were. These boxy ships all followed the same patterns.

Dagny started to drag, her body consuming her last dregs of adrenaline. They had walked nearly the entire length of the ship. Wouldn't be easy to sneak away on a shuttle when the hangar was a twenty minute very public walk away.

But they'd seen almost no people. None in the halls. A couple in the kitchen, three in the gym. All dark jackets and dark pants. Even dark gym shorts. Dagny thought the Light's scientists all dressed the same, but Beloved Spring's people had them beat.

At last, they stopped at a gray door that looked like all the others they had passed.

"Your new quarters," Aria said. She pressed her palm to the access panel, set the code for new key (4-3-2-1, duh), and moved to give Dagny the space to press her own palm on the panel.

The door stuttered open. Needed some axle grease. Dagny stepped through, and could see why.

Someone had been pounding on it.

The air that greeted her carried an unexpected blend of scents: the usual sharp ozone mixed with a faint, spicy aroma that reminded her of ginger and cloves. An oddly comforting smell, from a place that looked rather stark.

A bunk room, utilitarian, designed for four humans. Two sets of bunk beds bolted to opposite walls. One set had soft-looking bedding, dark blues. Standard standing metal wardrobes flanking each end of the beds, alto bolted to the wall. Four flexible-height desks. Three magnetic-wheeled chairs. Mini-kitchen on one side of the back wall. Door to the facilities on the other side.

The space was slightly larger than her old room but felt more transient, as if its occupants were always ready to leave at a moment's notice. Dagny felt as if she'd been transported back to first year at university.

But soft, amber-tinted lights cast a warm glow over every-thing. The harsh lighting was only for the hallways, appar-ently. The walls were a muted blue-gray, their surface slightly textured, providing a subtle grip under her fingers as she steadied herself.

On the other side of each wardrobe, the desks also showed a little personality. The one without a chair bore a series of tiny, colorful paint splatters that formed an accidental abstract pattern. Another had a small, hand-drawn map of constellations etched into its surface, barely visible unless you knew to look for it.

The wardrobe closest to the painted desk carried some stray magnets with words on them. Terrorists enjoyed magnetic poetry, too.

To Dagny's right, in the corner, sat a small round metal table painted cream. Tall, closed metal shelves bolted to the wall behind it probably held basic tools and playing cards. A half-finished origami crane, deep burgundy, sat on top of the shelves, too high or too dark to be captured by the cleaning mechs. On the table, a small clay-potted plant—some kind of hardy, alien succulent—was the only green in the room.

On the other side of the entrance the obligatory "porthole," a space on the wall for a display of the stars outside or visions of home, was currently blank. But someone had stuck glow-in-the-dark stars around its edges, creating a playful frame for the real stars beyond.

The steady hum of the ship's systems was familiar, but not exactly right. The barely perceptible vibration seemed off a half-beat. Not entirely unpleasant, more like a deep, mechanical purr.

As Dagny sank onto the lower bunk of the nearest bed that had bedding, her hand brushed against the blanket.Unexpectedly soft, almost silky, its a slight weight felt comforting. The mattress beneath was firm but responsive, molding slightly to her body like always.

The small, personalized touches offered a flicker of warmth

in the cold expanse of space. They were all she would have for a while. It wasn't as if the crew of the Breaking Light would pack her room and send it over.

She should have grabbed her memory crystal.

And changed her clothes.

And not sabotaged the ship.

And never, never have suggested meeting up at a Galaxy George theme park.

That was what had started it all, after all.

Aria still stood in the entry. "I'll leave you to rest. Get settled in," she said. "We'll talk tomorrow."

The door crunched closed. Panic lanced through Dagny's mind. How long before she'd be the one pounding on the door?

She looked around the room wildly.

No problems to solve. No Remy to remind to check the backups. No Sally to skirt by.

No Raza to beat at Go. No Nova to wonder at.

No tea.

Well, there might be tea. Dagny looked toward the kitchenette counter. Yes, it had the standard metal teapot. The bunk beds might scream summer camp, but the rest of this place was university all over again.

A sound from the small attached bathroom made her freeze. Someone was there? Whatever they'd been doing had been silent indeed.

The door handle turned, and Dagny's heart leapt into her throat. Time seemed to slow as the door swung open.

There, framed in the doorway, was Osa.

Dagny's world narrowed to her daughter's face. The bruises she'd seen in the photo were fading, but dark circles under Osa's eyes spoke of sleepless nights. Her hair was limp, her posture defeated. But her eyes—those eyes that Dagny had looked into every day for years—carried a storm of emotions.

"Mom?" Osa's voice was small, uncertain, so unlike the confident young woman Dagny remembered.

A sob tore from Dagny's throat, raw and primal. All the fear, guilt, and desperate love she'd been holding back crashed over her, a tidal wave of emotion. She staggered to her feet, arms outstretched.

"Osa," she choked out, relief clogging her throat.

In two steps, she crossed the room and enveloped her daughter in a fierce embrace. Osa stiffened for a moment, then melted into her mother's arms, her face pressed against Dagny's shoulder.

They clung to each other, two survivors in a storm of their own making, as the Horizon's Edge carried them further into an uncertain future.

In that moment, nothing else mattered—not the Breaking Light, not Beloved Spring, not the troubles that surely lay ahead. For now, in this room that was home but not home, Dagny held her world in her arms once more.

And despite everything, despite the pain and betrayal and relentless uncertainty, Dagny felt a flicker of hope.

They were together. And maybe, just maybe, that would be enough.

CHAPTER
TWENTY-FIVE

THE AMBER-TINTED light of the bunk room cast a honeyed glow over Osa's face, softening the harsh lines of exhaustion etched into her young features. Dagny drank in the sight of her daughter, cataloging every detail with the desperation of a woman dying of thirst. She breathed in the scents: vanilla, coffee, Osa.

They stumbled over to the bunk, crashing onto the bed where Dagny had been sitting all alone before. The silky-soft blanket beneath them seemed to absorb the tension in the air, creating a small island of comfort in the vast sea of uncertainty surrounding them.

Their hands gripped so hard Dagny winced. Osa's dark thick wavy hair, so like her own, fell in front of her eyes. A habit that had once driven Dagny to distraction during those teenage years, now it felt achingly precious.

"You… you're okay?" Dagny finally broke the silence, her voice barely threatening to break. She reached out, hesitated, then gently tucked a strand of hair behind Osa's ear. Her fingers brushed against a small scar on her daughter's temple, one she didn't remember being there before.

She'd missed so much.

Osa flinched slightly at the touch but didn't pull away. The tiny movement felt like victory and heartbreak all at once.

"I'm fine, Mom," she said, her tone flat, guarded. "You didn't have to come here. I had everything under control."

The familiar stubbornness in Osa's voice transported Dagny back in time. Suddenly, she was looking at toddler Osa, arms crossed, declaring she could dress herself, even as she put her shoes on the wrong feet.

"Under control?" Dagny couldn't keep the disbelief from her voice. It came out harsher than she intended, sandpaper against her vocal cords. "You were kidnapped by terrorists. I saw the bruises, I—"

"It's not what you think," Osa interrupted, her eyes flashing with a mix of defiance and something else. Uncertainty? Fear? The complexity in her gaze reminded Dagny of the swirling nebulas she'd seen on deep space missions, beautiful and dangerous and utterly unknowable.

"They're not terrorists," Osa said. "They're revolutionaries. They have a cause. A true purpose."

The words slammed Dagny in the solar plexus, knocking all the air out of her. She recoiled slightly, her mind reeling. The room seemed to shiver, the glow-in-the-dark stars around the display wall swimming in her vision.

"A cause? What are you saying?"

Osa cast her mother's hands away and stood. She started to pace the length of the room. Her long, willowy frame seemed too big for the confined area, like a sapling that had outgrown its pot. Dagny watched her daughter move, struck by how fluid and graceful she'd become. When had that happened? When had her awkward, gangly teenager transformed into this poised young woman?

"You wouldn't understand," Osa said, running a hand through her hair in a gesture so like Dagny's own that it made her heart clench. If she hadn't seen Nova do it perfectly, she would have believed she had stepped out of time and was seeing her younger self.

But Osa was not Nova. Not Dagny. She needed to keep remembering that.

"You've always been so caught up in your perfect Alliance, your perfect ship," Osa pivoted near the star-wall and started to march back toward Dagny "You never saw the bigger picture."

The accusation stung, bringing back memories of countless arguments, of the growing distance between them that Dagny had been powerless to bridge.

"I gave up everything for you," Dagny said. The words tasted like ashes in her mouth, bitter and final. "My career, my reputation, my future. All of it, to get you safe."

She wrapped her hands around herself, tight. It hurt to look at Osa, but she couldn't look away.

Osa stopped pacing, close but out of reach. Her eyes went cloudy, then widened as the implications of Dagny's words sank in.

"What do you mean, you gave up everything?"

Dagny squeezed her middle. Her insides churned.

"I sabotaged the Breaking Light, Osa," she said, the words

tumbling out like escape pods jettisoning from a dying ship. "Gave it to Beloved Spring. I betrayed my crew, my friends. All to save you."

The silence that followed felt vaster than space itself. Dagny watched Osa's face cycle through a range of emotions. Shock, disbelief, anger, and finally, a dawning horror. Each expression another twist of an invisible knife in Dagny's gut.

"No," Osa said. She dropped to her knees in front of Dagny. "You couldn't have. Tell me you didn't?"

The dam broke. Tears spilled down Dagny's cheeks, hot and relentless. She leaned forward, chest almost on her thighs, so broken.

"What choice did I have? They wanted the ship. I wanted you."

"Me?" Osa still didn't seem to get it.

"You're my daughter, my whole world. I couldn't lose you, not again." Not like she'd lost her own mother. Death was final. Her mother could not reach out from the grave. But Dagny was still alive. She would never stop reaching out to her daughter.

The admission hung heavy with years of unspoken pain. Dagny had never told Osa about her grandmother's death in childbirth, about the gaping hole it had left in her life.

Osa sat back, on her heels, her own eyes glistening.

"But I never asked for that," she said. "I didn't want your sacrifice."

It was like they were back on Chang-ko, Dagny watching her thirteen-year-old daughter slip away from her all over again. The fresh bite of that memory mixed with the present moment, creating a maelstrom of emotion that threatened to pull her under.

"I know I made mistakes," Dagny said. She closed her eyes, remembering the moment she'd decided to create Osa, the overwhelming love and hope she'd felt. "I know I hurt you. But everything I've ever done, Osa, has been out of love for you. You were my dream, my miracle."

Osa's shoulders slumped, the fight seeming to drain out of her. She moved to sit beside Dagny, close enough that their shoulders touched.

"I remember," Osa said softly, her voice taking on a wistful tone that made her sound young again. "When I was little, you used to tell me that the stars were diamonds scattered by ancient space dragons. I believed every word."

A watery hiccup of a chuckle escaped Dagny's lips, the sound surprising them both.

"You were so curious, always asking questions. I could barely keep up. You wanted to know everything about the universe."

Osa's tone transported Dagny back to that night under alien stars. "Remember that time on Stryker, when we went camping in the desert? I wouldn't sleep under the stars because I was convinced the space dragons might come back for their diamonds."

Dagny nodded, the memory bittersweet. The taste of Stryker's pine and sand air seemed to fill her senses. "You insisted on building a fort out of our supplies. We ended up sleeping in a pile of thermal blankets and ration packs."

She could almost feel the gritty sand between her toes, hear the whisper of the dune wind. A night of pure joy, untainted by what would come later.

"You were so stubborn," Dagny continued, a fond smile tugging at her lips. "You wouldn't rest until every crack in our makeshift shelter was sealed. 'No dragons allowed,' you kept saying."

Osa let out a soft laugh, the sound like music to Dagny's ears. "I was terrified, but I didn't want you to know. I thought if I acted brave enough, I could keep us both safe."

The irony of that statement hung in the air between them, unspoken but palpable. Dagny felt a lump form in her throat, thinking of all the times she'd tried to be brave for Osa, to shield her from the harsh realities of the universe.

They lapsed into silence, the shared memory a fragile bridge across the years of hurt and misunderstanding. The weight of exhaustion pressed down on Dagny, the events of the past days catching up all at once. Her body felt heavy, as if she were standing on a high-gravity planet.

The bunk room seemed to pulse around them, the amber light creating a cocoon of warmth. The silky call of the blanket pulled at Dagny.

As her eyes began to droop, she felt Osa shift beside her. "Mom?" her daughter's voice was hesitant, almost child-like. It reminded Dagny of countless nights when a young Osa would crawl into her bed, seeking comfort from nightmares. "I'm glad you're here. Even if I don't understand why you did it."

Dagny lay back. She managed a small smile, her eyes already closing. "I'll always come for you, Osa. Always."

As sleep claimed her, Dagny felt Osa's hand slip into hers. The gesture was so achingly familiar it brought fresh tears to her eyes. Osa's skin was soft, but Dagny could feel the calluses that spoke of her daughter's work as a xenobiologist. Even in sleep, Dagny marveled at how much Osa had grown, how much she had missed.

Somewhere in the vast, uncaring void of space, perhaps the ancient space dragons watched over them, scattering diamonds in their wake.

"Wait," she heard Osa say, from far away. "Is that my sweater?"

CHAPTER
TWENTY-SIX

THE SCENT of cinnamon and nutmeg wafted through Dagny's dreams, gently tugging her back to consciousness. For a moment, she was a child again, waking up to one of her father's rare attempts at breakfast. But as she opened her eyes, the unfamiliar contours of the bunk room came into focus, and reality set in.

Osa sat cross-legged on the floor, a tray of food balanced precariously on her knees. The sight of her daughter, illuminated by the soft amber light, made Dagny's heart stutter. It was a scene so domestic, so normal, that it felt out of place in this new, foreign world.

"Morning," Osa said around a bite of the biggest breakfast pastry Dagny had ever seen. "I brought breakfast. Or dinner. Or whatever meal your belly says this is."

Dagny sat up slowly, her muscles protesting after hours of stillness. The silky blanket slid off her shoulders, even across the nubbly arms of Osa's sweater. She inhaled deeply, letting the aroma of the food fill her senses.

"Smells fantastic," she said, her voice still rough with sleep. "Like the spice markets on Chang-ka-ko."

Osa's eyes lit up at the mention of the moon. "Remember that vendor who sold those star-shaped pastries? The ones that changed flavor with every bite?"

"How could I forget? You were so excited, you nearly knocked over the entire cart trying to get a closer look."

Osa broke the pastry in half, setting the other half on a pale green ceramic plate. As she handed Dagny the plate, their fingers brushed. Dagny sighed.

The food looked as good as it smelled—the flaky pastry filled with what appeared to be savory protein and vegetables. One bite and flavor exploded across her tongue. Rich and complex, the layers of spice reminded her of distant worlds and long-ago adventures. For a moment, she could almost forget where they were, what had brought them here.

But reality was never far away. As they ate in companionable silence, Dagny studied her daughter's face, searching for signs of the passionate revolutionary she'd glimpsed earlier. What she saw instead was uncertainty, a flicker of doubt in those dreamy eyes so like her own.

Nova could shape up a reasonable Dagny shape, but the Iridah hadn't gotten that detail right.

"Osa," Dagny began cautiously, setting her plate aside. "Tell me about Beloved Spring. Are you really with them?"

Osa's shoulders tensed slightly, but she met Dagny's gaze.

"They talked about change, about breaking down the barriers between worlds." She set her piece of pastry on the large serving plate. "Xenobiologists, you know, we see first-hand how rigid and unfair some Alliance policies can be. The Spring promised a new way forward."

Her words lacked the fervor of true belief, sounding more like a rehearsed speech than a heartfelt conviction.

Dagny pressed gently, "And now? After being here, seeing how they operate?"

Osa's gaze dropped to her plate. She pushed a piece of pastry around with her finger, leaving a trail like a comet's tail.

"Not what I expected," she admitted. "They're not as different from the Alliance as they claim to be. Maybe even worse, in some ways."

Dagny reached out, placing her hand over Osa's, stopping the comet's path. "Tell me more."

Osa pulled her hand away. "It's like, you know how some nebulae look beautiful from a distance, all swirling colors and cosmic majesty? But when you get close, you realize it's just dust and radiation? Completely hostile to life."

Did she ever. "That's an insightful way to put it," she finally said.

"I thought I was joining a revolution," Osa said, her voice gaining strength. "But it's just another group of people who think they know best, who are willing to hurt others to get what they want. And they're not wearing masks around us, Mom. Around me. Around you. Do you know what that means?"

Dagny had not thought of it before. In her mouth, the savory pastry turned to dust.

She choked the bite down. "They don't intend to let us go," she said. "Either of us."

Osa's eyes widened, as if hearing the words aloud made the reality of their situation sink in.

"I'm so sorry, Mom. I never meant for any of this to happen. I just wanted to, I don't know. Make a difference." She looked away, toward the door. Her mouth drooped the way it used to before two-year-old Osa started to wail.

"Oh, sweetie" Dagny said, her voice thick. She dropped to the floor to sit beside her daughter, leaning on the side of the bed and wrapping an arm around her shoulders. Osa leaned into the embrace, and for a moment, Dagny was transported back in time, comforting a much younger Osa after a nightmare.

"You know," Osa said softly, "I had this whole speech prepared for you at the diner. Galaxy George! You remembered my obsession, when I barely did anymore."

She smiled into the crook of Dagny's arm. "I was going to talk about how I'd realized you weren't a horrible mother, that you'd done what you needed to do to have me.

Dagny's breath caught. Unwarranted hope rose. "You were?"

"Traveling, studying other cultures, it showed me a lot. Of course not everyone thinks like the people on Chang-ko. I was going to tell you that I understood, finally. That I was glad you made the choice you did."

Dagny didn't know what to say. She'd noticed none of this at the diner. Osa had seemed overwhelmed, had acted stiff and unwelcoming.

Because she was about to do something hard.

Her girl was always prickly before a performance. Dance recitals, major exams. Idly, Dagny wondered who Osa had taken her nerves out on before her dissertation defense. Wouldn't wanted to be that person.

Osa lifted her head, looking straight at Dagny. "But then someone from the Spring approached me outside the bathroom. They said they needed to pick me up right away, right now. It was urgent. And everything spiraled from there."

The started to speak, but had no words. All this time, all this pain, and they had been so close to reconciliation.

The cruelty of the timing made her want to scream at the universe.

Instead, she held her daughter tighter, feeling Osa's tears soaking into her shirt. Her own tears wetted her daughter's wayward curls.

"I'm here now," Dagny murmured into Osa's hair. "We're together, and we'll figure this out."

As they clung to each other, Dagny's mind raced. The knowledge that Osa hadn't willingly thrown in her lot with terrorists was a relief, but it didn't change the gravity of their situation. They were still prisoners, pawns in a game whose rules she didn't fully understand.

Osa pulled back slightly, her eyes distant, as if reliving a memory. "There's something else," she said, her voice low and troubled. "Earlier, in the kitchen with Aria... it was strange, Mom. The way they looked at me, talked around me. It was like I wasn't really welcome, like I'd never earn a place here."

Goosebumps rose on Dagny's arms despite the room's warmth. She waited for Osa to continue.

Osa's brow furrowed, her hands twisting in her lap. "It's hard to explain. Like... you know how some plants on exoplanets look almost identical to Earth species, but there's always something just slightly off? That's how it felt. They smiled, but their eyes were cold. They talked about plans, but clammed up when I got too close. It's like they know I'm already having second thoughts."

Dagny nodded slowly, pieces clicking into place in her

mind like a complex encryption finally breaking. "Like you said, they're not wearing masks."

Osa's eyes widened, the implication sinking in. "But they didn't say you'd be hurt! They said you wouldn't be involved at all. That once we had the comms device…"

"The comms device?" Dagny interrupted. "They never said anything to me about the comms device. They wanted the ship itself. The Breaking Light."

The color drained from Osa's face, her freckles standing out starkly against suddenly pale skin. "Shit," she whispered. "Shit! How could I be so stupid."

Dagny reached out, taking Osa's trembling hands in her own. "Not stupid," she said firmly. "Deceived. We both were."

Osa shook her head, her hair falling forward to curtain her face. "No, you don't understand. It's worse than that." She pulled her hands away so she could drag them through her hair. "I overheard them talking. The Spring, they've gotten their hands on some new map. They're going to use it to plant traps at the jump-tunnel exits in this sector of space."

The words blew through Dagny. Her mind immediately leapt to the consequences, the danger not just to them but to everyone in Alliance space.

Shit, indeed.

She started to work the problem

"We have to warn the Light," she said. "The rescue ship that they'll send for the Breaking Light—it might stumble on one of those traps."

"How?" Osa's voice cracked. "We're stuck here, Mom. How can we possibly get a message out?"

Dagny's gaze dropped to her wrist, where her comms unit sat innocuously. Then her eyes flicked to Osa's wrist, where an identical device rested. They must have given it back after securing Dagny's help.

A spark of an idea flared in her mind, growing rapidly into a blazing plan.

They were still called comm units, but they were far more than that. Packed with sensors and powerful apps, they were designed to send and receive data in all sorts of environments. Including hostile ones.

"You've thought of something," Osa said.

Dagny nodded, her mind tracking the possibilities, the challenges, the risks. "Might work. We have the tool, but we need the portal."

A familiar thrill run through Dagny's veins. This was what she was made for—solving impossible problems, finding ways to connect across the vast emptiness of space. For the first time in a week, she felt like herself again.

Osa's set her shoulders, determination in her eyes. "Tell me what to do. I want to help."

Looking at her daughter, Dagny saw not just the child she'd raised. Not the stranger she'd become. But a partner. An equal. Pride swelled in her chest, fierce and bright as a newborn star.

"Alright," Dagny said, her mind mapping out the steps they'd need to take. "What here are you allergic to?"

CHAPTER
TWENTY-SEVEN

SEATED on the floor in front of their shared bunk, Dagny's hands trembled as she tipped the tin of curry over the last bit of flaky breakfast pastry. They'd eaten most of the head-sized savory delicacy, but there was this little bit left.

And the poison.

She looked at Osa, next to her on the floor. Her daughter's face was set in grim determination.

"You're sure you want to do this?" Dagny said. "We could just pretend."

Osa shook her head, her dark hair falling across her eyes. She flicked it back with a practiced head shake.

"No, mom. It has to be real." She reached out and took the pastry from Dagny's reluctant grasp. "We've got the inhaler. And besides, it's not like I haven't gone through this before."

The casual reference to past incidents sent a pang through Dagny's heart. How many times had Osa faced this alone, without her mother there to help?

"Just. Be careful," Dagny said. Lame, she knew

Osa jammed the whole thing into her mouth. For a moment, nothing happened. Osa chewed slowly, her expression neutral. Dagny held her breath, a part of her hoping that maybe, just maybe, Osa had outgrown the allergy.

Then it began.

Osa's face puffed red. Her eyes closed, either to hide her panic or because they were starting to swell.

"Happening," Osa gasped, her voice already growing raspy. "Too fast."

Dagny was moving before Osa could finish, her body responding to a fear as old and deep as motherhood itself. She caught Osa as she slumped forward, lowering her gently back to the floor. The silky blanket from the bunk tangled around their feet as Dagny cradled her daughter's head.

"It's okay, baby," Dagny murmured, her voice steadier than she felt. "I'm here. Just like we planned, right?"

But this was worse than they had anticipated. Much worse.

Osa's breath came in short, wheezing gasps, each one a knife in Dagny's heart. Her skin was clammy to the touch, a sheen of sweat making her look otherworldly in the amber light of the bunk room. Dagny brushed Osa's dark hair back from her forehead, the gesture as automatic as breathing.

This was too much.

Dagny pulled the inhaler out of the pocket of her sweater. It was sleek and unfamiliar, nothing like the clunky medical dispenser they'd used when Osa was small. Must be one of the emergency-room kinds, with extras. She clicked it open and a weblike mask shook out, too.

Dagny stretched the mask to cover Osa's nose and her

mouth. But when she went to set it on her daughter's face, Osa rolled away.

"No! Make the call."

Dagny swallowed hard, hating herself for what she was about to do. Every instinct screamed at her to help her daughter, to ease her suffering. But they both knew this was their only chance.

She ran to the door and banged on the control panel beside it. Behind her, Osa's breaths were a thin scream. Dagny pushed the too-slow sliding door open.

"Help!" she screamed. The fear in her voice was real.

"What is the problem?" The sterile voice filled the hallway. This ship's AI was no match for Sally.

"Medical emergency!" Dagny lifted her foot and reached back, slipping the inhaler into her boot. The cool metal pressed against her ankle like a guilty secret. "My daughter! She's having convulsions. I think she's going to pass out."

"Help is on the way," the ship said. "Please prepare the patient."

Something metal clanged at the end of the hallway. Dagny ran back to Osa. Her daughter's color was nearing raw beets. Cooked beets was critical, so they still had some time.

She kicked the breakfast tray out of the way, grabbed her daughter under armpits, and started dragging her toward the hall. Osa's breathing deepened. The movement must be helping her lungs.

A basic metal gurney rolled down the hall toward them. As it neared, it sank on its supports until it was knee high. Easy for Dagny to lift-roll Osa onto its long, tan cushion. As soon as she was settled, the gurney pushed itself to waist height and raised its side rails. It had only simple scanners, heart, breath, temperature. Which all signaled red.

"Please step away from the gurney," the ship said.

"I need to stay with my daughter!"

A pause, and then, "You may accompany your daughter to the medical bay."

Step One, complete.

CHAPTER
TWENTY-EIGHT

THE CORRIDORS of the Horizon's Edge seemed to stretch endlessly, the slow whoop of the gurney's hydraulics on the rubber decking a counterpoint to the tympanic stutter of Dagny's heart. She recognized the route, with its junctions and access panels—standard issue boxy ship. Still, she catalogued every details, trying to distract from screaming in her head to focus solely on Osa.

Her daughter was not in real danger, so long as Dagny and the inhaler were with her. No matter how terrifyingly red she looked.

They burst into a small space far more advanced than Dagny had expected. Sleek diagnostic equipment lined the walls, their displays coming to life as Osa was transferred to an examination bed. The air here was cooler, tinged with the sharp scent of disinfectant that cut through the lingering aroma of spices clinging to Dagny's clothes.

The medical suite must be a warren, if all the rooms were so small. A doctor—or at least someone officious—appeared as if by magic, pushing through a clear plastic curtain over a door opposite the one they came in through. Dagny found herself pushed to the side, a spectator in her own daughter's drama.

"Sinuses, esophagus, stomach. What did she eat?" the doctor demanded, not looking up from where she was pressing sensors to Osa's pale skin.

"A pastry," Dagny said, her voice sounding distant to her own ears. "There was cardamom in it, but she's not allergic to that.

"Not cardamom," the doctor muttered, tapping rapidly on a data pad and clucking her tongue. "Curry powder. Uncommon, but not unheard of. We can handle this."

Got it right in one. Relief washed over Dagny, so powerful it made her knees weak. She sagged against a nearby console, her fingers gripping the edge to keep herself upright. The cool metal beneath her hands was an anchor, reminding her that this was real, that Osa would be okay.

"Deep though," the doctor set her hand on Osa's solar plexus. "Gonna need to sedate her. Slow the process of the spice." She looked at Dagny. "Okay, mom?"

Why didn't she ask Osa for permission? Her daughter was an adult.

Because her daughter was completely limp.

"Do it!" Dagny said. "Now!"

On the opposite side of the bed from the doctor, Dagny took one of Osa's limp hands in her own. For once, her hand was warmer.

As the medico worked on Osa, Dagny's eyes darted around the room, taking in every detail. There, in the corner, the familiar shape of a comms interface. Inactive, screen dark, but still. Access.

The door burst open, flooding the room with harsh light from the corridor. Aria stood framed in the doorway, her expression shifting from annoyance to alarm in the space of a heartbeat.

"What happened?" she demanded, striding into the room.

"I don't know," Dagny said, letting real panic seep into her voice. "Something she ate."

Aria's pale gaze scoured Dagny and found her wanting. "Most people take their allergy treatments as children."

"It wasn't offered where we lived," Dagny said. She turned her head, supposedly to look at Osa but in reality hiding any tell of her lies. "It was never this bad before."

Aria sighed, and leaned against the wall beside the door. She crossed one foot over the other.

"She'll be fine," she said. Dagny looked up at her, surprised. Aria's arms were crossed, her expression unreadable. "Our medical facilities are top-notch. Have to be."

Dagny could only nod. She watched as the doctor administered some kind of hypospray to Osa's neck. Almost immediately, her daughter's breathing eased, the terrible wheezing fading to normal respiration.

"She'll sleep for a while," the doctor said, looking up at Dagny. "While the drip clears the irritant. The spray will keep her under for at least an hour. You can stay with her if you like. You don't need to.

"I'll stay right here." Dagny's relief was so great she worried Aria would think it was faked.

Aria's hand on her shoulder startled her. "Stay," she said,

her voice softer than Dagny had ever heard it. "Call if you need anything."

The medico doublechecked the sensors, nodded to herself, and then left.

Dagny allowed herself a moment to simply breathe. The antiseptic smell of the medical bay burned in her nostril. The aftertaste fear lingered in the back of her throat, metallic and bitter.

Osa was safe. For now. But the real work was just beginning.

The outer door hissed open. Aria about to leave.

Dagny's fingers ghosted over Osa's arm, tracing the outline of a fading bruise. The discoloration here and on her face stood out starkly against her daughter's pale skin, a painful reminder of how this all began.

"Aria," Dagny called out. "Wait."

Aria paused in the doorway. She turned, both eyebrows raised.

Dagny swallowed hard, steeling herself. "The bruises on Osa. When I saw them in that photo you sent." She shivered despite herself. "What happened?"

Aria's smile was cold. She leaned against the doorframe, arms crossed, the soft swish of fabric against fabric audible in the quiet room.

"Forgot to strap in right in the shuttle," Aria said, her tone casual, almost bored. "Gravity's a bitch."

The explanation hung in the air between them, simple yet loaded with implications. Dagny's hand tightened on the edge of Osa's bed, its sharp edge biting into her palm.

"That's it?" Dagny pressed, not quite believing.

Aria shrugged, the movement causing a slight creak in her

leather jacket. "That's it. Your daughter's smart, but some-times she forgets the basics." Her eyes flicked to Osa's sleeping form, then back to Dagny. "Anything else?"

Dagny shook her head, not trusting herself to speak. Aria nodded once, then left, the door closing behind her.

Alone with her daughter, Dagny let out a shaky breath. The constant hum of medical equipment seemed to grow louder in the silence, punctuated by the steady beep of Osa's heart monitor. She ran her thumb over Osa's knuckles, the way she had when they were young.

She waited another five minutes, counting each second, before moving to the computer terminal.

Step Two.

Her hands flew over the old-fashioned interface, muscle memory taking over as she bypassed security protocols and delved deep into the ship's systems.

The touch of the keys under her fingers grounded her, focusing her mind on the task at hand. As the screen came to life, bathing her face in a soft sienna glow, Dagny pushed aside her lingering doubts and fears. There would be time for ques-tions later. Right now, they had a mission to complete.

The AI's presence was immediately apparent, far more sophisticated than she'd anticipated. It manifested as lines of code that seemed to shift and change even as she read them, adapting to her queries in real-time.

"Identify yourself," flashed across the screen.

Dagny hesitated for a fraction of a second before typing, "Chief Communications Engineer Dagny Novak, Breaking Light."

There was a pause, longer than should have been necessary for a computer to process the information. Then:

"Greetings, Chief Engineer Novak. Your credentials are not recognized, but your access patterns indicate advanced knowledge of Alliance systems. State your purpose."

The AI's "voice," as expressed through text, was formal and precise, with an underlying current of curiosity that Dagny found unsettling. This was no mere computer program. This was something more.

"I need further information," Dagny typed, her fingers flying over the keys. "About Beloved Spring's plans. About the new aliens. About the booby traps in this sector."

Another pause, this one even longer. Dagny glanced nervously at Osa, still peacefully asleep on the medical bed. The soft beep of monitoring equipment was the only sound in the room.

Finally, the AI responded:

"Your inquiry touches on matters of great sensitivity. Beloved Spring has classified this information at the highest levels. However, your presence here and your apparent lack of knowledge suggest a discrepancy that requires resolution. I will provide limited information to correct this discrepancy."

Dagny's heart raced. This was it. Their chance.

"Proceed," she typed.

The information that followed was a flood, each revelation more shocking than the last.

CHAPTER
TWENTY-NINE

IN A TINY TREATMENT room in the Horizon's Edge's medical suite, its machines washing the poison from her unconscious daughter's veins, Dagny learned the secrets of this galaxy.

The AI's response scrolled across the screen, each line of text sending a jolt of adrenaline through Dagny's system.

"Beloved Spring has made contact with a new sentient species in the Nebula NGC-4993, colloquially known as the 'Fog Nebula' due to its unique electromagnetic properties. First contact was established 237 standard days ago. The species, which calls itself Soumai, possesses technology significantly advanced beyond current Alliance capabilities."

First contact. Dagny's mind reeled. The dreamed-of goal of the Breaking Light, achieved not by the Alliance but by a group they considered terrorists.

The AI continued: "Beloved Spring has represented itself to the Soumai as the primary governing body of this sector of space. The existence of the Alliance has been deliberately omitted from all communications."

The AI obviously had a feeling about that.

A wave of nausea washed over her. The implications were staggering. What had Beloved Spring told these new people? Would these significantly advanced beings fight to protect their new friends, the enemies of the Alliance?

"The placement of mines at strategic jump points throughout the sector is intended to prevent Alliance interference in this delicate first contact situation. Beloved Spring leadership believes that Alliance involvement would jeopardize the peaceful relations established with the Soumai."

Dagny's hands shook as she typed her response: "But the deception can't last. What happens when the Soumai learn the truth?"

The AI's reply was not quite instantaneous: "That eventuality has been calculated. Beloved Spring intends to negotiate a separate peace treaty with the Soumai before the deception is discovered, positioning themselves as the intermediary between the new species and the 'newly discovered' Alliance."

Clever. Protecting themselves from retribution by the Alliance with the threat to choke off any new discoveries the Soumai might share.

She was about to inquire further when a new message flashed across the screen. Shipwide.

Warning: Alliance vessel detected entering the sector. Classification: Retribution-class gunship. Estimated time to weapons range: 37 minutes.

Dagny's blood ran cold. Retributions were heavily armed and designed for rapid response and overwhelming force. If it encountered the Horizon's Edge, there would be no negotiation, no chance for explanation. Just destruction.

There was no guarantee the Horizon's Edge was the only terrorist ship in this sector. Would the survivors sic their new Soumai friends after the Alliance?

Could the Alliance start a war it had no idea was even in the offing?

She typed frantically: "We need to warn them about the mines. And about the Soumai. How can we send a message?"

The AI's response was maddeningly calm: "Standard communications are monitored and restricted." Dagny groaned aloud. But then the AI continued.

"However, there is an override protocol accessible from the primary bridge console. It would allow a brief, encrypted burst transmission."

"How do I access the bridge?" Dagny typed.

"The bridge is currently locked down. All non-essential personnel are restricted to their quarters due to heightened security protocols."

Dagny glanced at Osa, still peacefully unconscious. The monitor beside her bed showed stable vital signs, but Dagny knew the medication wouldn't last forever. They were running out of time.

She turned back to the console: "Is there any other way to send a message? Anything at all?"

The AI's response was slow in coming; a full ten seconds. "There is an alternative. The ship's waste reclamation system includes a matter-energy conversion unit for processing organic waste. In theory, it could be repurposed to create a short-range pulse. This could potentially bypass traditional communication barriers."

Dagny's mind skimmed the data, piecing together the implications. It was brilliant, if completely disgusting. And incredibly dangerous. One misstep and they'd be atomized along with the ship's waste.

What choice did they have?

"How do I access the reclamation system?" she typed.

As the AI provided instructions, a soft moan from behind made Dagny whirl around. Osa was stirring, her eyelids fluttering.

Dagny dropped a packet of the data the AI had given her into the buffer of the waste-reclamation controls and then wiped and second-wiped the text of their conversation. She even purged the memory of the keyboard interface.

Dagny moved to her daughter's bedside. She gently brushed that wayward strand of hair from Osa's forehead. She looked so young, so easy. The last time Dagny had watched Osa sleep had been the night before she left for the Interplanetary Exchange Program. She'd had stood in the doorway of Osa's bedroom, memorizing every detail, knowing it might be the last time she got the chance.

Now, as Osa's eyes slowly opened, Dagny saw not just her little girl, but the strong, capable woman she'd become. A woman who had made mistakes, yes, but who was willing to risk everything to make things right.

"Mom?" Osa's voice was hoarse, whisper-soft. She sat up slowly. The sensors on her skin dropped off, unneeded.

Dagny pulled the needle for the saline drip out of the inside corner of Osa's elbow, pressing down on the spot so it would not bleed. She spoke toward the corner of the room. "It's okay, sweetheart. You had a reaction to the curry, but you're going to be just fine."

Osa knew that fake tone of voice. "Worked?" she whisper-croaked.

Dagny nodded, and squeezed Osa's arm again before letting her go. "We need to get back to our room," she said, still in that voice. "There's some trouble outside. Think you can walk?" She looked around. "Bet they can get us a chair if we ask."

"I'd like a chair," Osa said. "A hover one, not with wheels."

By the time she'd slowly slid off the bed and onto her feet on the floor, a JetChair had entered the room from the back door, pushing through its transparent plastic curtain.

Osa dropped gratefully into the white vinyl and plastic chair, scooped for comfort, which used a joystick instead of a touchpad control.

"Back to the bunk room?" she said.

"That's the plan," Dagny said. But her head moved side to side. No.

Osa grinned. "Got it. Not sure how we got here, though. You'll need to lead." She winked.

As they made their way to the door, Dagny's mind raced through the plan. Move quickly, avoid detection, and somehow reprogram a waste reclamation system into a pulse communicator. Within the next thirty-one minutes, before the Alliance gunship came into range. Ideally, way before.

It was insane. Impossible. And their only hope.

The fate of three civilizations rested on their shoulders, and the clock was ticking.

CHAPTER
THIRTY

THE WASTE RECLAMATION center assaulted Dagny's senses like a poorly maintained spaceport on a backwater moon. The acrid stench of industrial cleaners battled with the underlying funk of organic waste, creating a nauseating cocktail that made her eyes water. Harsh, utilitarian lighting cast everything into sickly yellow and threw deep shadows into corners where Dagny half-expected to see something skitter away.

As she stepped into the first of the processing rooms, the constant low hum of machinery vibrated through the soles of her feet, a raucous march of pumps, filters, and processors working tirelessly to keep the ship's waste from overwhelming its inhabitants. It was a far as they could get from the sterile, controlled environment of the medical bay they'd just left.

Osa wrinkled her nose, her hover chair whirring softly as she maneuvered into the room.

"Wow. No way we could just do this from the hallway?"

Dagny couldn't help but smile at her daughter's under-stated disgust. So familiar, so Osa. For a moment Dagny could almost forget the dire circumstances that had brought them here. Almost.

"Trust me, sweetheart, this isn't my idea of a fun family outing either," Dagny said, her eyes already scanning the room for the access panel she needed. The sooner they got this done, the better.

A wall of gauges, a wall of those cheap shelf desks that sagged as soon as someone leaned on them. No chairs, which would only make sitting on the desks more appealing. No people, which wasn't that surprising. Whatever could be done remotely was probably being done remotely.

There. On the far wall next to the door to the next, prob-ably smellier, room. A nondescript gray box that looked like it hadn't been touched in years.

As Dagny approached the box, she locked the door next to it. Then her hand went to her wrist, fingers ghosting over the comms unit. She scanned the screen that popped in front of her.

"All right," she said more to herself than Osa. "Let's see what we're working with here."

Her fingers flew over the interface, navigated through layers of brittle security protocols. It was like playing a complex melody on an instrument she'd never seen before, but whose music she knew by heart.

"Mom?" Osa's voice cut through her concentration. "What are you going to tell them?"

The Breaking Light, gliding along without its main engine. The warship, faster, bearing down on the both of them.

Dagny paused, her hands hovering over the controls. She turned to face her daughter.

"I'm warning Breaking Light and the Alliance warship about the mines in the system," she began, her voice steady despite the storm of emotions churning inside her. "I'm telling them that Beloved Spring already has the map. And…" She hesitated, knowing the affect her next words would have on her oh-so-curious daughter. "And that they've made first contact with a new species. The Soumai."

Osa's eyes widened, a spark of excitement igniting in their depths. The same look she'd had as a child listening to stories of far-off worlds and undiscovered wonders.

"First contact? Seriously? What else do you know about them?"

The hunger for knowledge in Osa's voice made Dagny's heart ache. This was what her daughter was meant for. Exploring. Discovering. Gaining understanding. Not being caught up in a deadly game of political intrigue and betrayal.

"Not enough for your taste, I'm afraid," Dagny said, turning back to the console, which was now responding to the commands on her screen. "The AI had more details. I'm sending everything. But I haven't had time to read it."

"Did you keep a copy?" Osa asked.

Dagny hadn't planned to. It was a big file, and wristcom storage wasn't infinite.

But she could easily slice the piece that referred to the Soumai out.

As the reclamation's system analyzed itself for her, Dagny sought out and copied the fog belt—the Fold—data. She set the file to send and touched her wristcom to Osa's. It shouldn't work—Osa should have had a firewall up and require permission to download—but the file dropped right in.

They'd have to have a talk about data safety later.

"Is there anything else you think I should include?" she asked instead. "Do you know how many people are on the ship? Anything like that?"

Osa was quiet for so long that Dagny turned to look at her. Her daughter frowned in thought. When she spoke, her voice carried a mix of awe and frustration.

"No, that covers it. But." She paused, and a dozen emotions chased each other on her face. "I can't believe how the Breaking Light people treated you. Why are you even helping them? They hurt your wrists! And for what? You were just trying to save me."

Dagny gasped, and then choked on the room's miasma. Osa didn't know the whole story. "No time for that, hon. Right now, we need to focus on preventing a disaster."

As if on cue, Aria's voice suddenly crackled through a nearby comm panel, tense and urgent: "What? Get us right the hell out of that target lock, now! I don't care what it does to the ship. Flip the blasted thing."

Dagny and Osa shared a look of alarm. The weight of their task, already heavy, seemed to double in an instant.

Osa scooted closer to the closed door to the outer hall. They'd seen no one in this part of the ship earlier, but that was no guarantee.

Dagny checked her screen. The data transfer seemed to crawl, each second stretching into eternity. She was acutely aware of every sound—the burble of the pipes, the hum of the cooling fans, the soft whir of Osa's chair. Her own pulse pounding in her ears.

Finally it was all across, into the reclamation system's buffer. Dagny compressed it yet again, opened the system's rudimentary comms link, now boosted by the targeting app on her wristcom, and blasted the data like buckshot toward the two Alliance ships. She didn't want to risk a second comms blast, so she spread the message wide, hoping both ships would catch it. Hoping at least one ship would recognize it.

Then, she shut down the reclamation system's comm channel entirely. But not before she sent the command, shut down system for maintenance.

Just as Dagny reached Osa at the door, footsteps echoed in the corridor outside. Osa reacted instantly, maneuvering her hover chair to block the doorway. Dagny pressed her back against the wall and held her breath.

Seeing Osa here would be odd enough. Seeing Dagny here would be a dead giveaway.

The door didn't open. The footsteps receded down the hall.

Dagny sagged against the wall. Osa put her hand to her heart.

"I don't think I'm built for this," she said.

Under the harsh yellow lights, breathing the sour air, Dagny smiled at her daughter.

"You're doing great."

CHAPTER
THIRTY-ONE

THE STENCH of industrial cleaners gave way to a more insidious odor as Dagny and Osa hurried out of the waste reclamation center. Dagny's nose wrinkled involuntarily, her mind conjuring images of long-forgotten compost heaps. Her sabotage was working, perhaps too well.

"Mom, what did you do?" Osa's voice was muffled, her free hand clamped over her nose as she steered her hover chair with the other.

Dagny's lips quirked in a humorless smile. "Gave them a problem they won't be able to ignore." The irony wasn't lost on her—she, Dagny Novak, once the paragon of reliability, had become disturbingly adept at sabotage.

The corridor stretched before them, its utilitarian gray walls a blur as they rushed towards their assigned quarters. Dagny didn't want to think about why their bunk room was in the same hallway as all the ship's refuse.

Osa's hover chair whirred beside her, a high-pitched counterpoint to the ship's usual bass rumble. "Do you think they got our message?" she asked, her voice tight with worry.

Before Dagny could respond, a new voice filled the air, unfamiliar and authoritative. It emanated from hidden speakers, filling the corridor with its chilling message:

"Unidentified vessel, this is the Alliance warship Nemesis. Prepare to be boarded. You have two minutes to power down your engines."

Or they'd shoot.

Dagny's hands went cold, her steps faltering. She exchanged a look of horror with Osa, seeing her own fear reflected in her daughter's eyes.

"They can't be serious," Dagny said.

The Nemesis wasn't just toying with the Beloved Spring ship. They didn't know this star system was inhabited. They didn't know the rules. What if those new people, the Soumai, thought that warring in their territory was a declaration of war against them?

Osa's face had gone pale, her suns-tinted freckles standing out starkly against her skin.

"They'll start a war we can't win!" she said. "Didn't they get our message?"

Apparently not. Maybe she wasn't considered a reliable narrator any more. But the AI-encoded data couldn't be faked. They had to believe that.

Or, worse, they did get the message and went ahead anyway. Hatred of Beloved Spring ran deep among the Alliance's warfighters.

The consequences of such willful blindness could be catastrophic.

"We need to get to an escape pod," Dagny said, her mind

already racing ahead, mapping out routes and contingencies. "There should be one at the end of the hall. Behind us."

They pivoted, Osa's chair spinning with surprising grace as they headed back the way they came. The ship's alarms began to blare, an atonal wail that set Dagny's teeth on edge. Red and purple emergency lights flashed, making the world look as if it were stuttering.

As they passed the closed door of the waste reclamation center, a series of ominous gurgles and clanks emanated from within. The smell had intensified, seeping through the seams of the door like a noxious fog. Dagny allowed herself a grim smile. At least that part of her plan was working.

Dagny's legs pumping hard to keep up with Osa's hover chair. The ship shuddered around them, the deck plates vibrating beneath Dagny's feet. Whether from weapons fire or the waste systems' imminent rebellion, she couldn't tell.

As they rounded a corner, they nearly collided with a trio of crew members rushing in the opposite direction. Dagny kept her head down, certain they'd be stopped, questioned, detained. But the crew barely spared them a glance, too focused on their own urgent tasks.

They reached the emergency stairwell, its entrance yawning before them like the maw of some great beast. Dagny hesitated, looking at Osa's hover chair.

But Osa was already moving, her fingers flying over the chair's controls. "No worries."

As if to prove her point, the chair rose smoothly into the air, maneuvering down the stairwell with ease. Dagny followed, taking the steps two at a time, her hand trailing along the railing for balance.

Halfway down, the ship rocked violently, nearly sending

Dagny sprawling. She caught herself against the wall, her palm stinging from the impact.

"You okay?" Osa called back, her chair stabilizing itself automatically.

"Fine," Dagny grunted, pushing off the wall. "Keep going!"

They burst out of the stairwell onto level C, the corridor here almost identical to the one they'd left. But Dagny's keen eyes spotted the differences—the slightly wider passageways, the additional safety markings. This level was designed for rapid evacuation.

And the escape pods were hard right of the stairwell. Six identical vertical doors, leading to six pods. Each with a basic push-panel to open.

Dagny punched the panel for the center-right pod.

Nothing.

Osa punched the one for center-left.

It slid open.

The doorway was almost two narrow for the chair. Rather than wait for Osa to maneuver. Dagny grabbed the back of the chair and wrestled it into the pod.

Behind them, Aria's voice filled the corridor. "Everyone, buckle up. Impact in six seconds."

Dagny clambered into the escape pod, closing first the outer hatch and then the inner. The pod was a miniature version of the shuttle that had brought her here. Two long padded benches facing each other, and a compact navigation system up-front.

The pod reeked of new plastic, stale cleaning fluid, and something else—a metallic tang that reminded her of blood. It clung to the back of her throat.

Osa had tipped up part of the bench closest to the navigation station and was tucking her hover chair into the locks built for it underneath the bench.

Dagny ran for the nav station. No way was she trusting the AI to drive this time.

The button to jettison the ship was the only physical control on the the control panel.

Dagny threw herself into the pilot's chair and slammed her hand on the button.

CHAPTER
THIRTY-TWO

THE ESCAPE POD shuddered violently as it detached from the Horizon's Edge. The vibrations traveled up Dagny's arms, rattling her bones and setting her teeth on edge. For a heart-stopping moment, they were in free-fall, the pit of Dagny's stomach lurching as if she'd missed a step in the dark.

Then the thrusters engaged with a roar that filled the small space, drowning out Dagny's yelp of surprise. She hadn't realized these pods even had such power. The force pushed them away from the Horizon's Edge, plastering Dagny against her chair, squeezing the air from her lungs. The pressure on her chest felt like grief made physical.

Then the thrusters clacked off, and all went quiet and floaty. Above the navigation panel, a plastic film of some kind started to roll up, exposing three wide windows. Dagny scanned the view.

No warship.

"Made it," Osa said on a sigh. Buckled into her hoverchair,

which was locked onto this minibus of a ship's hull, she didn't float much. Except for her halo of shiny black hair.

Dagny's must look the same. She forced a small smile, the bitterness of fear still sharp on her tongue.

"Not out of the woods yet, sweetheart." The old phrase, a remnant of a childhood spent planetside, felt hollow out here in the void.

She turned back to the navigation console, pulling up a screen.

"Good news," she said. "Nemesis is behind us. Horizon's Edge is between us and them."

"That's good news?" Osa leaned to the side, peering out one of the side windows. "Who's going to rescue us?"

Well.

Breaking Light wasn't going to welcome Dagny with open arms. They'd just polluted the Horizon's Edge. That left the warship.

"Plan is to get out of shooting range and then call the Nemesis." She didn't like the sound of that sentence.

Osa snapped her attention away from the window and onto Dagny.

"Not Breaking Light?"

Dagny didn't answer right away, busy getting the escape pod's sluggish navigation scans to figure out where all the ships were. Apparently, people were supposed to lock themselves into these tiny metal boxes and then just drift around, waiting for pickup. But then, why have a nav board in the first place?

Finally, it coughed up the coordinates. There was the Breaking Light, off to the right. A little micro-moon with a flat butt in front of the bright light of a distant sun. All the ships were traveling roughly the same speed. Quite the trick, with the Breaking Light on coast, the Nemesis on short burn. Not to mention the Horizon's Edge seeming to cartwheel like a drunken gymnast, trying to avoid being pummeled by the bombs the Nemesis was throwing at them.

At least they were bombs, meant to short out the power and electrical. Not those beams of death.

Now with all the coordinates she needed, Dagny quickly plotted a course away from the conflict. She set the instructions into the autopilot and turned in the pilot's seat to face Osa.

Who had not stopped staring at her.

"It's like this, sweetie," Dagny said. "Beloved Spring told me they had kidnapped you, right? And they wanted me to give them Breaking Light."

"Yes, but—"

Dagny held up a hand. "And they said I couldn't tell anyone or they'd hurt you." Although she had told someone, and nothing had happened. "When my first try messed up, they sent me a photo of you, all bruised up."

Osa's hand went to the greenish-yellow bruise at the top of her cheek. Her eyes went wide. So like Dagny's, and so unlike.

"I believed them. I sabotaged the ship." Dagny took in a shaky breath. "No one there is going to welcome me back."

Osa shook her head. Her hair-halo didn't move. "But how? You do the communications. Not engineering."

"You'd be surprised. But you're right. Both my tricky-tech tries failed."

"There's a non-techie way?"

Dagny glanced away. Breaking Light was behind the view

of the windows now, but its shadow lingered, a thinning cylinder.

She held up a fist, the top of her knuckles pointing at Osa. With the pointer finger of her other hand, she traced the circle, knuckles, thumb, back to knuckles. Then with her index finger and thumb, she "flicked" the bottom bit of the imaginary sphere away.

"Pop the main engine," she said. It's at the bottom pole of the ship. For safety."

Osa stared at Dagny's hand a moment. She blinked, and looked into Dagny's eyes. She actually looked impressed.

"Wow."

"Nobody got hurt," Dagny said quickly. "And we—" Dagny had to swallow. "And they could still get to where they were going, if the Dawn couldn't catch up to them. They just can't jump."

Osa had gone as pale as she had back in the reclamation room. "Oh, mom."

They sat in silence but for the chug-chug of the pod's little motorized fan of an engine. Dagny wished they had another of those giant pastries. With cherries, this time. She was getting hungry, but not yet hungry enough to break out the emergency ration packs.

Then Osa's head tilted, as if she were listening to something outside. She peered out the window closest to her. Her arms, now free from their launch restraints, floated up like willow branches in a light wind.

"Why aren't we going forwards?" she said.

Dagny swung back to the navigation console. Osa was right. With the rotor-engine-thing chugging in the back, the pod should be on a forward trajectory.

But the ship was moving sideways.

Toward the Breaking Light.

Dagny tapped into the instructions she'd given the autopilot. It was all correct. They just weren't following the plan. No gravity wells or other anomalies. It was as if—

Shit.

"Breaking Light has a tow on us. This is bad."

Osa shrugged. "They'd catch us eventually, anyways. One of them. Right?"

"But after all the shooting," Dagny said. She fought with the console to see if she could pull more power for the engine. "Now, we'd just be in the line of fire again." She did not want to trust the Nemesis to hit only its named target.

It wasn't working.

The readouts on the screen blurred before Dagny's eyes, fatigue and stress taking their toll. She blinked hard, wiping at her eyes before the tears started to float away. Willing her vision to clear. Just a little longer.

And a little longer after that.

Forever.

"Mom?" Osa's voice held a note of concern that cut straight to Dagny's heart.

She unbuckled and floated over to the bench beside Osa. She settled onto the bench, a foot around the anchor strap underneath to keep herself in place. She reached for Osa, wrapping her deep in a side hug. She ignored the pain of the hoverchair's short armrest against her hip.

Her strong willow girl hugged her back. She smelled so good, past the veneer of panic and reclamation center. Her core was vanilla chai. Dagny used to tease her that she was one-third chai, she drank so much. Still her girl.

Even with her eyes closed, breathing the soft scent of her daughter's hair, Dagny could picture the ships around them. The Horizon's Edge, cartwheeling, shedding escape pods. The Nemesis, hanging there like a buzzard, waiting for the jackals that were its bombs to harry the Horizon's Edge into submission.

"They always say they'd collect the escapees," Dagny muttered. The words tasted like ash in her mouth, the promise of rescue now feeling more like a threat.

Before Osa could respond, a violent impact rocked the pod. The force of it threw Dagny across the narrow aisle and into the hull. Or rather, she stayed still while the hull ran into her, she thought, dazed. She winced. Her shoulder didn't seem to be right in its socket.

A shrill chorus of alarms erupted. Warning lights bathed the pod's interior in a hellish glow. Osa, still mostly strapped in, looked okay except for the panic streaking across her face.

The acrid smell of burnt circuitry tainted the air. A hissing, barely audible over the alarms but terrifyingly distinct.

Oxygen leak.

"Alarms off!" Osa shouted.

The hissing filled the cabin.

"We're losing air!" Osa's eyes went wide. She quickly unstrapped herself from the chair.

Dagny was already moving, kicking over to her daughter, her body operating on instinct honed by years of emergency drills. Her hands reached for the emergency vacuum suits stored beneath the benches. The skinny packets cold and slick against her palms. Three on this side.

"Quick, put this on," she said, handing one to Osa. The suit felt insubstantial, inadequate. A flimsy barrier against the unforgiving vacuum of space.

Dagny grabbed a second suit but didn't put it on right away. If she could get the pod sealed up again, she wouldn't need to.

Then she looked at the other side of the pod.

The gash stretched at least two meters. The piece of metal —of the Horizon's Edge—that had made it was still jammed in the space.

Just not perfectly tight.

Time to put the suit on.

Time seemed to stretch and compress as they struggled into the suits, each second precious as their breathable air slowly seeped into the void. The suit's slick material clung to the nap of Dagny's sweater. But it was already getting cold in here; she wasn't taking the sweater off.

Her hands shook as she helped Osa seal her helmet, her own suit only half-donned. The fear of failing her daughter, of a mistake that could cost Osa her life, made Dagny's movements frantic yet precise.

Finally, with the hiss of pressurization, they were sealed in their protective cocoons. The sound of Dagny's own breathing, loud in the confines of her helmet, was both comforting and claustrophobic. She allowed herself a moment of relief before turning back to the problem at hand. Just a moment.

Dagny clicked the suit's comms on. "Osa?"

"I'm okay." She had her back to Dagny, heading toward the back of the pod. "Looking for some sealant."

"I'll find out how much air we have left."

How long they had left.

The navigation controls were sluggish under her gloved

hands, barely responding to her inputs. Dagny could taste her panic in every shallow breath.

They were drifting, now. The crash must have knocked them out of the Breaking Light's tow field or something.

Just when they needed a fast tow.

She found the Light, now directly behind them. Big U-turn and head straight there. How long could that take?

Dagny's mind raced, calculating distances and velocities almost as fast as the pod's snail of a nav board. Her brain felt on fire, working so fast it even brought sweat to her chilled forehead.

The air supply. Dagny checked and doublechecked.

Whatever Osa had found, it was doing the trick. The readings weren't dropping nearly as fast. And the suits would give them a couple hours, more if they put themselves to sleep.

The numbers scrolled through her mind, mixing with her planned trajectory. This engine couldn't give any more acceleration. Turning would burn off some of the little they had off. They didn't have to get all the way to the Light, but they had to get close enough to be noticed.

By a ship on cruising speed headed away from them.

The numbers weren't adding up right. They weren't even close.

There wasn't enough for both of them. Not nearly enough.

Dagny's too-loud breaths stopped.

The realization pounded the air out of her her lungs. For a moment, the only sound was the rasp of her own panicked breathing echoing inside her helmet. The sweat on her forehead froze, then drifted away.

Holding onto one of the nav board's grips, she turned to look for her daughter.

Inside her helmet, Osa's face was hidden in a cloud of dark hair. She passed her hand across the seal she had made, checking for leaks. She was on her second can of sealant. The other floated on the other side of her.

"We're not good on air, are we?" she said, not looking at Dagny. She tipped up the seats on this side. The slots for more vacuum suits were empty. "Cheap bastards."

As the full impact of their situation settled over her, Dagny felt an odd sense of calm descend. Soon she was cocooned in it, like standing in the eye of a storm, a moment of terrible clarity between bouts of chaos.

She looked at Osa, wrapped up silver tight. Her daughter, so brave, so brilliant. Her whole life ahead of her. It hurt, how much she loved her.

Dagny's own future, if they made it back to the Breaking Light, was far less rosy. Betrayal, sabotage—these weren't things easily forgiven, even if done for reasons people might agree with. The faces of her former crew flashed through her mind—Saanvi's disappointment, Raza's anger, Mira's stoicism. Remy's bewilderment. They all deserved better.

She would do better.

A flash in the window beside her. The Horizon's Edge. The pod was finishing its U-turn.

With hands as steady as her heartbeat, Dagny set the nav controls for a direct course to the Breaking Light. She bumped the speed past safe. If the engine blew, the momentum would still stay true. She hoped.

"Mom?" Osa's voice crackled through the suit's comm system. She was at Dagny's shoulder. "What's the plan?"

Dagny swallowed hard, the lump in her throat threatening to choke her. She forced a lightness into her voice that she didn't feel, a final act of protection. Her swirling hair would hide her expression. She hoped.

"Heading for the Light. They will take good care of you." The words tasted bitter, a half-truth that felt like betrayal.

"Of us," Osa corrected.

Dagny slid past her daughter to get to the storage compartment that still had suits in it. She pulled out the two remaining. The material slipped through her gloved fingers, eerily reminiscent of the silky blankets Osa had loved as a child.

"Can you get back in the chair?" she said. "With the suit on? That's safest."

It took three tries, and an assist from Dagny, but Osa managed it. Dagny strapped her daughter in.

With methodical care, she tied the two suits to the armrest of the chair, where Osa could easily reach them. Each movement felt like a farewell. A benediction.

"Have you done this before?" Dagny said. Osa shook her head no. "Then listen." Dagny's voice took on the tone she'd used when teaching Osa her first lessons about the stars. The familiarity of it made her heart ache. "When your air gets low, you'll need to swap out the tanks. Like this." She demonstrated the process, her movements slow and deliberate. The click of the air tank connecting was unnaturally loud in the confined space, a sound that Dagny knew would haunt her.

Osa nodded, her eyes following Dagny's hands. She was focused on the task, not noticing as Dagny reached out to wipe the top of her helmet, a final, tender caress. Her wayward hair, so close, so impossible to reach.

Dagny patted Osa's shoulder twice—all good—and pushed herself over to the airlock.

"I looked back there already," Osa said. "No more suits."

Dagny pressed the panel to open the inner airlock door. Trapped air escaped into the pod. Another few minutes' grace for her daughter.

"What are you doing?"

Dagny made the mistake of looking back. Osa speared her with her gaze. The dawning realization in her daughter's eyes was like a knife to Dagny's heart.

"No." Osa struggled with the chair's restraints.

Dagny pulled herself into the airlock.

"I love you, Osa. More than anything in this universe, or the next." The words felt inadequate, a pale reflection of the depth of the feelings roiling inside her.

"Don't you dare!" Osa's voice rang with panic the sound tearing at Dagny's resolve. "We can figure this out. We're Novaks, dammit."

The inner door of the airlock slid shut with a click, but it didn't cut off Osa's pleas. In the small space of the airlock, Dagny's breathing rasped. Her hand hovered over the outer door control, her resolve wavering for just a moment.

She could do this.

The stiff metal of the button was ridged under her gloved fingertip, one last link to the world of the living. Tears blurred her vision, turning the airlock controls into a smear of color.

"I'm so proud of you," she said. Each whispered word torn from her soul. "My brilliant girl."

On the comms line, Osa sucked in a breath. Before she could respond, before Dagny's own courage could fail her, Dagny hit the control.

The outer door lifted. Space reached for her like a long-lost lover, infinite black velvet waiting to embrace her.

Dagny stepped out.

CHAPTER
THIRTY-THREE

THE SILENT BUZZY energy of space enveloped Dagny as she grabbed the handhold on the hull next to the outer airlock door. She watched the door drop closed, accompanied by the steadying rhythm of her breath.

Then she let go.

The cosmos unfolded around her, a vast, star-speckled flower. A black tulip.

Osa's voice floated through the comm, a melody of pleading and anger and desperation and love. Each word a note in a bittersweet symphony that tugged at Dagny's heart.

"Mom. Please. Don't do this. We need you." A sob. "I need you."

Dagny let the music of her daughter's pleas wash over her, savoring each syllable like the last drops of a precious elixir. With fingers that felt both leaden and gossamer-light, she reached for the comm control.

"Star light, star-bright girl," she whispered, her voice a single thread connecting them one last time. "Shine on."

She clicked off the comms. End of one movement and the beginning of another.

Silence soaked into her her like a warm bath after a long day. The frantic beating of her heart started to slow. A wry thought bubbled up—she, Dagny Novak, expert at interstellar communication, voluntarily severing her final connection. The irony tasted of lemon and stardust.

The air-clock on her visor pulsed gently, its numbers counting down like a lullaby. The suit puffed around her knees and elbows. A second skin that didn't quite fit, much like her role in recent events. At least it was a little extra air.

The pod, looking even smaller now that she was out of it, left her behind. Distances in space were hard to judge, but the Breaking Light didn't look that far away at all.

Osa would make it.

To one side of her, the battle unfolded like a cosmic morality play. One massive ship, darker than the vacuum, bullying its neighbors. Tiny pods and boxy shuttles fleeing towards the Breaking Light like fireflies chasing after a lantern in a storm.

Time became fluid, stretching and contracting like taffy pulled by unseen hands. Reality shimmered at the edges, a mirage in the desert of space.

A wayward piece of debris, a tiny, near invisible player in this grand performance, hit her in the shoulder. At least it was the bad shoulder, the one she'd already bashed up.

The impact set her spinning, transforming the universe into a kaleidoscope of trailing lights. For a heartbeat, Dagny was a child again, twirling under the stars of her home world, dizzy with the joy of a summer's day.

Then she saw it—a gossamer trail of vapor escaping from

her suit. The debris was deadly accurate today. The tempo of the countdown in the corner of her visor quickened. Minutes evaporating like morning mist under twin suns.

In a dreamy haze, Dagny grasped the broken hose in her glove-thick fingers. She used it as a painter might use a brush, against the spin, slowly bringing the chaos of her back into order. The stars settled back into their celestial canvas, the play and its players once again in focus.

Dagny used a tiny puff of the last of her air to spin away from all the ships and their busy-ness.

She wanted to see the galaxy, serene.

Space blanketed her, cold and indifferent. Yet somehow comforting, in its vast, uncaring beauty. Was she looking towards the Fold, with its Soumai, those mysterious new players in the cosmic ballet? She couldn't be sure, but the possibility sang in her veins.

So much left to discover, so many wonders Osa would witness.

As the chill started to creep in, Dagny remembered eight-year-old Osa's lopsided grin. Her mouth not big enough for the adult teeth that were starting to come in. Running on the sand, the hottest day of the year. Getting steamed up, she said, so she could throw herself into the lake and cool off.

Something pushed on her back, but didn't make her spin.

Dagny smiled, content.

Around her, the galaxy faded to pink.

CHAPTER
THIRTY-FOUR

CONSCIOUSNESS RETURNED to Dagny like a tide creeping up a shore, each wave bringing with it fragments of sensation and memory.

The first thing she registered was the smell—antiseptic and sterile, with an undercurrent of ozone that whispered "ship" to her trained senses.

Iron on her tongue. Blood, old.

Then the light. Not the warm yellow of the cabins or the easy-on-the-eyes blue tint in the comms suite, but loud and bright white. She could see the veins in her eyelids, which weren't ready to open yet.

Machine humming, slow as a sleeping heartbeat. Human humming, that "wiggle your butt" song all the rage back at Exeter Station.

She hated that song, and now it was back, stuck in her head again.

She turned her head away from the humming. She pressed one ear into the soft pillow, trying to block the song. No joy.

She tried to open her eyelids. It took more effort than usual, all gooped up with something. She squinted against the harsh white light that wanted to stab right into her brain.

A small medical room came into focus. It was oppressively compact, the walls too close, the ceiling too low. Not gray, like the Horizon's Edge. White, like the Breaking Light.

She closed her eyes again.

But she'd been made.

A warm hand wrapped around Dagny's left hand. A very much cooler hand took her right. She opened her eyes again.

Where there had been the tiniest aisle between her bed and the medical cabinets, Nova shimmered into view. The Iridah took her childlike form, the cartoony round eyes, the bright pink tube dress, the pale pink swirl of hair.

Pink.

"Friend Dagny," she said, her large eyes blinking slowly, "it gladdens my heart to see you awake." She looked up and across.

Dagny turned her head.

Osa's face was a canvas vivid with emotion—joy, anger, love, fear, relief.

"Mom," Osa's voice cracked on the single syllable. Her hand squeezed her relief. The touch was electric, grounding Dagny in a reality she wasn't entirely sure she was ready to face.

She cleared her throat. Her tongue was swollen dry.

"How?"

"Your friend." Osa reached for Nova's free hand. The connection closed the chain. "She went out to get you."

"But—" How could she say this with Osa here? But wasn't your "I can live in a vacuum" trick a Great Iridah secret?

"But how did I know where you were?" Nova said. "Your Kipi friends. They put a tracking device on your boot. They were going to challenge you to hide-and-seek, or something, I didn't understand exactly. But when your child called the ship, all emergency, Kipi told me the secret. They gave me the coordinates."

"But—"

"You have many friends here, friend Dagny."

Dagny wasn't sure the Kipi actually were friends, if they planned to cheat her at an alleged game. But before she could summon up something coherent to say, the door hissed open.

Chief Mira Patel entered first, her hair smoothed back violently as usual, her height dwarfing the already small room. Security Chief Raza followed, their bulk making pretty much filling the rest of the space.

The tension in the room ratcheted up several notches, pressing down on Dagny like a physical weight. She tried to sit up, her body protesting every movement. Everything ached. What had happened?

"Dagny Novak," Patel's voice was cool, professional, but Dagny could hear the undercurrent of... what? Disappointment? Anger? "I see you've decided to rejoin us."

The medical bay's recycled air suddenly felt thick, almost suffocating.

Raza's gaze was hard, their eyes boring into Dagny with an intensity that made her want to shrink into the bed.

"We need to discuss your future on this ship," they said. "Or lack thereof."

The words slapped her. Dagny grabbed onto the hands she had clasped in hers, and squeezed. The steady beep of the heart monitor quickened, betraying her rising panic.

"Leave her alone!" Osa let go of Nova and Dagny, a loss Dagny felt in her gut. "She just woke up. She doesn't even know what happened."

"Osa," Patel said, not unkindly. "Please step outside. Ambassador Nova, we would request you, too, to step outside."

"No," Osa said, chin lifting in familiar defiance. "We're staying right here."

Nova nodded, her large eyes never leaving Dagny's face. "Friends support each other in times of need. This is such a time."

Pride, panic, and gratitude swirled in Dagny's chest. Her brave, stubborn girl and her unlikely alien friend.

But this wasn't a battle they should be fighting.

Patel's lips thinned, but she didn't argue. Instead, she turned her attention back to Dagny.

"Your actions put this ship, its crew, and our entire mission at risk. We cannot simply overlook that."

"You can't just blame her!" Osa interjected, her voice sharp. "She was trying to save me. Any of you would have done the same for your child!"

The words hung there, heavy and accusatory. Dagny saw Patel flinch, just slightly, while Raza's expression hardened further.

"Yes," Dagny croaked. She couldn't seem to push her voice above a whisper. "I understand the gravity of what I've done. I had to save my daughter. I had to."

Patel's eyes narrowed, her jaw clenching. "And in doing so, you betrayed everything we stand for. The Alliance, this ship, your crew—we trusted you, Dagny."

The disappointment in Patel's voice cut deeper than any

anger could have. Tears pricked at the corners of Dagny's eyes, the salty sting a counterpoint to the antiseptic smell of the room.

"What would you have had me do?" Dagny asked, her voice cracking. "Leave her to die?"

Raza stepped forward, their bulk casting a shadow over the bed. "There are protocols, procedures. You of all people should know that."

The room seemed to shrink further, the walls closing in. Dagny could not catch her breath. The heart monitor's beeping grew more frantic.

"Enough!" Nova's voice, usually so calm, cut through the tension like a knife. "Can you not see the toll this is taking? Friend Dagny needs rest, not interrogation."

Patel hesitated, conflict clear on her face. The mission chief looked exhausted, her lips pale, the circles under her eyes dark as bruises. For a long moment, she simply stared at Dagny.

"Here's what's going to happen," she finally said. "Dagny Novak, you will remain under medical supervision for the next forty-eight hours. You will wear an ankle monitor. Sally will monitor you at all times. Your access to ship systems is severely restricted."

Dagny's heart plummeted, each word more mass pressing her down.

"After that," Patel continued, "you will be on probationary status. Your future on this ship will depend on your actions in the coming days, especially during our encounter with the Fold."

She paused, her gaze softening slightly. "I understand why you did what you did, Dagny. But understanding doesn't negate consequences. You've lost our trust. It's up to you to earn it back."

With that, Patel turned to leave, Raza following close behind. As the door hissed shut behind them, the tension in the room eased slightly, leaving behind a heavy silence.

Osa's gripped Dagny's hand again, her voice thick with emotion. "We'll get through this, Mom. Together."

The tears fell. At least they would wash away whatever goop was on her lashes.

Dagny lifted her hand to rub at her eyes. Nova's hand came with it.

Nova let go, smiling that quirky Iridah idea of a human smile. "Indeed. The path ahead may be difficult, but you do not walk it alone."

The future was uncertain, fraught with challenges. But with Osa and Nova by her side, Dagny could face it. Probably.

Surely.

At worst, Dagny was done on Breaking Light. Done in the Alliance altogether. At best, Osa might get her dream job— joining an expedition in search of new friends. She was so close, now. Already here, ready to make a good impression on the xeno teams downstairs.

Dagny would do all in her power to make Osa's dream come true.

Exhaustion washed over her. But hunger growled at her louder.

"You wouldn't happen to have a savory pastry on you, would you?" she asked her daughter.

CHAPTER
THIRTY-FIVE

TWENTY HOURS and three warm meals later, Dagny opened the humans' door to the newly created performance space the Zarks had created. And stopped, gaping.

A startling fusion of Zark aesthetics and Alliance practicality, the space looked as if a cosmic wind had swept through the Breaking Light, rearranging its innards into this improbable theater.

The ceiling soared impossibly high, a good ten meters above her head, creating an illusion of vastness that made Dagny's breath catch. Soft, amber lighting suffused the space, reminiscent of the bioluminescent caves on Stryker IV, the Zark home world. The walls, no longer basic gray, had been doused with shimmering paints, swirls of deep purples and blues. The edges of the paints caught the light and scattered it like starlight through a nebula.

Rows of mismatched seating stretched in semicircles before her, a hodgepodge of Alliance-standard chairs interspersed with what looked like repurposed acceleration couches hastily reworked into benches. The variety spoke volumes about the crew's ingenuity and determination to make this work, despite the tight time frame and the usual communication and artistic differences.

Underneath it all, a low, rhythmic thrumming that she recognized as the baseline to a more-popular form of Zark music.

At the far end of the room, a raised platform served as a stage. Its surface gleamed with a polished sheen that seemed to absorb and reflect light in equal measure. Was this some new Zark tech? More important, was it slippery?

Now that she was newly part of the theater "management," she felt responsible.

Dagny had slept another half a day in the tiny recovery room before feeling herself again. Doc Shaw said it was time to get up and at 'em, clicked on the ankle bracelet, and shooed Dagny out the door.

Where she didn't know where to go. What was she to do, hide in her room?

Osa was shadowing one of the lead xenos, hoping to impress her enough to let her stay at least through first contact. She didn't need to worry—at this point, they were all staying for first contact. The coordinates weren't two days away.

Dagny had been told to join the diplomatic briefing tomorrow morning, apparently because she'd collected the data, or found the original signal, or something. But she was off the schedule today. Totally free.

Which meant she couldn't exactly say no when Zark Ambassador Xalara, in the person of green-grass-scented assistant Krim, asked her to help manage the "front of the house." No ticket-taking, Krim promised, just making sure everyone had a comfortable place to rest and enjoy the show.

So here she was, in a clean gray jumpsuit and her favorite thick boots, her thick hair corralled by a wide purple headband. Ready to assist, whatever that meant.

Inside the performance space, the air carried what she hoped was Kipi incense and something else, sharp and alien, that must be from the Zark. And also the mighty bustle that was Theater.

The clatter of last-minute set preparations, the rise and fall of murmuring—people rehearsing, or discussing where the backgrounds should go, or voices starting to rise while discussing the height of the tables in the back row.

Dagny hurried toward that discussion. As she got further into the room, she felt the weight of uncertain gazes upon her. Most of the humans looked to be from security or engineering. In their expressions, she saw curiosity, wariness, and in some cases, outright hostility. Another reminder of how precarious her position was, balanced on the knife-edge between redemption and exile.

She didn't say hello to any of them.

"Tch! Specialist Novak, there you are." Ambassador Xalara's voice boomed from behind one of the tall tables. The Zark easily leaped over the table to loom over her, their silver-gold exoskeleton gleaming under the amber lights. "Your expertise is required. These accommodations are not ideal."

She nodded and smiled, lips only. "Of course, Ambassador. Xalara, excuse me. How can I help?"

They waved their two left arms back at the table they had just hurdled. "Just look how short these tables are!"

The tops of the tables came to Dagny's chin. "I see what you mean," she said.

"And the acoustics! Tch." Xalara launched into a detailed critique of the room's acoustics, with the tables somehow taking a large part of the blame. Not a problem that new tables and a bunch of baffles couldn't solve. She looked around for the sound console.

But before she could find it, Dagny's attention was drawn to a flash of movement near the lower, human-height seating. The Kipis, Ambassador Myli and Consort Belle, were scampering about, circling each other and moving forward at the same time. Their riotous pastel fur blurred as they darted among the seats, leaving what looked suspiciously like small devices in their wake.

Dagny's heart sank. Whatever the Kipi were planning, it was bound to complicate an already delicate situation. She made a mental note to warn Raza, assuming the security chief would even listen to her now.

"Are you listening, Specialist?" Xalara's sharp tone snapped Dagny back to the present.

"My great apologies," she said smoothly, still scanning the room. Where was the other Zark, Krim? They could reason with the ambassador. "I was just considering potential solutions to the acoustic issues you mentioned. Perhaps if we adjusted the placement of those stunning fabric panels near the ceiling…"

As she immersed herself in problem-solving mode, Dagny felt a familiar presence at her side. Nova had materialized next to her, currently mimicking the form of a pink Zark, complete with the necklace/rebreather pendant, also pink.

"Tch," Xalara said, crossing their top pair of arms. "Inappropriate, Ambassador Nova. Extremely." They looked at Dagny for confirmation.

Dagny thought Nova looked rather fetching as a giant pink Zark. Gave a more-cheery aspect to the Zarks' typical looming stance.

"But this form works better for my performance." Nova had some narrow woodwind in one of her arms. "Duet for one, from *Zark Classics for Everyone*."

Xalara reared back. The back of their head jammed itself into their carapace.

"You would not."

Nova tilted her head, pink-tinted multifaceted eyes whirring. "It's such a gorgeous piece. And short. I hope I can do it justice."

"Krim!" The trumpet blare of a shout made Dagny's ears ring. Nova grabbed her arm, her spiky pink fingers the only thing keeping Dagny from reeling.

A commotion began on the stage, behind the set piece that looked like a giant blue round-capped mushroom, or maybe a really bushy tree. A flash of a bronze pair of multifaceted eyes above the crest of the mushroom-tree. A breeze blew past Dagny and settled into Assistant Krim, at his ambassador's side.

Krim wore a poncho made of gold felt, armholes, and pockets, some of which had paint splatters on them. One of Krim's narrow bronze feet was currently as blue as the mush-room-tree.

"Explain to the ambassador the meaning of *Zark Classics*."

Krim, in his usual hunch before his ambassador, turned to look at Nova. Without warning, he grabbed the woodwind out of Nova's hands. It disappeared into one of the pockets.

"Experts only," Krim said. Before Nova could do more than blink, he hurried on. "We need another drummer." He pulled a hand drum in the rough shape of an hourglass out of another pocket. "This is mine."

Nova took it wonderingly. "Won't you need it?" She tipped it to the side, tapping it gently. One side rattled, as if beads were just under the face of the drum. The other side boomed.

Krim glanced back at his ambassador, grimacing. "Too busy." He tapped the rattling side twice, as if telling the drum to behave.

Xalara's head tilted into its usual position. "You don't need to look Zark to play the drums."

Dagny wasn't sure about that. This drum was tuned for the agile, strong, bony hands of a Zark. It would sound different under human hands.

Nova smiled in that terrifying Zark way—all teeth. Then her form wavered, shrinking to Dagny height. Dagny-plus again, only pink.

But now with an extra pair of Zarkish arms. She waved hello to the Zarks.

"For the drums," she said.

The Zark ambassador reared up, legs extended, to their full three meters. Their spinning eyes landed on Krim. "Tch!" Then they scuttled away, past the seating, past the audio console— there it was—and out the far door. Into the Zarks-only hallway.

Krim calmly considered Nova.

"Did the Kipi put you up to that?" he said.

Nova's Dagny-style eyebrows arched. "How did you know?"

Krim couldn't exactly roll his eyes, but the way the colors

swirled in them gave the same impression. "That instrument is for royalty only."

"But it's so easy to play!" Nova turned to Dagny. "It didn't take me an hour to sound just like the recording."

"Because royals don't have time to practice. But no one is allowed to play better than they do on the oohlek. So no one else plays."

"Stick with the drum." He nodded and took his leave, back to the blue fields on stage.

"Kipi, huh?" Dagny scanned the lower tiers of seating. "I have to go check something." Nova followed behind.

"Friend Dagny," Nova said softly, her Dagny-sized eyes filled with concern. "Are you certain you wish to participate in this spectacle? Given your current status—"

Dagny cut her off with a gentle shake of her hand. She bent to peer under the first set of padded theater benches.

"It's fine, Nova. What I do here isn't going to affect the chief's opinion of me. Unless she sees corralling ambassadors as serving the mission." There, stuck under the bench, a lumpy round something that shouldn't be there. Dagny touched it— no shock, no sting—and then gently pulled it free from the bench.

"You know, Chief Patel might, actually, consider this a help." She set the walnut-sized roundish lump of clay in the palm of her hand. She showed it to Nova. "Give me a hand? Look under all the seats for more of these."

"What are they?" Nova said, peering with Dagny-plus's eyes.

"Dunno," Dagny said, crawling farther down the benches. Another one, there. "We'll figure it out once we get them all out of here."

Nova moved to the row in front of Dagny's. As she knelt down, her form shimmered slightly, a physical manifestation of her unease.

"And if it's not enough? If Chief Patel is still angry. What then?"

The question hung between them. Dagny moved on to the next set of benches before she trusted herself to speak.

"Then, well, I suppose I'll have to trust that the universe has other plans for me."

"You could join the Iridah delegation," Nova said, not looking at Dagny as she searched under the next bench.

What?

"But I'm not even Iridah." Dagny tried for a light tone, but her voice sounded mildly dyspeptic instead. Or just plain confused.

Nova popped up, another squishy square in her hand. She handed it to Dagny.

"We have a station, that circles one of our moons. The Alliance always has humans there. I could request one of them be you."

Dagny didn't know what to say.

Then she did.

"I don't want to take someone else's job. Especially not one of our Iridah experts."

"No such thing," Nova said airily.

"But thank you," Dagny rattled on. "It means so much. You wanting to help."

Nova's hand, warm and slightly gelatinous, slipped into Dagny's, squeezing gently. She'd molted back to her half-formed practice-person shape.

"Whatever happens, friend Dagny, know that you are not alone."

The simple gesture, so human yet so alien, nearly undid Dagny. Two tears dropped as she squeezed Nova's hand in return. So unexpected. So welcome.

"Tch!" Xalara had returned, apparently fully recovered from whatever had startled them. "If you two are quite finished with your sentimental display," they said, mandibles clicking in irritation, "we have a performance to prepare. The fate of interstellar diplomacy may well rest on its success."

As Dagny allowed herself to be pulled into the whirlwind of final preparations, she couldn't shake the feeling that Xalara's words held more truth than the ambassador knew. With the Soumai waiting at the end of their journey, this performance did feel like more than just a standard cultural exchange.

It was a test, a chance to prove that different species could come together in harmony. For Dagny, a last opportunity to show that despite her recent behavior, she still belonged here.

As she moved through the improvised theater, the controlled chaos around her ratcheted up a notch.

"No, no, no!" Xalara's voice cut through the din, their multifaceted eyes flashing with irritation. "The resonance crystals must be aligned precisely. How do you humans manage to build starships when you can't even grasp basic acoustics?"

Dagny stepped in, her hands raised in a placating gesture. "Ambassador, perhaps if we—"

A sudden yelp of surprise from one of the people hanging the backdrops interrupted her, followed by burst of high-pitched giggling. Dagny turned to see Belle, the smaller of the two Kipi, cartwheeling gleefully away from the scene. The human—systems engineer Spencer—hung by her hands from a hoverchair that had somehow turned itself upside-down.

"Oops!" Belle trilled, not sounding sorry at all. "I thought it needed a little lift!"

Dagny pinched the bridge of her nose, feeling a headache building.

"Remy," she called out, spotting her gangly former assistant on the stage, reaching out to help Spencer. Without thinking, she gave him an order. "Could you please help make sure all the chairs are, ah, properly grounded?"

Remy only nodded, his expression a mix of amusement and exasperation. As he moved to address the floating furniture situation, Dagny felt a pang of longing for the easy camaraderie they once shared. Would he ever trust her again?

She was about to turn her attention back to Xalara when she felt a gentle tug on her sleeve. Looking down, she found Myli, the Kipi ambassador, gazing up at her with those impossibly large eyes.

"Specialist Dagny," Myli chirped, his voice a melody of false innocence. "We were wondering if you might help us with a small addition to the performance?"

Dagny raised an eyebrow, suspicion immediately prickling at the back of her neck. Why ask her? Where was Krim?

"What kind of addition?"

Myli's fur rippled in what Dagny had come to recognize as their version of a shrug. "Nothing much. Just a little surprise to make things more festive."

Before Dagny could probe further, a commotion near the audio console drew her attention. Osa was here! And already arguing with Xalara.

That was fast.

"—absolutely not!" Osa was saying, her cheeks flushed with indignation. "You can't expect the human performers—much less the audience—to withstand those frequencies. It could cause permanent damage to their auditory systems!"

Xalara's mandibles clicked rapidly, a sign of agitation. "But without the full range, the emotional impact of the piece will be lost! Surely your primitive physiology can adapt—"

Dagny hurried over. "Whoa, let's all take a breath here," she said, positioning herself between Osa and Xalara. "I'm sure we can find a compromise that preserves the integrity of the performance without risking anyone's health."

As she worked to smooth over the situation between Osa and Xalara, she was almost swept away by a swirl of conflicting emotions. If this was to be Dagny's final performance, her last duty on the Breaking Light, at least she could share it with her daughter.

Such a gift.

As the argument settled into a grudging compromise, Osa took Dagny's arm and pulled her aside, her eyes bright.

"Mom, guess what?" she said. "I'll be watching the first-contact briefing tomorrow morning along with most of the xenos. We'll be on video from the labs down-level, so we have access to all the references and materials you could want in the meeting."

"That's wonderful, sweetheart." Dagny smiled, her heart still aswirl, now with added pride and wistfulness. "You know, you should really be taking my place at that meeting. You already know so much more about the Soumai, and you helped get us the data, too."

She meant it as a joke, but also as a compliment. In her mind, Dagny could see it clearly—Osa, confidently presenting information, impressing the senior staff. A golden opportunity for her daughter to shine.

But to Dagny's surprise, Osa's face clouded over with anger. "That's your spot, Mom," she said, her voice tight. "You've earned it. If people on the Breaking Light are so stupid they can't appreciate you, then maybe this isn't the place for me, either."

Dagny blinked, taken aback by the vehemence in Osa's tone. "Sweetie, I didn't mean—"

But Osa had already turned away, marching back towards the audio console with quick, angry strides.

Reeling, Dagny sought out a moment alone. Apart from the controlled chaos of the makeshift theater, Dagny found a quiet corner in the back. She leaned against the wall, prickly with the reflective paint that shimmered like stars in the right light. She took a deep breath as she surveyed the scene before her. Xalara—and now Krim—debating acoustics with Osa, Kipi scampering between the audio hubbub and the set-design hubbub. Humans and non-humans alike working to create something beautiful together.

A microcosm of what the Alliance hoped to achieve on a galactic scale.

But could this even work? The Kipi's mysterious devices— Nova said they were called "fart bombs" in the reference literature. The Iridah's own near-faux pas with the royal instrument. The yellow brick of food that so incensed the Zark. The Iridah's so many lies of omission. On and on. An undercurrent of tension always seemed to run beneath every interaction. Always, that sense of unease.

As if sensing her thoughts, Belle appeared at her side. The

Kipi consort's large eyes gleamed with manic intensity. Her whole body seemed to be purring.

"All is well, Specialist Dagny?" she chirped.

Dagny's smile wobbled. "Just thinking about tomorrow's meeting," she replied, changing topics in her mind so she could be truthful.

Belle's fur rippled in what might have been amusement. She looked just so squeezable. "Ah yes, the great planning session," she said. "So much to consider."

She paused, tilting her head. "We can never know what surprises might arise during first contact, do we?"

Before Dagny could respond, Belle had scampered off. That boded ill. Or did it?

There likely would, indeed, be surprises in store, no matter how much everyone planned.

With a sigh, Dagny pushed off from the wall. She had a performance to help steer. With plenty of feathers to unruffle, so to speak.

And a fraught, galaxy-altering meeting in the morning.

CHAPTER
THIRTY-SIX

THE NEXT MORNING, Diplomacy Meeting Room Two hummed with nervous energy. Holographic displays floated above the nearly circular table, showing views of the fog belt from along varied spectra: ultralight, gravity, sound, and just plain camera vision.

The warm lights were dimmed a bit from the last time Dagny had been here. Then, she'd felt like a convict being interrogated. Now, she wasn't even at the table.

She sat on one of the benches against the long walls of the oval room. The wall on the other side of the room showed star charts and a large screen full of excited xenobiologists. On Dagny's side, the wall displayed a camera's view of the outside of the ship, deep-space grays and blacks. If she leaned back to rest against the wall, it would look like she was falling into space.

The air carried a dizzying cocktail of strawberry shampoo, curried grass, chalk, green tea, coffee, and smoke. Dagny and Nova had missed one of the Kipi's "smoke bombs" yesterday afternoon, to the bitter surprise of poor Deputy Security Head Nell. She had scrubbed herself so far that her pale face carried tiny red scratches, and yet smoke still wafted off her.

The sound of Chief Patel clearing her throat ended all conversation. "Alright, people. Thank you, ambassadors, for attending. We are merely hours from our encounter with the Fold. Let's go over what we know."

Patel nodded at Dagny. She felt every gaze—curious, distrusting, speculative—turn toward her. "Specialist Novak," the chief said, "please share the information you retrieved from the Horizon's Edge."

Swallowing hard, Dagny stepped forward. The familiar act of presenting data felt foreign now, tainted by recent events. By what she'd done. Her precarious position was painfully clear.

She wore an ankle bracelet. No longer a trusted specialist, but not yet an outcast. The weight of proving herself, of clawing back some semblance of respect, weighed heavy on her mind.

Yet beneath the anxiety and shame, a flame of excitement still burned. They were about to uncover the unknown, to push the boundaries of human knowledge. Even if she was now on the fringes, she was still part of this monumental discovery.

She was still here.

For now.

Dagny touched her wristcom, and a new set of holograms sprang to life. A little off, compare to the others, because they were lifted from a different system. She hadn't had time—or access to her workstation—to smooth everything out.

"The Soumai are physically unlike any species we've

encountered," Dagny began, her voice surprisingly steady. "They exist simultaneously in our dimension and in others we can't perceive. Their technology is so advanced it might appear to us as magic."

She gestured to a swirling, nebulous image. "As we approach, we'll enter what's been termed the 'fog belt.' Our sensors and visual data will become increasingly unreliable. Standard navigation systems will struggle."

Raza leaned forward, their brow furrowed. "So we just coast in, with no engine, thanks to you. And no idea how to get out? Not a great plan," the security chief said.

"This is where it gets interesting," Dagny continued, a hint of excitement creeping into her voice despite herself. "The fog isn't just buzzy interference. It's a complex, information-rich environment. As we get closer, patterns will emerge." She pushed touched the nebula's image controls, dissolving the visual into lines of data.

Saanvi leaned in. She pointed something out to one of her deputy engineers. "Looks like fractals, yes?" she said softly. "Pull up refs for that."

Dagny took a breath before saying the next part. "In fact," she said, "the Soumai might even guide us in."

Everyone's eyes pivoted back to her. Dagny's mouth went dry. She had to swallow hard.

"This is what the Horizon's Edge believes happened to it," she said. "They entered at one point, talked with the people of the Fold, as they called them, and exited a day later and three days' travel away from where they started. And the whole thing felt like less than an hour."

Chief Patel tapped a finger on her lip. "What else did they say about biological effects? Should we be concerned about exposure to this—what? multidimensional?—environment?"

"Individual differences. The data suggests some crew members might experience temporal dissonance or even psychic impressions."

"I'll get a monitor update to everyone's wristcoms" Remy said. "Doc Shaw's working on it now." He glanced worriedly at Dagny under the swath of hair across his forehead. She might need to help him with that. "The comms can't fix you if you have a problem," he continued, "but they can keep a record."

"Great," Saanvi said. The engineering chief's voice was tinged with skepticism. "This all sounds rather fantastical. Are we certain this information is reliable?"

Hot shame burnt up Dagny's cheeks. "I understand your doubt. But both the Horizon's Edge AI and our Sally could double confirm most of it. Beloved Spring didn't expect this data to fall into anyone's hands."

"Hah." Khan chuckled. "The thieves didn't expect anyone to steal from them. Typical."

An uncomfortable silence fell over the room.

So Saanvi thought she was a thief.

So be it.

Nova, who had been silent until now, suddenly shimmered, drawing the room's attention away from Dagny. The Iridah was her original-human shape, pink hair poufed high above her big, round, adorable eyes.

"If I may," she said, her voice melodious, "the Soumai's nature aligns with certain aspects of my own people. We also exist in a state not entirely bound by your perceptions of space and time."

Another lie of omission from the Iridah. So much of what was commonly accepted about them wasn't true. Entire books would need to be rewritten. The xenos onboard must be salivating at the idea of their names and findings in the top science and diplomatic journals.

Patel nodded slowly. "Thank you, Ambassador. Your insight is invaluable. I hope you will join us tomorrow. "

"I would be delighted."

Xalara tch-ed. "Of course, we will all be there. No one wants to be the last to meet our new friends."

Patel nodded again. "We'll proceed with caution, but we'll take this information into account. Remy, get that update out. I want full biometric monitoring on every crew member. If anyone starts experiencing anything unusual, I want to know immediately."

"We should establish clear safety protocols," Raza said. "If we meet with these 'reality bubbles' or 'impossible geometries,' we need a plan to extract our people quickly."

"Right," Patel said. "Saanvi, see what you can do to shore up our navigation systems."

"Break out the sextants, you mean?"

"Whatever works," Patel did not smile at the joke. "We need redundancies for every system. Saanvi, I want you to work on boosting our subspace beacon strength. If we lose standard comms, we need a way to punch through the interference."

"And navigation?" Raza asked. "If we can't trust our sensors, how do we avoid collisions?"

Saanvi leaned forward, her earlier skepticism giving way to problem-solving mode. 'We could deploy a network of micro-buoys as we enter the fog. They'd create a breadcrumb trail of fixed points we could use for triangulation."

"Good," Patel said. "And let's prep the long-range shuttles. We might want to leave someone out there to call for help."

As the meeting continued, Dagny was forgotten on the sidelines. Watching as the crew she once worked with now worked around her.

At least the Kipi hadn't stink-bombed this meeting.

Remy caught Dagny's eye. She read concern in his face, worry, and something else—a hint of the camaraderie they once shared. It was a lifeline in a sea of distrust, and Dagny clung to it. She offered him a small, grateful smile. Maybe, just maybe, not all bridges had been burned.

"Look behind you," he whispered.

At the edge of the wall showing the star field outside the ship, the first tendrils of the cosmic fog floated into view. The thinnest of clouds, but where no cloud could ever be. The star field gave way to swirling patterns of light and shadow, it alien complexity scary beautiful.

The room went silent.

This was it.

"That view is ten hours from us," Saanvi said, checking her scans. She looked back up, her dark face aglow. "Beautiful."

Chief Patel had to clear her throat.

"You know what you have to do," she said. "Let's go do it."

This time, the chief smiled.

"This is going to be amazing."

CHAPTER
THIRTY-SEVEN

WHEN THE BREAKING Light reached edges of the odd cosmic fog, reality started to shimmer around them like heat waves on a desert horizon.

The usual folks were back in Diplomacy Meeting Room Two. Cold snacks on the counter, warm drinks scenting the air. The rest of the xenobiologists were in their big auditorium down on Level Six, watching the biggest screen on the ship. The engineers were in their auditorium on Level Eight, watching the second-biggest screen. Support staff had massed in the Observation bubble on Level One, making them the only ones with an actual window view.

They'd all corralled themselves more effectively than Beloved Spring could have ever dreamed.

Except now the people of the Beloved Spring ship Horizon's Edge couldn't take advantage of it. They were even more effectively corralled: In the brig of the warship Nemesis.

Dagny stood near the center of the oval table. Saanvi had chosen to join her crew downstairs. The chief of the xenobiologists also had made way, for Osa. Her daughter, the resident Soumai expert.

Dagny's hands gripped the back of the chair, afraid that if she took the time to sit, she'd miss everything.

The familiar hum of the ship's systems was muted, replaced by an eerie, almost musical resonance that seemed to reach into the ship from the swirling mists outside.

"Approaching coordinates," Remy announced, his voice tight with concentration. The nav console in front of him flickered, numbers and trajectory lines appearing and disappearing like fireflies in twilight.

Dagny's eyes were drawn to the main view screen—the wall across from her—where the fog was transforming. What had been amorphous clouds now coalesced into intricate, fractal-like patterns. It was as if they were flying through the synapses of a cosmic brain, each tendril of light a thought made manifest.

She hoped they weren't breaking into anyone's thoughts.

"Remarkable," Osa breathed, her gaze darting between two floating screens and the big wall of space. "The patterns… they look like they're responding to our presence. Adapting. It's almost as if the space itself is alive!"

A shiver ran down Dagny's spine. This was beyond anything she had imagined, even with the information gleaned from the Horizon's Edge. She felt like a child again, wide-eyed with wonder at the vastness of the universe.

Suddenly, the ship shuddered. Dagny stumbled, catching herself on the chair as a wave of vertigo washed over her. For a heartbeat, she saw double—no, triple.

Multiple versions of the meeting room overlapped, each slightly different. In one, Patel wore a captain's uniform she'd never seen. In another, Raza stood where Remy should be.

"Spatial distortion!" Saanvi's voice cut through the disorientation. "Compensating!"

As quickly as it began, the effect faded. Dagny blinked, her singular reality reasserting itself. She caught Osa's eye, seeing her own mix of heady exhilaration mirrored in her daughter's face.

"Chief Patel," Nova's voice sang out, tinged with awe. "I believe we're being invited."

Before anyone could ask for clarification, they saw fog before them parting like a curtain drawn back. A structure shimmered into existence—a massive archway that crafted from light and mathematical equations given form. It hurt Dagny's eyes to look at it directly, her mind struggling to process its impossible geometries.

"Oh, my," Patel murmured, her usual stoic demeanor cracking.

Raza's voice came like a shout in the awed silence. "Chief, I don't like this. Energy readings are off the charts." They looked up, at the swirls on the wall. "And the spatial dimensions around that archway—they don't make any sense."

Saanvi's voice crackled from the ceiling. "Ship's systems are going haywire, but nothing is in the purple. No danger detected. It's like we're interfacing with a completely different level of technology."

A voice—no, a chorus of voices speaking as one—resonated not through the ship's comm systems, but directly in their minds:

"Welcome, travelers. You have reached The Fold."

Dagny felt a presence brush against her consciousness,

alien yet oddly familiar. It was like standing at the edge of a vast ocean, aware of unfathomable depths just beyond her perception. A flood of information and emotion that, if she stepped into it, might sweep her forever away.

A figure materialized in the corner of the room. It shifted form constantly, at times appearing as a tall, luminous humanoid with skin that shimmered with galaxies, at others as a being of pure energy. Then a giant Kipi. A Zark. A human.

Its multiple eyes—sometimes two, sometimes dozens—regarded them with ancient wisdom and childlike curiosity.

"I am the Interface," they said, its voice a harmony of tones. "Created to bridge the gap between your perception and ours. We have long awaited this moment."

Chief Patel stepped forward, her deep voice rock steady.

"I am Mira Patel of the Alliance ship Breaking Light. We come in peace, seeking knowledge and friendship."

The Interface's form rippled, a gesture that might have been a nod. "Your intentions are clear to us, Mira Patel. But it is not you we've been waiting for." Their gaze, somehow both piercing and gentle, turned to Dagny.

"Step forward, Dagny Novak."

It felt as if all the air had been sucked from her lungs. She moved on trembling legs, acutely aware of the surprised looks from the diplomats and from her crewmates.

Her mind raced, trying to make sense of this impossible situation. Why her? After everything that had happened, how could she be at the center of this cosmic drama?

When she got within arm's reach of the being, it spoke again.

"You decoded our message," the Interface said. "You understood what the others could not. And when faced with a choice between your corporeal being and the greater good, you chose to warn your people of danger."

Realization dawned. "The map," she said. "The warning about the mines. You were watching?"

The Interface's form shimmered with what might have been amusement. This close, she could catch a glimpse of the edges of the continual blending and unblending. Like Nova's changes, times a thousand.

"We observe much, across many realities," the Interface said. "The group you know as Beloved Spring sought to manipulate us, to position themselves as the sole representatives of your sector. This deception was clear to us."

Dagny's mind raced. "So the message. The map. It was a test?"

"A catalyst," the Interface said. "An opportunity for truth to emerge. And you, Dagny Novak, proved to be the pivot upon which much turned."

"Wow, mom." The sauciness in Osa's voice rang true. "Who knew?"

The import of her actions dropped over Dagny like a cloak made of wet sand. Pride at being chosen warred with a gnawing self-doubt. After all her mistakes, how could she be worthy of this? Fear clawed at her throat—fear of the unknown, fear of failing, fear of losing herself in something so vast and incomprehensible. Yet beneath it all, that familiar flicker of curiosity. The puzzle-solver in her, the part that had driven her across the stars, yearned to understand, to explore. But at what cost? Her gaze flicked to Osa. What would this mean for her daughter, for the life she'd known?

And how could her actions, born of desperation and love

for her daughter, had unknowingly shaped the course of inter-stellar relations?

Impossible.

And yet.

Osa stepped forward, her scientific curiosity overcoming her awe. "Excuse me," she said, her voice quavering slightly. "But how is this possible? The level of technology required to manipulate space-time on this scale, to observe multiple reali-ties, it's… it's stellar."

The Interface turned its attention to Osa, its form shifting to something that resembled a friendly nebula given humanoid shape.

"Your understanding of the universe is still in its infancy, Osa Novak. What you call technology, we simply call exis-tence. We are as much a part of the cosmic fabric, the warp and the woof, as the stars themselves."

Nova moved closer, her form shimmering in a way that seemed to resonate with the Interface. "I sense a kinship," she said softly. "My people have long known that reality is more fluid than most believe. But this." She spread her hands. "Is this what we should aspire to?"

The Interface's attention shifted to Nova, their form rippling with interest. "Your species walks a path that may one day lead to an existence similar to ours. But that journey is long, and not without peril."

Okay, now the Interface was starting to sound like a bad video game.

Dagny pinched her thigh, hard.

The being was still there.

Patel did not step forward. It was getting crowded here in the corner. "We are honored by your attention," the mission chief said. "And grateful for your wisdom in seeing through Beloved Spring's deception. We hope this can be the beginning of a fruitful exchange between our peoples."

The Interface's form shifted again, this time resembling a shimmering constellation in vaguely humanoid shape. "That is our hope as well, Chief Patel. But first, a choice must be made." They turned back to Dagny.

"You stand at a crossroads, Dagny Novak. Your actions have brought you here, to the threshold of something greater than yourself. Are you prepared to take the next step?"

Dagny could feel the weight of every gaze in the room. She glanced at Chief Patel, whose usual stoic demeanor had cracked, revealing a mix of awe and concern. The chief's eyes darted between Dagny and the Interface, clearly trying to gauge the implications for her mission, her ship, her crew.

Remy sat frozen in his chair, his expression a twist of wonder and fear, hands hovering uncertainly over an interface that suddenly seemed obsolete faced with such advanced beings.

Osa's nervous excitement

Nova's serene encouragement.

Dagny thought of all that had led to this moment. Her desperation. Her mistakes. Her decisions.

Her sacrifices.

"I'm not sure what you mean?" she said. She winced in advance of some angry response.

The Interface's form blazed with light, and suddenly the room on the Breaking Light seemed to dissolve around them. Dagny gasped as she found herself suspended in what appeared to be the heart of a galaxy, stars wheeling around her in a cosmic dance far faster than humans had ever observed.

"We offer knowledge," the Interface's voice resonated from everywhere and nowhere. "We offer a glimpse into the true nature of reality. But be warned: Such knowledge comes at a price. To understand us, you must be willing to let go of your current perception of existence."

Images flashed before Dagny's eyes. Impossible structures that seemed to exist in more than three dimensions, beings of pure energy moving through the cosmos like fish through water, entire universes blossoming and fading in the span of a heartbeat.

"Mom", Osa's voice came from somewhere nearby, filled with wonder and a good dollop of fear. "Are you seeing this?"

"Yes," Dagny said, her voice shaking. "Beautiful. Too much."

The cosmic vision faded, and they found themselves back on the bridge. But something had changed. The air seemed to shimmer with potential, reality itself feeling thin and malleable.

The Interface regarded Dagny with their multi-formed gaze. "The choice is yours, Dagny Novak. Will you step into the unknown, to serve as a bridge between your people and ours? Or will you turn back, content with the reality you know?"

CHAPTER
THIRTY-EIGHT

THE FAMILIAR CONTOURS of the Breaking Light's Meeting Room Two seemed shallow and arbitrary to Dagny now, viewed through a prism of her newfound cosmic awareness. The long oval table, once a symbol of fairness and balance, now appeared to Dagny as an arbitrary construct, a futile attempt to impose structure on the fluid nature of existence.

No time had passed. Or a half a day had passed. She wasn't sure.

Dagny sat midway down one side of the table, facing the long wall that showed the very shallowest of views of the fog belt outside. Her fingers traced abstract patterns on the table's smooth surface. Her mind still rang from the shock of the encounter with the Soumai. Visions of impossible geometries and multifactorial realities washed through her, bright as sound.

The lingering sensation of cosmic vastness made the room feel claustrophobic, or that may have been the swamp's worth of sweat and old pheromones the air system could not clear away fast enough. No matter, the walls might collapse under the weight of the infinite at any moment.

Around the table sat a diverse assembly that would have been unimaginable mere days ago. Chief Mira Patel sat across the table from Dagny, her posture rigid, hands clasped, forearms resting on the table, her gaze a wash of awe and uncertainty. Beside her, the ever-changing form of the Interface, not needing a chair, their presence a continuous shock. A steady reminder of the profound shift in their understanding of the universe.

Further along the table from Dagny, Xalara, the Zark ambassador, chittered softly to themselves, their compound eyes darting nervously between the Interface and the rest of the group. Next to them, the Kipi representatives, Myli and Belle, for once seemed subdued. Their fur only slowly rippled, a pale reflection of the chiaroscuro that was the Interface.

Nova sat next to Dagny, holding her hand. The Iridah's hand was warm and firm, but the rest of her felt more fluid—more ethereal—than usual. It was as if her encounter with the Soumai had awakened something primordial within her.

Osa, to Dagny's left, practically vibrated, her excitement barely contained. Her data screens blank, gone to sleep, forgotten. She'd seen the folds of the universe, too, but had recovered quicker.

Kids.

The rest of the seats were filled with humans, their expressions ranging from wonder to apprehension. The air in the room felt charged, crackling with potential and the weight of decisions yet to be made.

Chief Patel cleared her throat, the sound startlingly ordinary.

"We're here to discuss recent events and their implications for our mission. For our alliances. And," she paused, glancing at the Interface and then quickly away, "our understanding of the universe itself."

Dagny felt the weight of eyes upon her, a familiar sensation that now carried new meaning. She was no longer just Dagny Novak, disgraced communications officer. She was a potential bridge between worlds, a cosmic translator of sorts.

"Specialist Novak," Patel continued, her voice over-carefully neutral, "perhaps you could summarize your experience for those who weren't present in the room."

Dagny took a deep breath, searching for words to describe the indescribable.

"There's so many edges to the universe," she began, her voice soft but steady. "No, more like layers, each self contained but also sharing the same moments. Kind of like knots. Maybe?" She frowned. Her mind was still trying to get its arms around it all. Far too soon to be able to share it with beings who could not share the levels of her thought.

She tried again, simpler. "I do know that the Soumai exist on a level beyond our current understanding. But they've chosen to reach out to us. They've been watching, waiting for the right moment to say hi."

"Seriously?" said Khan, sitting on the other side of Osa. Wonder and disbelief warred in their voice. "And that moment hinged on something you did. You alone?"

Osa glared at him. Under the table, she grabbed Dagny's hand in her overheated one.

"Yes," Dagny said to Khan. To them all. Pride, humility,

guilt, despair, hope, every other emotion seemed to be swirling in the universe inside her. "My decision to send the warning message about the mines the Dawn planted. To prioritize the greater good over my own concerns"—her own safety—"helped them decide to reveal themselves now. But you would have gotten the map no matter what."

The Interface's form shimmered, their ever-changing collection of eyes appearing to scan the room. More than a few of the humans shifted in their seats, uncomfortable.

"We regret the error in giving the earlier humans the system map, as you call it," they said. "We wanted to even the field of play, that was all. But Dagny Novak's choice surprised us. It signaled a critical juncture, a moment where the potential futures of your species and ours aligned in a significant way."

Xalara's mandibles clicked rapidly. "Tch! Are we to understand that the fate of interstellar relations rested on the actions of a solitary small human? One who, might I add, had recently betrayed her own crew?"

The words stung, but Dagny made herself meet the Zark ambassador's gaze.

"I caused harm, yes," she admitted, her voice firm despite the knotting of her stomach. "I was desperate. But when I had to choose between personal gain and the greater good, I chose the latter. The Soumai saw value in that choice."

"Indeed," the Interface reverberated. "It is in moments of great pressure that a true nature of beings is revealed. Dagny Novak's actions, motivations aside, demonstrated a capacity for selflessness and a commitment to the greater good that aligns with our hopes for your species."

Nova's form shimmered, her voice carrying a new resonance that seemed to echo the Interface's multidimensional nature. "Among my people, we have a saying: 'The star that burns brightest is forged in the heart of chaos.' Perhaps my friend Dagny's tribulations were necessary to bring us to this point."

Raza Khan leaned forward, their brow furrowed. "While I appreciate the cosmic perspective, we still have very real, practical concerns to address. Dagny's status on this ship, the security implications of her actions, the potential risks and benefits of this new relationship with the Soumai—"

"If I may," Osa cut in. As all eyes turned to her her cheeks flushed pink. "From a scientific standpoint, the opportunity the Fold presents is unprecedented. Mom's—I mean, Specialist Novak's—unique connection to the Soumai could be invaluable. To dismiss her now would be to squander a resource we can't afford to lose."

A surge of pride and love for her daughter, tempered by a pang of regret for the years they'd lost. And the years they might lose in the future, if she took the Interface's offer and stayed here in the fog belt.

She squeezed Osa's hand under the table. Osa smelled of strawberries, tea, and love.

Dagny tried to remember what the Fold had smelled like.

Like nothing she knew.

Myli, the Kipi ambassador, bounced slightly in his seat. "Yes, yes! New friends, new knowledge. Much to gain, much to learn. Why cling to old grudges when the universe has opened its arms to us?"

Consort Belle nodded vigorously, adding, "Besides, it's so much more fun with Dagny around. Things were so dull without her."

A ripple of nervous laughter ran through the room, breaking some of the tension. Dagny felt a glimmer of hope, fragile but real.

The Interface's form shifted, taking on an aspect that somehow incorporated elements of every species present without being creepy.

"We propose a solution," they said. "Dagny Novak's unique perspective and connection to us make her an ideal liaison between your people and the Soumai. From now, we can speak to her wherever she is in the universe. On this vessel, or any other vessel. Let her serve in this capacity, bridging the gap between our realities."

Patel's eyebrows rose. "A new position."

"Why not?" Remy chimed in, his eyes alight with possibility. "We're in uncharted territory here. Our old structures, our old ways of thinking—they may not serve us in this new reality."

Khan frowned, but their voice held a note of consideration rather than outright rejection. "It would allow us to keep a close eye on her, while also utilizing her so-called unique qualifications."

Dagny felt as if she stood at the edge of a black hole, the immensity of the moment threatening to pull her in.

Was this what she wanted?

Was she even allowed to ask that question?

It had not been her dream to be a bridge between universes.

She just wanted to solve puzzles. Enjoy her friends. Love her daughter.

She watched Chief Patel roll the idea about in her mind.

The chief was quiet for a long moment. Her gaze traveled from face to face around the table. Finally, she nodded.

"Very well. Dagny Novak, I hereby appoint you as our official liaison to the Soumai, conditional on the eventual agreement of the Greater Alliance. You will retain your rank of Specialist, but your duties will be focused on facilitating communication and understanding between our peoples."

Dagny gasped. Reinstatement! Doing the most mind-blowing job in the universe.

Marvelous.

Astounding.

But.

But this was not her dream.

Never her dream.

It was somebody else's.

Under the table, she squeezed her daughter's hand.

"I am honored—" she started.

Patel leaned back in her chair, satisfied. She almost put her arm on the armrest, but then caught herself. That space had been ceded to the Interface.

Dagny went on. "But I was not the only one shown the wonders of the Fold. And I am not the best choice for this role."

Patel froze.

Osa gasped.

"Mom. This is your dream."

Dagny turned to the messy-haired, freckle-faced child of her heart. She drank in the love she saw in those round brown eyes.

"Remember back on Chang-ko? You staring out at the

stars, dreaming of the future?" With a finger, she touched her daughter's heart.

"Your dream. Well," she swept her hand away from Osa and toward the Interface. "There it is."

Patel looked terrified. She turned toward the Interface, surreptitiously pushing her chair in the opposite direction.

But the Interface had not changed—or had not stopped changing.

"We did entertain this possibility," they said. "Two were shown The Way. We will accept either."

The room fell silent. Nobody seemed to even blink. For a moment, it seemed as if time itself had paused, allowing everyone to process the shock of what Dagny had done. Again.

Patel seemed to be taking this all in little slower than usual.

"Let me get this straight." She squinted at Osa. "Osa Novak, you, too, went on the, ah, journey?"

Osa nodded so hard her hair bounced. Dagny could see the hope become real behind her daughter's eyes. Her skin seemed to glow.

"It was amazing," Osa said. "With a capital A."

"And you, ah, study other cultures?"

"Xenobiologist, yeah. I know the lingo. It would be easy for me to translate. Well," she amended, "not really easy, you know. The whole thing is kind of mind-blowing. But in a good way," she quickly added, looking at the Interface.

Patel took that all in with a very slow blink. Then she shifted her gaze to Dagny.

"And you. You do not care to serve the Alliance?"

Ow. Dagny searched for words.

Nova's hand in hers heated, then cooled, then heated again.

Yes, exactly.

"I would be honored to serve the Alliance," Dagny said, her voice thick. "But my skills and abilities"—and friendship —"would find a better fit not with the Soumai, but with the Iridah."

She clasped Nova's hand tight.

Dagny turned from Patel to fully face the Interface.

"Interface for the Soumai, you honor me with your invitation. You honor all of us."

"I understand," chimed the Interface. "This is acceptable."

A wave of relief washed over Dagny, so intense it left her lightheaded.

"Yes!" Osa whispered. She pumped her fist in the air. Then quickly slipped it into her lap.

Nova's form wriggled with what Dagny had come to recognize as joy. "If I may interrupt," she said, her voice a clear bell, "the Iridah would be delighted to host Dagny Novak on our home world. We have honored no one in this way, in all the years of the Alliance. But in light of recent events, and the great example of our new friends the Soumai, we feel the time is right."

Across the table, the Interface's form began to waver more intensely.

"We leave you now to rest," they said in their heady harmony of tones. Beside them, Patel's face eased, her jaw popping at the release of tension.

The Interface did not remark on that. Their shimmers somehow melted, into motes of light that themselves seemed to melt.

Osa touched her temple. "They'll be back tomorrow midday. Our time."

The room erupted in excited chatter. First contact! Voices crossed and recrossed—congratulating one another, trying to explain the universe, dictating messages to go out as soon as the temporal anomalies faded.

Khan's brow furrowed as they discussed the security implications of these new arrangements with Nell. Xalara tched at the Kipi, who were circling them like demented tumbleweeds. Nova's edges shivered with barely contained joy at the prospect of Dagny meeting her people. Every one in the room, and on the Breaking Light—and soon, in the known universe —began to start to grapple with the monumental shift in their place in the universe.

The noise level was already high when Saanvi shouted over the intercom.

"We're out of the fog!" she crowed. "And there's the main drive! Just waiting right here for us."

Dagny felt as if she were floating, buoyed by a sea of second chances and new beginnings.

Remy had cornered Osa, peppering her with questions about what she'd seen. As she passed behind them on the way to confer with Chief Patel, Dagny caught Osa's eye. Her daughter's smile, bright and unguarded, was a comet of happiness slamming deep into Dagny's heart.

Patel was tugging at the elastic that held her tight bun in place.

"Need help?" Dagny asked.

"Nah." The great swath of blond hair was briefly free—so glossy!—and then tightly bound once again. Patel waved Dagny to the seat beside her. "Sit, sit. I don't know what I expected. Well, actually I do. We came up with so many scenarios! And none of it matched."

She shook her head. Her hair did not move.

"You'll have to go through channels. Get properly approved. But I can't see how the brass could say no. They'd have to face the ire of two peoples."

Dagny tried to laugh, but it came out a whisper of a huff.

"I think I'm going to need to sleep for two days straight just to figure out what-all happened this week."

"You and me both."

They looked across the table, at the ambassadors and humans all chattering away. Behind them, the screen showing the xeno auditorium was happy pandemonium. The scientists looked like they were playing some clumping game. First one set of clumps of people, then another.

Chief Patel set a hand on Dagny's knee. "We're going to miss you, you know." She grinned. "Sally was right."

"Sally?" Dagny said, voice rising. Her nemesis.

"She said you wouldn't stay long. You were too good for us, she said."

"Sally? The ship? Said that?" The ship's AI didn't hate her?

That was the biggest surprise of all.

CHAPTER
THIRTY-NINE

THE PERFORMANCE SPACE hummed with anticipation, a palpable energy that reminded Dagny of the moments before a star goes supernova. The makeshift theater, once a chaotic jumble of mismatched chairs and hastily erected platforms, had evolved into a harmonious blend of function and alien aesthetics. Dagny marveled at how the space seemed to capture the essence of their recent cosmic journey—a fusion of the familiar and the extraordinary.

The show must go on, Xalara had declared, even if it was only twelve hours since the entire universe had changed. Not to mention, everyone needed a break.

The ship's engineers had carefully maneuvered the main engine back into its slot at the south pole of the sphere. First time anyone had done that outside of a shipyard. The xenobiologists had split into teams: one parsing every moment of the Interface's visit, one collecting the wristcom data and verbal reports of people's experiences of the space-time anomalies.

And one group of twelve that devoted themselves entirely to wringing information out of poor Osa.

They wanted to probe Dagny, too, but she'd begged off. She promised to give them all they wanted tomorrow and reminded them that Osa might be gone to the Fold at any moment. As soon as they heard that, Dagny was forgotten. She'd gone to her cozy room and turned her comms off. Under her soft blue blanket, she'd slept for ten solid hours.

But she was up in time for her front-of-the-house duties here. For the Grand Evening of Galaxy Entertainment.

Soft, amber lighting turned this bare shuttle hangar of a room into something almost romantic. The walls, with their optical illusion shimmer paint, and the draperies behind the slightly raised stage, made of a fabric that seemed to ripple with a life of its own, transformed the space into something almost sacred.

The mismatched chairs and hastily constructed benches and tables, frantically arranged—was it just yesterday?—were so ingeniously integrated into the design they looked like intentional artistic choices rather than last-minute solutions.

The seating arrangement itself told a story of interspecies cooperation. Refurbished acceleration couches for the humans ranged in concentric half-circles. Behind them the single very tall table and perches for the Zark. A nest of plush cushions in front of the humans awaited the pair of Kipi.

Who should be there already.

As Dagny did one last sweep of the room, she heard the cheep-rush-giggle of madly dashing Kipi coming from behind the tall screen at the back of the bare stage. Belle ricocheted softly off Dagny's shin on her way to the cushions. Ambassador Myli stopped himself by using Osa's knees, getting a tuft of fur on her black jumpsuit. Osa only laughed, and reached out to stroke his pastel cloud of fur. Myli tilted his head, silently demanding his round fuzzy ears get scritches. Dagny was impressed; Osa wasn't a toucher. But who could resist the cartoony teddy bear of a Kipi.

"Dagny!" Belle chirped. "Did you hear? The mushroom tree isn't blue anymore! Somebody made it all orange." As Belle snuggled herself between a pair of cushions, Dagny spotted a speck of orange on the top of Belle's back foot.

"Orange is a nice color," Dagny said. "Sunny."

Belle trilled a laugh. "Oh, no! Orange is for mourning for Zark. Ab-so-lute-ly in-ap-propriate. Tch!"

So that's why no blue mushroom-tree.

As Dagny settled into her seat, Belle snuggled up to her shins.

"You know, you could sit closer to the center," she told the Kipi. Dagny had to sit on the far left of the first row, ready to leap up at any problem.

Belle looked down the row. She shook her little head, the blue-brown tufts on her ears swiveling.

"Patel and Khan? Too stiff and skinny. You're plush!" She snuggled deeper into Dagny's velvety skirt. It was nice to dress up sometimes.

How far they'd all come. The air, once thick with tension and puzzled misunderstanding, now buzzed with excited murmurs and handsigns.

"Can't believe this is the same place," Osa said. "All our work on those acoustic baffles really paid off. And we only blew out one of the big printers making the curtains."

Dagny smiled agreement, bumping her daughter's shoulder softly. The scent of popcorn wafted from a bench behind her. She'd have to grab some of her own during intermission. If they had intermission.

A hush fell over the audience as Ambassador Xalara stepped onto the stage, their chitinous exoskeleton gleaming gold under the spotlight. Dagny was struck by the change in the Zark's demeanor—gone was the impatient, demanding diplomat. In their place stood an artist, poised and quietly confident.

Quite the transformation. Just yesterday, Xalara had been all mandible clicks and impatient demands, their every movement a study in barely contained frustration. Now, under warm lights and in front of an eager audience, there was a new grace to their carriage that Dagny had never seen before. And a new depth to their vocal range.

"Esteemed colleagues, honored guests," Xalara began, their voice pushing into deep their lower register. "We gather here not merely as different species, but as fellow travelers in the grand cosmic dance. Through art, we bridge the gaps between worlds, between dimensions, between hearts."

As Xalara spoke, Dagny noticed subtle movements in the audience. The Kipi, true to form, were up to something. But instead of the mischievous sabotage she half-expected, she saw Myli discreetly passing out small devices to those seated nearby. Dagny cautiously accepted one when it was offered to her.

But it wasn't one of those "stink bombs" the Kipi had been planting earlier. Made of the same clay-putty material, this device had evolved into something beautiful and unifying.

The vaguely square object, no larger than her palm,

hummed softly as the performance began. Xalara, now with long wide ribbons in each of their four hands took the stage to the accompaniment of Nova on the hand drum. There was a diplomatic détente Dagny would not have predicted.

Xalara's movements, strangely sinuous, blended dance and a form of sign language. As they moved, Dagny felt a gentle vibration from the device, translating the visual poetry into tactile sensations that seemed to resonate in Dagny's very marrow.

"Oh, wow," Osa breathed beside her. "It's like I can feel the story they're telling. About journey and discovery. About home."

Suddenly, Krim appeared at Dagny's side. His movement was noticed from the stage, only a meter away. Xalara somehow included a glare at their assistant in the rhythmic flow of their performance.

Krim sank down on his haunches. Trying to be less obvious. His voice was a low, urgent whisper.

"Specialist Novak, there's been a complication." His compound eyes darted nervously towards the Kipi. "The song isn't really about home, or home-equivalents. The Kipi have altered the translation in the devices."

Darcy groaned silently.

Of course.

"So, what's it really about?" she whispered back.

Krim's mandibles clicked in what might have been embarrassment. "It's about the mating habits of a species from the far reaches of Zark space. The painful birth of the Zark empire, so to speak."

Dagny stifled a laugh, torn between amusement and worry. She glanced down at the Kipi, cuddling close to each other, snuggled hard against her skirt. At Osa, still enraptured by the performance. Then back at Krim.

"Should we do something?"

The Zark assistant clicked to himself a moment, not-so-surreptitiously scanned the audience, and then looked back at her.

"Probably best to let it play out. The sentiment seems to be having a positive effect, regardless of the actual content. Just don't tell the ambassador."

Good luck with that.

As Krim headed back to his perch, Dagny sighed. Even now, in a moment of interspecies harmony, the Kipi couldn't resist adding their unique flavor of chaos to the mix.

And, in their way, they had actually kept the peace. Dagny could just picture Chief Patel and Security Head Khan drawing back farther and farther during what Dagny could see clearly now was an evocation of foreplay, Zark-style.

The show flowed relatively seamlessly from one group to the next, each species contributing their unique take on performance art. A Kipi song that painted colors in the air, a human instrumental piece that sank deep into the bones. A lovely Iridah poem that made Dagny cry for three different reasons.

Throughout it all, Dagny was acutely aware of the subtle orchestrations happening behind the scenes. Remy, at a discreet control panel, expertly balanced the sound and environmental controls to keep each species comfortable. Saanvi's ingenious holographic interfaces allowed for real-time translations and sensory adaptations. Even Nell, standing guard at the back, was swaying to the harmony unfolding before her. Lucky for her, Khan seemed just as taken; they hadn't scanned the scene every ten seconds for nearly an hour.

As the final act approached, Dagny felt a familiar cool presence materialize beside her. Nova, in her preferred pink-skinned form, leaned in close.

"Friend Dagny," she burbled. "Wish me luck!"

The finale was a collaborative piece, with representatives from each people on stage. Krim provided a rhythmic backing hand drums, while Belle's fur rippled in complex patterns that pushed themselves into the very air, dancing. Two humans in the blue and orange of Specter School, the most-exclusive music academy in the sector, wove an intricate counterpoint that sent shivers down Dagny's spine.

And at the center of it all, a shimmering Iridah form served as a living conduit, pulling all the elements together in a colorful, breathtaking display of unity.

For a moment, there was a discordant note as the Zark rhythm faltered, nearly throwing off the rest of the players. Dagny tensed, remembering the earlier squabbles over frequencies and volume. But then, almost miraculously, the other performers adjusted, weaving the mistake into the fabric of the song. Working together. How far they'd all come.

As the performance reached its crescendo, Dagny felt a shift in the air, a sense of expansion that went beyond the physical. For a moment—just a moment—she could have sworn she glimpsed the infinite realities of the Fold superimposed over their own, as if the boundaries between dimensions had become as thin as gossamer.

The final note lingered, resonating not just in the room but seemingly across realities. As it faded, there was a heartbeat of absolute silence—and then the audience erupted in thunderous applause, chittering, stomping, laughing, and every other form of appreciation.

Dagny cheered and finger-clicked, shedding happy tears. Beside her, Osa also was cry-smiling. Even the usually stoic Patel was smiling broadly. Khan just stood there, stunned.

The performers on stage joined hands (and various appendages) to take their somewhat Alliance-style bows. As the applause began to die down, Xalara stepped forward once more.

"Fellow cosmic travelers," they said, their voice thick with emotion, "tonight we have created something beautiful together. Something that speaks to the very essence of what it means to explore, to connect, to grow beyond our individual limitations."

Dagny felt the truth of those words in her soul. This performance, born from chaos and misunderstanding, had blossomed into a testament to the power of cooperation and open-mindedness. It was a microcosm of their entire journey—from conflict and suspicion to harmony and mutual appreciation.

As the final echoes of applause faded and people moved to the snack tables in the back of the room, now visible once the curtains had been pulled aside, the makeshift theater began to transform once again.

Crew members efficiently cleared the stage while others rearranged the seating area, creating space for mingling. The air hummed with excited chatter as the audience, a small group around each performer, shared their experience of the performance.

Dagny found herself at the center of her own small gathering. Khan, Saanvi, and Osa all congregated around her, their faces alight with the kind of joy that comes from witnessing something transcendent.

"Well, Dagny," Saanvi said, with a warmth in the chief

engineer's voice that Dagny hadn't heard in a long time. "You seem to have a knack for bringing people together."

Dagny felt a blush creep up her cheeks. "Not just me. This was a true group effort."

Saanvi had gone all out, sartorially. Her statuesque form and beautiful dark skin was shown to best advantage by a bright pink hourglass-shaped bubble dress that clung to her like a lover. Her braids had ribbons of the pink fabric twined through them. Dagny felt positively dowdy in her high school prom-style long velvet and matching velvet headband.

"Perhaps," Saanvi conceded. "Now, where's that delicious popcorn that's been taunting me all evening?"

Khan, dressed as always in black on black, her short blond hair exactly right, cleared her throat. She spoke to Dagny but looked at Osa.

"Heard from the Nemesis. No need for you—either of you—to give more testimony on the Beloved Spring affair."

Osa looked at Dagny. Her daughter didn't dare speak. Once Osa got started on the many flaws in the Alliance penal codes, she often couldn't stop.

"Summary judgment, then?" Dagny slid in.

"Turncoat," Khan growled. "Leader spilled her guts. Guess she thought they'd treat it like a business deal gone bad."

"Good luck with that."

"Didn't realize she was building the case against herself single-handed." Khan shook their head, still focused on Osa. "At least the people against us are stupid." A ghost of a glance at Dagny and quickly away. "Usually."

Before she could respond, Osa tugged Dagny out the group and over to the snacks. Wise move.

The popcorn smell she'd salivated over for an hour

couldn't hold a candle to the taste of the chocolate torte. Someone must have made it from scratch.

"Aria wasn't so bad—," Osa said before throwing a handful of popcorn in her mouth and crunching down.

Dagny said nothing for a moment. Aria and the Beloved Spring stole her daughter. Or at least brought her in under false pretenses. They stole Dagny herself. They tried to steal this ship.

"—for a terrorist," Osa finished once she'd swallowed. "Want another fancy piece of cake?"

As the night wore on, filled with laughter, music, and the excited chatter of beings discovering new common ground, Dagny couldn't stop smiling. The universe, vast and mysterious, had led them all to this moment of connection and understanding. Whatever challenges lay ahead in their exploration of the Fold and beyond, they would face them together. A harmony of diverse voices, united in the grand cosmic symphony.

As the evening's festivities began to wind down, Dagny was drawn to the pillows that had been the Kipis' nest. The pillows were in relative shadow, now that the stage lighting was off, and quiet, now that all the various amplifiers were tuned down. The excitement of the performances still hummed around her, but here, in this pocket of relative calm, she could finally take a moment to process all that had happened.

Osa joined her, two steaming mugs of tea in hand. "Thought you might need this," she said, offering one to Dagny.

Dagny accepted the mug gratefully, inhaling the familiar aroma of her favorite blend. Remy must have told her. A small comfort, a touch of the familiar in a world that had become extraordinarily unfamiliar.

"Thanks, sweetheart," she murmured.

They sat in companionable silence for a moment, sipping their tea and watching the mingling crowd. The Kipi had bowed out early, pleading exhaustion. Dagny was suspicious, but nothing had farted yet. Xalara was still holding forth next to the refreshment table. Krim and one of Dagny's comms interns were animatedly discussing something about how the curtains were made.

"You know," Osa said softly, "I keep thinking about that day at Galaxy George. How angry and lost I felt. If someone had told me then that we'd end up here." She shook her head, a wry smile playing on her lips. "I would have laughed in their face. Or tch-ed."

Dagny snorted. "That's my girl."

Osa turned to face her mother, laughter, hope, pain, and a multifactorial universe in her eyes. Dagny set down her mug and pulled Osa into a tight embrace.

"Oh, my star-bright girl," she said. "You've grown so much. I can't wait to see where this journey takes us next."

How far she had come from that desperate mother who had made a fateful choice in a theme park. The universe had tested her, broken her down, and forced her to build herself into something stronger.

The weight of their new roles settled over her. Such purpose, her daughter had. Such an opportunity, for Dagny. There would be challenges ahead, dangers and wonders, sure. But for the first time in years, she felt truly, completely alive.

"Mom?" Osa's voice pulled her from her reverie. "What are you thinking?"

Dagny turned to her daughter, a smile playing on her lips. "I'm thinking we're in for quite an adventure, sweetheart. Are you ready?"

Osa's answering grin was brighter than any star.

"Together," she said. "Forever."

CHAPTER
FORTY

DAGNY STOOD at the sandy threshold, her hand hovering close to the shimmering membrane that separated her sanctuary from the alien world beyond.

Eliah, the first home of the Iridah.

The membrane, a dome that sheltered a rambling one-story clay-brick house, a near-circle of a running track, and not much else, pulsed with a soft, bluish light. Its living tissues happily filtered the atmosphere to create a bubble of Earth-like conditions in this decidedly un-Earthlike place.

"Ready?" Nova's voice sang with excitement.

Dagny took a deep breath. She was a month behind.

At least her lungs were working now.

When she'd first arrived on Eliah, stepping off the ship had been like walking into a dream—and then a nightmare. The colors, amazing. The temperature, balmy. The atmosphere, vicious.

The very air had seemed to resist her, its strange composition making her dizzy and nauseous. The fluctuating gravity had sent her stumbling, and the kaleidoscopic sky had left her disoriented and reeling.

Nova had been her anchor. While Dagny retreated to the shuttle that had brought them down to the planet. Nova had quickly devised and, with the help of her people, created this island dome-home. A safe haven where Dagny could adapt gradually.

Now, after too many weeks of carefully controlled exposure and some minor biological adjustments, she was finally ready to step out.

"Ready," Dagny said.

She hoped.

They should have tested this before inviting Nova's family to visit. Well, they would have, but Dagny had relapsed.

She couldn't relapse today.

Nova's form wavered, taking on the pink-skinned, elf-like appearance that Dagny had come to associate with moments of affection.

"I am right here with you. That is the correct reassurance, yes?"

Dagny hid a smile at her friend's endless earnestness.

She pressed her palm against the membrane. It parted like a curtain of water, cool and tingly against her skin. She stepped through.

The first thing that hit her was the smell—a crash of surf, chalk, and overripe fruit. The air felt thick, almost gelatinous, but she found she could breathe it easily now.

It was sand here, too, beach. A dozen meters away flowed one of the liquid parts of this world. Ninety percent of Eliah was liquid. Nova said Dagny should feel honored to be loaned this tiny island. They'd wanted her to stay in their capital city, a floating coral-style structure. Even with the new body enhancements, she wasn't ready for a fully-floating life.

Mist swirled around her feet, the last taste of the dawn. The water glowed faintly in response to her cautious excitement. Nova had shown her that property of the dew already.

Dagny looked up, and gasped. The sky was alive with colors, auroras dancing across a backdrop of glittery clouds. Three moons hung low on the horizon this early morning, their combined gravitational pull creating visible ripples in the liquid landscape stretching out before her.

"Wow," was all she could think of to say.

Nova smiled, her form now blending seamlessly with the environment, her legs blurring into the mist.

"Welcome to Iridah, Dagny. Truly welcome, this time."

As if on cue, swaths of the colors in the sky flowed directly toward them. They started taking shape. At first, Dagny thought it was just another quirk of this strange world, but then she saw the eyes—hundreds of them, mostly in pairs, in every color imaginable. Blinking into existence.

The Iridah were here.

They came in a dizzying array of forms—some humanoid, others completely not. Some flowed like living mercury, while others floated like luminous jellyfish. But all of them radiated a sense of warmth and welcome that transcended their range of appearances.

One Iridah, shimmering in hues of deep purple and gold, approached. Its form rippled, and suddenly Dagny was looking at a mirror image of herself.

You'd think she'd have gotten used to that.

"Greetings, Dagny Novak," they said, their voice a thick blend of tones. "We are glad you are well."

As some two dozen Iridah crowded around, their bodies creating a living, breathing tapestry of color and movement, Dagny felt Nova's hand slip into hers. She leaned into Nova's shoulder.

A year ago, a little more, she'd sat in a Galaxy George diner, feeling like the loneliest human alive. Now she was the only human on this huge planet, and yet far, far from lonely.

This week, the xenobiologists were holding their annual conference. Osa had called her last night. No longer the wide-eyed audience member from last year, but a featured speaker, sharing insights gleaned from her unprecedented access to the Fold. She'd be giving both a workshop and a keynote lecture.

Her little girl.

"What amuses you?" Nova asked, already smiling in empathy before Dagny even opened her mouth.

"Just thinking about Osa." She paused, considering. "Wondering if she'll take time out to hit the local amusement park. Silly idea, I know."

Nova shrugged. "The universe has a way of taking us where we need to be, even if we don't know it at the time. Is that not the human saying?"

"You're so right," Dagny said.

From a desperate attempt to save her daughter to letting her go again, watching her take up the challenge of being a bridge between worlds, every step had led to this moment.

Her own challenges—starting with how they were all going to sit in a circle on this tiny spit of land—were real. And daunting. But for the first time in a long while, Dagny felt truly, completely ready.

After all, she was home.

ALSO BY NICKY PENTTILA

Cosmic Weave

Cooperative Realm: Frankie's Journeys

Cargo Trouble

Frankie Takes a Holiday

Frankie Takes a Dive

Frankie Finds a Dot

Frankie Takes a Bow

Cargo & Chaos: Frankie books 1 & 2

Cooperative Realm: The Arkhide Chronicles

Hidden Planet

The Listeners

The Elders of Arkhide

Tales of Arkhide story collection

Short Stories

Here: Earthbound Fantasies and Futures

There: Journeys to Imagined Realms

Historical Fiction

A Note of Scandal

An Untitled Lady

The Spanish Patriot

ABOUT THE AUTHOR

Nicky Penttila wrote her first story, a Mayan murder mystery, in seventh grade. But then came gymnastics, math team, and boyfriends. Later came husband, car payments, and a sleep-depriving work schedule at newspapers across the country. Then came a second career as a science writer. But the fiction kept trickling out, a story here, a novella there, and finally, a real live novel. And she hasn't stopped.

Find more great reads at nickypenttila.com